THE CANTICLE'S PATH

The Songcycle Chronicles

J.G. Flora

ISBN-13: 9798703940402
ISBN-10: 1477123456

Library of Congress Control Number: 2018675309
Printed in the United States of America

For Those Who Chose:
- to build up and not tear down
- to love and not hate
- to face the madness and not run away
- to listen and not judge

GRATITUDE

Thank you to my many supporters and friends, Nicole and Maria, especially for your invaluable, professional support. To my early test readers (Chrystal, Katie, Dawn, and Dolly), I appreciate your patience, encouragement, and critiques.

Graphic Design by Maria Guevara, @mariaillustration1

Copy Editing by Marja Consulting, LLC

CONTENTS

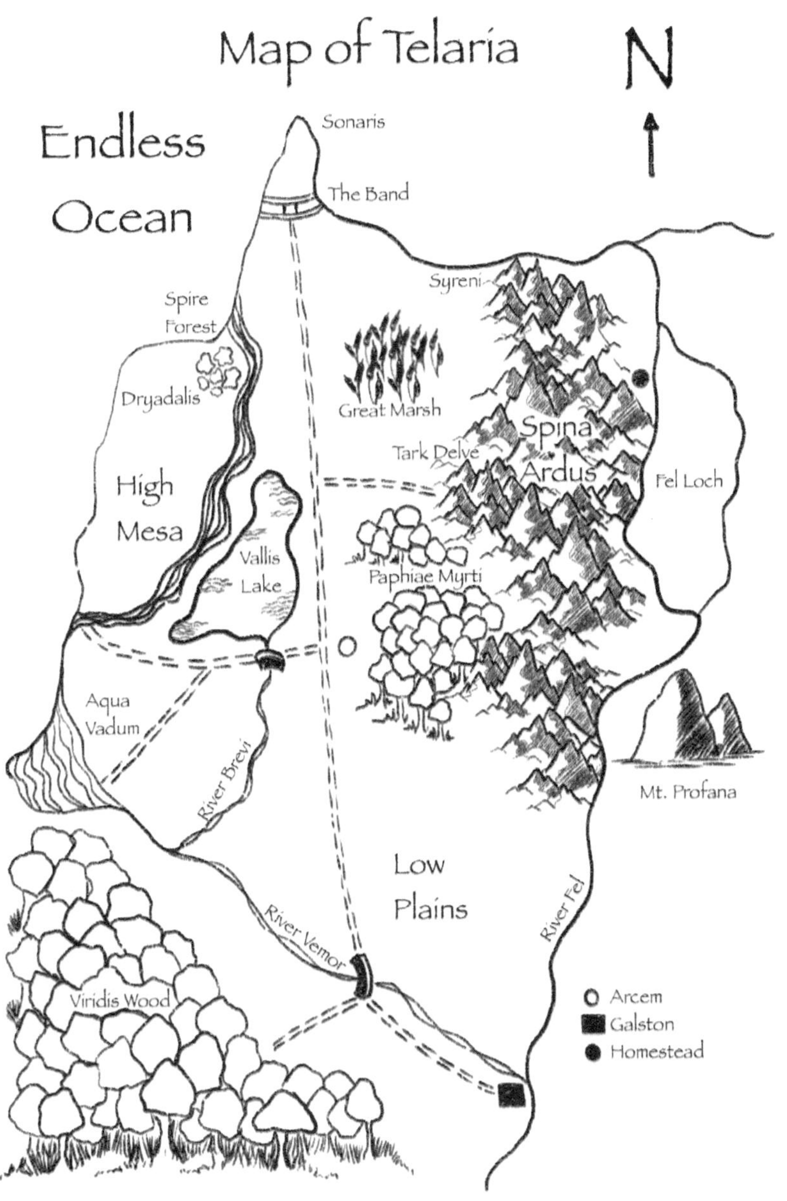

Map of Telaria
N
Endless Ocean
Sonaris
The Band
Syreni
Spire Forest
Dryadalis
Great Marsh
Tark Delve
Spina Ardus
Fel Loch
High Mesa
Vallis Lake
Paphiae Myrti
Aqua Vadum
River Brevi
Mt. Profana
Low Plains
River Fel
River Vemor
Viridis Wood
Arcem
Galston
Homestead

CHAPTER 1

"Girls! Girls! Come and say goodbye to Papa before he leaves this morning. You won't see him for another two days." Jael shouted up the stairs to the children, as Aries shouldered his pack. He glanced around the rustic living area to be sure he had not forgotten any necessary items. Reaching just to his left, he grabbed a roll from the rough hewn trestle table and wandered past the fire place to stand next to Jael, as she leaned over the bannister.

"Just let them sleep. I'll be back soon and they have a full day ahead of them without starting an hour earlier than normal." Aries gave a smile and kissed his wife on the cheek. "Don't worry about the barn roof. I'll patch it first thing when I get back. Promise." He leaned back against the solid stone of the fireplace and pulled his wife into his embrace.

The sound of scurrying feet interrupted his assurances, as his three girls tumbled down the stairs, which wrapped up and around the stone chimney piece to the girls' bedroom and school room on the second floor. As always, Ryl and Iyna moved in tandem, so fast that he was almost upended in a mass of giggles and braids, one head dark as night and the other white as moonlight. They forced him back onto the bench by the table and climbed into his lap. Safara came tromping good naturedly down the stairs, her brown hair in a tangled mess around her shoulders. She gave a yawn and plopped down on the hearth and leaned against her mother. All three girls looked remarkably different, other than sharing fair skin and wide eyes. Aries motioned to all three and advised them to stay on their mother's good side while he was away. "Mama is a hard task master, but good girls will be in for a treat when I return. We will all be taking a trip to the coast this fall, so we need to have things ship-shape around here before we go." Ear splitting squeals almost deafened Aries and he laughed as Jael did her best to rein in the twins. She sent Iyna to fetch the plates from the cupboard and Ryl to let the cat in. Safara covered her ears and rolled her eyes at her father's tactics. He slowly stood up across from her and tousled her hair. He noisily kissed each of his girls on the cheek as they came his way making them giggle and run away.

"If you are going to get them all worked up like that, you may as well go!" Jael gave him a light shove out the door and slammed it behind him in mock indignation, as Aries jogged down the steps with a chuckle. The barn was directly out the front door of the house and the large, timber structure housed their horse, Parsifal, two cows, an ox, and a dozen or so chickens. Aries moved purposefully toward the paddock on the left side of the barn. "Watch out for the ladies for me, Par," he requested. The horse whinnied in response and bobbed his head up and down. Aries hummed a little melody as he crossed the barn yard and passed the well. Tuning into the Song around him, Aries used it to manipulate the surrounding flora. As he focused on the plants, his tune wove a wreath of roses for Jael from those nearby. She loved the tiny pink rosebuds and encouraged them to grow up the stone foundation of the building and on up to the roof. Feeling his song from inside the house, Jael added her melody to build a cairn of rocks for it near where Aries was standing. Aries chuckled. She was cheeky; she knew he could not manipulate earth without the foundation of her song. With a loving glance and a jaunty wink, he deposited his gift and strolled out of the clearing toward his trap line.

After watching him out of sight, Jael turned to the children. "All right. First breakfast. Help yourselves to the bread and milk from yesterday, girls. Iyna, you and Ryl gather whatever berries are in the bushes by the spring once we finish. Fara, could you please clean up after breakfast and get started on your lessons? I am going to gather the laundry after we eat."

"Yes, Mama," all three girls chorused, as they tucked into their meal. Jael smiled and joined them. Ryl's dark hair fell on her face as she chattered about the coast and wanting to meet a Mer. "Just think! They can live underwater for days at a time without surfacing. Their skin must get awful pruney."

"Don't be dense. They don't get pruney from the water. They were made for water." Iyna corrected her twin. "But they are blue. Right, Mama?"

"Yes, they can be blue, but not all are. Be careful of your tone with your sister. Her skin gets wrinkly in the water, so why wouldn't she think the same of the Mer? Human bodies are different from mer, but she has never met one to compare." Jael admonished her youngest and wiped her face before turning to her eldest. "Fara, what are you looking forward to seeing?"

"Anything," answered Safara shortly. She disliked the morning and although she was never in a bad mood, it was rare to get more than a sentence out of her until after breakfast. She reached for a second roll and tried her best to sleep as she ate.

The meal continued on with chatter between the twins, no noise from Safara, and the occasional redirection from Jael. With a sigh, Jael brushed the crumbs from her hands and excused herself from the table and puttered around the house tidying as she went. The girls scooted around her and charged up the stairs to play. As they ran past, she kissed each of the children on the head and reminded them of their chores before moving through the door, shooing the cat out in the process. She heard the back door slam and the twins scamper off in the direction of the stream. She nearly fell down the steps as the world seemed to tilt on its edge before quickly righting itself. Jael shook her head and staggered to the laundry line to one side of the well. An intense, high-pitched whine sounded in her mind. Involuntary shivers raced down her neck, trailing icy fingers of fear along her entire body. As she began pulling down a pair of tiny leggings, she felt Aries' harmony in the distance, but it was wrong.

❋ ❋ ❋

Aries headed south from the homestead to check the trap lines. The sunlight was dappled through the trees and an early morning mist clung to the underside of the forest canopy. This was his favorite time of day; mornings held so much promise. It had been a week or so since he set the line and he was hoping to have a nice haul of pelts to take to the coast to trade. The Song of Creation pervaded everything around him. High, steady lyric notes wafted by on a breeze. The deep thrumming of the earth soaked up through the soles of his boots. The heat of the sun cut through the morning haze with a controlled vibrato. Through it all, Aries focused most on the plant life, his strength. Aries picked up on the melody of the ferns around him, gently pushing them out of the way as he passed. As a Canticle, he could manipulate existing systems and enhance them with his harmony. Swirling invisibly around him, the soaring score of the forest slowly faded.

With a sinking sensation in his gut, he stopped abruptly and surveyed the forest around him. The plants around him looked wilted and jaundiced. The Song in this portion of the forest was flat and, in places, eerily quiet. He shook off the feeling of foreboding, mistaking it for missing his girls already. As a Vocalist and with her elemental affinities, Jael was far better equipped than he to defend the house, but she was not a fighter by nature. She craved peace and security above all other things. That was the reason why he agreed to leave their training and the school at Sonaris behind. The Masters of the school all recognized her abilities, but did not fully appreciate her retiring nature. They all mistakenly thought she would gain the confidence needed to face their perpetual enemy if she bonded, which would increase her capabilities exponentially. However, the reverse happened. She wanted even less to fight. Once bonded, Jael's fear of losing her bondpartner instantly made her want to flee. For almost a year, Aries resisted her, but the intimate mental connection between bondpartners meant most feelings and instincts were communicated subconsciously, especially in close proximity. The influence of one partner over the other could only deepen over time. In the end, they fled the school with Parsifal under cover of night. The alarm that went up the next morning could be heard all the way to The Band, but not before they shot through the gates, as they were opening for morning trade. The guards tried to follow on foot, but Parsifal was able to carry them to the edge of the Great Marsh before they had to stop and rest for the day.

After a mile or two, the uneasy feeling went from a faint impression to an active concern. Aries felt like he was being tracked and herded. Two seasons ago, he stumbled onto a detachment of three sycop troops, who followed him for almost a week before he managed to deal with them all. The sensation was similar, but more urgent. He took off faster through the trees hoping to escape up the ridge, or force his followers into a clearing off to one side. Aries cut through the forest changing directions often. Each time he felt pressure from the new direction steadily pushing him south. Without warning, he heard someone alter the Song around him and almost fell when a pit opened up directly ahead, cutting him off from the trail up into the mountains, where he could lose his pursuers. Whoever it was, they were trying to capture, not kill him. Nervous sweat poured down his face and body as he tried to recall his training prior to running away. He had only been at Sonaris for two years before Jael convinced him to leave and he had only trained on his own for one of those before they bonded. The smell of freshly turned earth mixed with fear stank in his nostrils.

"Show yourself! You may as well come out and face me. I will not run like some terrified mouse." Aries postured defiantly as he burst into the clearing filled with low ferns ringed on three sides by towering trees, hoping to force his attacker into the open. Looking north, the smoke from his home faintly curled away into the breeze, and he backed slowly to the far side of the grass. He knew from previous trips that the mountain sheared away into the lake below behind him. No one would be approaching from his back, but there was no way out. He was trapped between an hundred foot fall and his pursuers. He could feel them on all sides, but whoever was manipulating the Song was directly in front of him. Between him and home.

The birds stopped calling and the clouds gathered overhead, even the Song, which had been a constant hum in his head since his earliest memory, was suppressed. He was truly alone facing a challenge for which he was not prepared. The throbbing silence was deafening and he almost wept when a weathered, old man pushed through the brambles. He whistled a chaotic tune and the ground on either side of Aries fell away, leaving a slim finger of land between the two, even as groups of sycops appeared to his right and left. "What are you?" whispered Aries, almost enthralled in his terror.

"You know who I am. Anyone who hears the Song must know who I am. My brother may have gifted the races, but I am the reason he did it. " The man smiled assessingly. His confidence was overwhelming and for a moment, Aries felt calm before he realized his opponent was humming him to sleep.

"No, I will not go so easily," Aries shouted, shaking his head to dispel his opponent's work. He tried to find a thread of the Song to offset the stranger's pull. He began his own melody slowly and found a counterpoint to his sleepiness. Even as he regained his faculties, Aries knew that he was lost. He feared for his family. At best, his life was forfeit. At worst, they would end up with this monster. The canticle realized with horrifying clarity that he was facing Rasulo, the Angelic who was bound within the Cycles by Stahd himself. "Merciful Stahd! I know you.

How are you here? It is too early. It has only been five years since the last fall," Aries whispered.

"Do not mention that traitor before me, worm," Rasulo spat. "The last cycle pairing was a joke, but perhaps I have you to thank for that? I am only recently freed from their pathetic attempt at incarceration." Rasulo smoothed out his wrinkled, dirty robes thoughtfully. "I sense that you are a Canticle, if under trained, and there are only ever a handful of those in a generation. But your bondmate...she is the powerful one. You have a spark of defiance about you, so one must assume that she convinced you to abandon your work. My thanks." He bowed to Aries and began a slow march in that direction. "We will work well together, I think. A Canticle is not a gift that I will just leave in the wilderness by Loch Fel. No, no. I have use for you."

Meanwhile, Aries was working within the plants around him. Without Jael to lay a foundation for him, he was vulnerable. On his own, he could only manipulate flora. With limited options, he reached within himself and put every ounce of love for his family into one hit at the large oak to his right. He lashed out a tone in a quick grab at its canopy and brought the entire tree crashing down as a barrier between Rasulo and himself, planning to run and jump the fissure to his right. In response, Rasulo carelessly pushed the tree out his way, but it swung like a door by its roots and hit Aries mid-stride. The force swept him off the cliff onto the rocks below. The canticle's shout echoed off the rock walls as he fell and he sent a final pulse of warning to Jael through their bond. It was a combination of surprise, regret, danger, and most of all his love for her and the children. Rasulo moved to the edge of the cliff and sniffed, "Pity."

❊ ❊ ❊

Snap

Jael fell over her laundry basket and tumbled to her

knees in agony. A silent shriek tore from her mouth as she realized that she could no longer feel Aries. There was just a void where his thread of the Song had tumbled about in her head not a minute earlier. The last pulses over their bond projected overwhelming danger. She sat still for a full minute: numb, mute, and in shock. Repressing her grief, she sprang into action, gathered several sets of clothes from the line, and sprinted to the house. If Aries were gone, then someone had killed him and no ordinary traveler would be a match for him. If they were hunting Hearers, then the girls would be the next target. Outside of Sonaris, Hearers and Users were rare enough that they were hunted, sold, and used by any one that could pay for them. That was part of the reason that anyone who tested as proficient was brought to Sonaris for training. It doubled as protection. It was always a mystery how Aries managed to avoid capture and was free to move around Telaria until he was sixteen and decided to seek sanctuary in Sonaris. Now she had three Hearers and likely powerful Users under her protection without her bondmate.

When Jael reached the house, Iyna and Ryl were already off doing their morning chores leaving Safara as the only occupant. "Fara, listen carefully. You have five minutes to gather whatever food you can find and get out to the barn. Call Parsifal into his stall so that I can saddle him. Go!" Safara looked scared, but scurried to do her mother's bidding. Jael ran across the living space to her bedroom and grabbed several blankets and a fire-starter, shoving them into a satchel with her stock of clothing. As an afterthought, she grabbed her journal, hoping to keep her identity and the girls' lineage a secret. She raced to the barn just as Parsifal came thundering up at Safara's call. As her mother hurriedly saddled the horse, Safara dumped the satchel and the food into the saddle bags and waited for her mother to lift them onto the horse's back.

"We don't have much time, sweetling. Please do as I say. Go find the girls and take them to the lake. I will join you before midday. We must all leave this place and head to Sonaris. Do you understand me? If anything happens to me, you must get the girls to Sonaris. The school will take you girls in and keep you safe." Jael hugged her daughter close.

"Yes, Mama," came the muffled reply. As Safara's arms crept around her waist, Jael blinked back the tears and turned her head to Parsifal.

"You know the way. Keep them safe. Do not come back here for me. Go home." Jael gave a hard look at her faithful friend, who snuffled at her forehead in response and waited for her to lift Safara onto his back. Jael took one precious moment with her girl before peeling her arms away and hoisting her eight year-old atop the horse. "Go. I love you." With that she tapped the horse on the rump and they were out of sight in a moment headed past the well, toward the spring.

* * *

"Your turn to carry the basket, Ryl." Iyna handed it to her twin as they wandered to the blackberry bush. The mist was burning away in the sunlight, turning the morning uncomfortably warm and humid. This early in the season, the bush nearest the spring had a few small early season berries peeking out from under the leaves. Otherwise, it was covered in the remnants of the flowers from weeks before.

"Mama said to get all the berries we could, but there are barely any," said Ryl with disappointment. She could barely wait for the jam that Jael was sure to make. She plopped down on the ground and tossed the basket off to the side of the bush.

"We could make there be more! A whole bush full!" Iyna practically burst with enthusiasm at the idea. "Mama and Papa always sing to make things do what they want. Why can't we? You sing like Papa and I'll sing like Mama. I know it will work!"

Iyna bounced around to the far side of the bush. "I'll start, Ryl. You fill in." She started to hum at the bush and thought about berries and jam. Her song was sweet and unfocused, as she started to repeat the melody created from listening to the Song around her. Soon Ryl joined in, finding a place to add her own harmony to the melody. Her tone was a third below her sister's and a pleasant addition. After a few minutes of singing together, the bush responded. It grew and pushed out slightly. The girls giggled and continued on eagerly. Ryl tried to match her sister's song better and soon her harmony encouraged the bush to ripen its fruit. The berries grew heavy on the bush and were the biggest that either girl had ever seen. With a nod to each other, they increased their volume and focus with a rush, the bush almost cracked in its haste to grow. It shot out in all directions pushing the girls apart and trapping Iyna within its brambles. At the same time, both felt the other fall in sync and a bond beyond that of sisters or even being twins snapped into alignment.

Both girls were slammed to the ground. Ryl was pushed yards away back toward the stream. "Iyna! Where are you?" Ryl called over and over again each time more desperately. She could hear Iyna calling for her, but it was in her head and very quiet. Confused, she yelled to her sister, "I'm going to get Mama! Stay there! I'm coming back for you." Ryl rushed off back to the house with a swirl of dark hair as fast as her short, five year-old legs could carry her.

Just as she rounded the corner of the path, a small dark carriage rumbled up from the other direction, branches and smaller foliage making way as it passed. A rather dirty man of indeterminate age stepped out. He smiled at the blackberry bramble and popped a few of the ripened berries into his mouth as he pushed the thorns and branches back with his song. *A child*, he thought, *one of the urchins off that idiot from this morning. Not a total waste after all. It's always better to train them from an early age.* Rasulo hummed Iyna into a deep sleep and carried her to the carriage. He signaled to the driver. "Follow the track ahead. That Canticle's home can't be too far. Let's see what other spoils we can find." He smiled and sank back into the cushions with a small smile of anticipation on his lips.

❊ ❊ ❊

Jael watched Safara and Parsifal to the edge of the clearing and then ran to release all of the animals from their pens and enclosures. Once they were all clear, she began to gather her song and moved between the house and barn. The home she had built with Aries, her bondmate and father of her children. She wept and put every fiber of her being into calling down two massive columns of fire to consume the structures on each side of her. Fire songs always came easily to her. Her confusion manifested best as an open flame. She watched in anguish as her life burnt down around her. She fed the flames with her grief and screamed until her voice was raw and spent. Within minutes, the entire house and barnyard were gone, leaving only Aries' wreath and the ashes floating around her as a witness to their home.

As she extinguished the flames, Rasulo's carriage rattled up into the yard behind her surrounded by his guard of pale, mute sycops. Through the haze of smoke and ash, Jael turned to face the intruders, her hair flaring out in a red arc around her. The grieved Vocalist instinctively knew that this was the reason for her loss. She might have been fearful, but she had always been smart. Her chest heaved taking in huge gulps of air. Soot streaked her face and hair, with her tears leaving tracks in their wake. She felt trapped and alone; the essence of her worst nightmares come to life.

"Leave. I know who you are. Just leave. You have already taken everything from me." Jael lashed out as Rasulo slowly climbed down from the carriage, knocking out three of the guards that had advanced on her with a push of wind song.

"Now, that is no way to greet me. We were always destined to meet. I think I prefer this way to the one intended by your precious masters, don't you?" he said soothingly. The Angelic knew she was emotionally spent, but also volatile and keyed up for a fight. He appreciated talent and did not want to lose a second acquisition in one day. Considering his weakened state, she was more than a match for him. Five years of maintaining the weight of a mountain on top of him had drained most of his reserves. Instead, he opted for purely mental warfare.

Rasulo stood blocking the open door of the carriage and taunted his quarry. "You are the most powerful Vocalist I have encountered in over a hundred years. Now, that Canticle of yours, he was nothing special. With training, he could have been formidable, but as it was, he barely lasted five minutes and most of that was pleading. Come along with me, I have work for you." He gestured to the open carriage door behind him with a mild wave of his hand.

With every word, Jael felt rage boiling up inside of her focusing on the figure before her. Just as she called fire with her song, Rasulo swept to the side and revealed Iyna, asleep on the floor of the carriage. Instinctively, Jael painfully tamped down the fire she had called, redirecting it toward herself, as she was unable to extinguish it completely. The aborted song combined with fear for her child and the torment of not avenging herself on Aries' killer, burnt her soul from the inside out. For a brief moment as she burned, she felt relief and welcomed the fire. She would not have to live without her bondmate. Then she saw Iyna, small and alone in the carriage. Willing herself out of her fatalistic bent, Jael screamed out to the earth and encased herself in a shower of dirt and stone. The earth did its work and smothered the fire, but a moment too late.

❈ ❈ ❈

Safara tore through the forest in search of her sisters. Shortly, she came upon an exhausted Ryl crying for their mother and yelling about Iyna being trapped in a pokey place. Parsifal began to slow as soon as he saw Ryl and Safara half fell from the horse as soon as he stopped.

"Ryl! I'm here. Mama sent me," she said, trying to calm her sister down with a hug. "Show me where Iyna is."

"She's stuck, Fara. And our bush pokeded me. I couldn't get her." Ryl sobbed as she held out her bloodied, chubby hands for her sister to see. "We sang to the bush and it 'sploded so fast and ate Iyna. You can get her!" With that pronouncement, the tiny girl pulled her sister in the direction from which she had come. Parsifal followed along, never letting the girls out of his sight and keeping an eye on their surroundings. The forest felt too quiet.

As they rounded the bend in the path near the bush, Ryl cried out. "The bush is torn!" She pointed to a gash in the foliage the size of a person. In the middle of the bush, they found a few pieces of white blond hair stuck to a thorn and Iyna's basket with its berries scattered on the ground.

"Iyna! Where are you? Come here!" Both girls called out variants of the refrain over and over until they were hoarse. By noon, it was obvious that Iyna was nowhere to be found and she was gone. Safara pulled Ryl under the shade of a big tree where they collapsed into tears.

"We need Mama," Ryl sniffed. "Why hasn't she come to find us?"

"I don't know, Ryl," responded her sister. "She sent me to find you both and said she would meet us by the lake. Maybe we should go find her."

"But what about Iyna?"

"She isn't here, Ryl. Mama will know what to do. Come

on." With a heavy sigh, Safara pulled Ryl over to a rock and helped her climb it. Parsifal waited patiently as both girls clambered on his back. Once they were settled, he headed for the lake at a brisk walk. He was still on edge. The forest was back to normal, but he grieved for Iyna and knew Jael would be inconsolable.

At the lake's edge, the girls automatically headed for a small dock their father maintained for fishing. A few supplies were stowed in the benches along the sides of the dock, which were mostly used on camping trips during the summer. The girls scanned up and down the coast for a sign of their mother, by this time it was late afternoon and both knew better than to be in the woods at night. Safara slid off Parsifal's back.

"Mama said she would meet us here by midday. Something is wrong. We have to go home!" Safara talked more to herself than anyone else. She started home, but was blocked by Parsifal. He whinnied reproachfully at her and attempted to herd her back to the dock, stamping his feet in protest the whole time. "Move, Par! Let me go! I want my Mama. I want my Papa. I want my Iyna!!" She wailed at the horse trying to get around him. But he would not let her pass. She backed up to the dock and started to throw rocks and driftwood at the horse. Ryl stared at her sister and started to cry from her perch on Parsifal's back.

"MaaaaaaaMaaaaaa! Help! Please find us," she screamed facing the woods. When no answer came, she turned to her older sister. "Why won't he take us back?"

"Mama told him not to. She said to never come back and that we were supposed to go to her school to be safe. That they would help us. But she was supposed to come and take us with her. We can't leave without her or Papa or Iyna." With each statement, the older girl's voice became higher pitched and more desperate. Overwhelmed, Safara collapsed to her knees and threw up. At that, Ryl jumped down from Parsifal and ran to her.

"Don't be upset, Fara. Mama will find us. She always does and she will bring Papa with her." Ryl crooned to her sister and held her hand. "Mama said to go to school. She prolly has Iyna and is coming with her, too." Ryl's hopeful personality peaked through despite their horrible situation. Parsifal knelt in the sand and sniffed at each girl's head reminding them that he would not leave them. Both turned and leaned against him. Exhausted and spent, all three slept until morning.

CHAPTER 2

The sun rose on the eastern horizon, gently touching the tops of the trees before disturbing the rest of the sleepers on the beach. A slow fog drifted off the lake as dawn changed to early morning. Ryl was the first to wake, confused as she brushed the pebbles and sand from her face and clothing. With a jolt, she remembered why she was not in her warm bed and drew her knees to her face with a muffled sob. This was the first morning she ever greeted without Iyna by her side and she felt the loss keenly. Just wanting to be alone, Ryl quietly crawled away from Safara and Parsifal. Once clear of their small huddle, she took off toward her favorite tree. It had a hollow trunk and huge arching branches that swept around the trunk in all directions. Some touched the earth and others soared far above. The tree was the largest in the area by far and the entrance to the hollow was obscured by a large knot in the trunk. She and Iyna spent many afternoons hiding from Safara and their parents, playing games inside and telling secrets. A wave of homesickness overtook her as she climbed within. She always felt safe here. Hidden, but protected. Not only because her parents and sisters were around her, but something about the tree felt comfortable. She often heard bells or a tinkling noise, which made her laugh. It always felt like the tree was singing to her or trying to play. Ryl and Iyna used to parrot back at the tree and tell it their silly jokes and stories. But today, she climbed in alone and cried.

From above, she heard a faraway tinkling noise, it sounded like a question. Ryl was not in the mood to play, so she ignored the noise and wiped her nose against her sleeve with a great sniff. Her eyes were red and blotchy and her hair was matted with sand and mud from sleeping on the beach. The questioning noise moved closer and became more insistent. Finally, she looked up and thought she saw movement. Curious, she squinted deeper into the dark interior.

"Tree? Iyna is gone. I know she is gone. I can't hear her. Mama and Papa are gone, too. Fara and Par are still asleep on the beach. How will we get to school from here like Mama said to? Why did we have to leave? Parsifal won't let us go back. Fara said Mama said not to, but I don't want to be here without them. What if they don't find us?" Ryl wailed, the words tumbling rapidly from her trembling lips. Her voice crackled with anxiety and fear. She felt a whisper of a touch on her cheek followed by a comforting chirp not an inch from her face. Ryl shrieked and scooted back, but the light touch and noise repeated. In the weak morning light filtering in through the opening, she saw a tiny black figure with translucent smoky wings extending from behind its petite shoulders. Stunned, she stopped crying and after a moment reached out asking, "Do you make the songs for me?" A small encouraging chime was the answer. Momentarily distracted, Ryl held out a hand and the small creature landed gently. His body was no larger than an apple with his beautiful wings spanning his full height in either direction. They sparkled gently in the light and had every shade from brilliant white to coal black in their shifting pattern. The ends spun off into curling mist at the top and bottom that trailed behind him when he flew. His skin was deep ebony, as was his hair. The diminutive face that peered back at her was both kind and wise with small grey eyes that appear to look straight through to her innermost thoughts.

He reached forward with his hands and placed one on either cheek leaning forward and resting his forehead against Ryl's nose. His light chime reached into her heart and she felt his emotions. He was grieving with her. Iyna was his friend, too, and he felt her loss. A single tear slipped down her cheek and he caught it with his small hand.

"I miss her," Ryl whispered.

The little being nodded and chimed in agreement. After a moment, he shrugged his shoulders and indicated to Ryl to wait for him. In a flash, he shot up to the top of the hollow and through a crack.

"Come back...don't go, too," the little girl whimpered. Her plea was met with the chiming of hundreds of bells. Not so loud as to overwhelm her with noise, but enough to let her know that she was not alone. With a shuddering sigh, she sat back down reassured upon realizing that there was more than one being in the tree with her.

In fact, Ryl and Iyna had made their hideaway inside a Faerydae colony. The inhabitants were fascinated by the small humans and often played with them using callback songs while keeping themselves hidden from view. The Faerydae did not like humans as a rule and avoided all contact when possible. The girls were a rare exception because of their connection to the Song and their ability to manipulate it at such a young age. Even their parents and Safara were considered undesirable by the Faerydae, as they lacked the uninhibited playfulness of the twins. Upon seeing only one of their pets and in response to her obvious distress, one individual revealed himself to comfort the child.

Within moments, the chiming reduced back to just one bell, which came winging back to her. The creature stopped abruptly and hovered in front of Ryl, as if considering his choices. He squared his shoulders and opened his hand palm up. She reached forward with one finger and rested it in his light grasp. She felt a jolt and slight warmth whip up her arm and into her face. He smiled and she felt his thoughts hazily.

"Nyx? Is that your name?" Ryl thought back with childlike intuition. She was rewarded with a short laugh from the faery-

dae. Intrigued into temporary distraction, she spoke out loud, not realizing that their previous communication was telepathic.

"How come you haven't talked before? Why did you hide?" Her dark eyes were wide with suspense as she pushed the black tangle of hair out of her face with a grubby, pudgy hand. Nyx indicated that his people rarely spoke to humans and his village was so enchanted with her that while they wanted to communicate, they feared exposure. "I wouldn't hurt you, any of you. Never!" proclaimed Ryl with wide, honest eyes. "Fara and Iyna wouldn't either." Her twin's name reminded her of her loss and she teared up again. At that moment, a scream echoed around the lake.

"Ryl! RYYYYYYYYYLLLL! Where did you go?"

The call was quickly followed by a very upset whinny from Parsifal. His cries were louder and just as insistent as those from Safara. Both seemed to be beside themselves and on the brink of a meltdown. Nyx urged Ryl to climb out of the tree and practically drug her through the brush to the edge of the lake. Ryl tripped over a root and almost fell on her face, but Nyx grabbed her shirt and held her body several inches from the ground. *I'll be carefuller,* Ryl thought at her new guardian. He released her as soon as she was supporting her own weight. She clambered to her feet and took off for the beach again. The faerydae followed closely with his smoky wings leaving a fading trail behind them.

"Fara! I'm here. I'm here!" Ryl screamed to her sister, not slowing her pace until she could throw herself at her remaining family. Parsifal nickered at her and snuffled both their hair until he noticed the addition to their circle. He unsuccessfully attempted to insert himself between his girls and the faerydae, but Nyx nimbly flew between his legs with an offended chime and landed on Ryl's shoulder. He held on by her ear to indicate his intention of accompanying the younger girl. When

Safara pulled back to look her sister in the eye, she was greeted by the face of the tiny, black creature, who viewed her as the interloper. She yelled. While she was trying to fight him off, Ryl tried to mediate, but it was an inauspicious beginning to say the least.

"No, no, no, Fara! He's a friend!" Ryl pushed her sister back and waved Nyx out of her sister's reach. "He lives in my tree over there. He heared me crying and wants to help."

"What is it?" asked Safara with a confused look on her face.

"He's mine. I dunno what he is, but he is mine." Ryl stated firmly with her arms crossed over her body. Nyx landed nimbly on her shoulder and nodded. He tinkled at her reassuringly. His beady eyes regarded the girl and horse across from his self-appointed ward warily. He was ready to fight for his right to stay with his pet.

"If he is nice, he can stay, but we need to find Mama, Ryl," Safara reminded her sister unsure if they were fighting.

"Mama!" The familiar wail started up from Ryl. She sat heavily on the pebbled beach; her shoulders heaving as she gulped in as much air as possible. Nyx chirped at her and tried to calm her. Safara joined her quietly on the other side and they held hands waiting for their mother to arrive. After trying to calm them, Nyx finally succeeded in getting Ryl's attention.

"He will go look for Mama at home, since he knows we are supposed to wait here." Without waiting for permission, he zipped away through the trees following the path taken the prior day.

"I guess we can just wait here then." Safara said, feeling a little better. Not understanding what kind of creature had attached itself to them, she was just glad he was gone for the moment. Her heart hurt as she looked out over the water of Fel Loch. The morning mist melted away quickly and the day looked bright and cheerful, unlike her mood. The roiling emotions within her made her want to run downstream as fast as she could or scream; she could not tell which. She settled for gathering as many fist sized stones as she could find and hurling them into the lake from the end of the pier. Each splash, thunk, and spray relieved some of the pressure on her heart until she felt like she could breathe again. After a few minutes, Ryl joined her and they spent most of the morning alternating between gathering and throwing stones. Parsifal regarded them mournfully, but other than making sure they did not go out of his line of vision, he let them grieve as they wanted. By midday, they were famished and sat on the side of the dock to have some bread and cheese from the saddlebags. Their steed had been grazing all morning and was impatient for something to do.

The sound of bells came from the direction of the trail. It was faint at first and gradually increased until both girls noticed. Exchanging a glance, they both silently agreed to check out the noise. Within minutes, Nyx flew down the trail. Upon seeing Ryl, he immediately slowed and landed on her shoulder, chittering so fast it sounded like a continuous note. The tired girl started crying as her confused sister tried to get her attention.

"Ryl. What is it? You have to tell me what is going on?" Safara begged her sister tugging on her arm to pull them face to face.

Ryl sobbed. "Home is gone. All gone! Nyx thinks it burned up. No Mama, no Papa, no Iyna!"

Safara hugged her sister and Parsifal crowded close and nuzzled both heads. Jael had been his trainer and familiar, a bond that ran as deep as blood. A familiar connection through the Song joined a User and an animal on an instinctual level, enabling either half to know what the other was feeling and pick up impressions of their thoughts. It was similar to the connection of a bondpair, but fainter. His first memories were of a gangly, red haired teen offering him a carrot inside a paddock at Sonaris and they were inseparable after that. His heart broke for her loss, but the horse knew his first responsibility was to the children in front of him. He gently herded both out toward their camp and nudged Safara until she met his eyes.

"What do we do, Par?" she asked. He looked pointedly at the gear and then pranced in place. "We can't just leave!" Safara shouted angrily. "My Momma isn't here!"

Parsifal repeated the gesture until both girls finally calmed down enough to gather their possessions. Even Nyx helped by hauling the water skins off shore to be filled and returned them to be strapped onto the saddle. Using the dock as a mounting block, the girls managed to saddle and mount their guardian. The faerydae settled between the horses ears and chimed quietly at him. Both seemed to understand each other and for the time being they were only concerned with getting the children to Sonaris, as instructed by their mother.

It was late afternoon, as they started north along the western bank of Fel Loch. The summer afternoon was warm, but with the mountains to their left, they quickly lost both light and heat. The sun faded below the mountain line winking in and out in a cheery manner, not appreciated by Ryl or Safara. With a shuddering sigh, Safara secured her sister in her embrace and held on to the saddle horn. There was no need for her to use the reins, as Parsifal was the only one who knew the direction they should go. Within a couple of hours, they made the decision to camp at the base of a mountain by a stream. As they gathered wood for a fire, Parsifal grazed nearby and then rested once Nyx had it lit. All four huddled in a pile staring into the flames as Safara passed out the last of the bread and cheese. Fortunately for them, most of the route was dotted with streams and rivers, so water would not be a problem. Food was the primary concern. With Nyx's help finding seasonal berries and nuts pilfered from the local squirrel population, the journey was uncomfortable, but manageable.

After four long days of following little more than a deer track from the homestead, they came to the mountain pass. Aries had always been very careful to vary his route, as he did not want to risk being followed home on his biannual trips to the coast. However, there was only one good route through the Spina Ardus at the northern end of the range. The east and west sides were connected by a tunnel built cycles ago by the Sonaran Chorale. The wide grey stone road wound up the mountainside for a mile before leading into a tunnel nestled between the joint of two mountains. The space within was wide enough for two carts to pass comfortably. Perfectly smooth walls arched gracefully overhead meeting at the center in a slight point. Veins of ore appeared to be melted smooth, marbling the surface in a mesmerizing pattern. Silver, gold, copper, and the occasional gem winked out in the summer sun, locked and protected by the original song used in its creation. The walls were dotted at regular intervals with sunken mirrors of burnished metal, which refracted the light along the walls. If there was any significant light outside, it would dimly fill the length of the passage.

Ryl clasped tight around Safara's waist and her mouth formed a perfect "o" of surprise as she leaned to the side to see around her sister. Never before had either girl seen such a magnificent structure. Safara was no less awed. As they passed through the entrance, she leaned to the side of the saddle to run her fingers along the smooth stone. The surface was cold and still as a frozen lake. She half expected to be able to see her own reflection on the surface. Even Nyx seemed impressed. His people never worked with stone and lived almost exclusively in trees, but he appreciated the sheer scope of the accomplishment.

"What is dis?" whispered Ryl. The tunnel seemed an almost sacred place, so she spoke softly. Her dark eyes were wide under the thick black fringe of her hair.

"Papa said that he took a tunnel to Syreni on the coast every year. This must be it. It's..." Safara's answer drifted off as her mind tried to determine a word to describe their surroundings. "It's the most beautiful ever," she finally finished.

Ryl agreed emphatically. Her volume grew and evened out at a normal volume as she grew accustomed to their surroundings. No other travelers were in the tunnel at the moment. The path was not straight and level, so their exit was not visible. After the entrance disappeared around a corner, Safara remembered her father saying that it took him more than a day to pass through. The light would not last and they would be in the dark overnight, she thought suddenly afraid.

"What will we do when the light goes away?" she asked Parsifal. Their guardian flicked his ears in response, as though thinking.

"Why will it go?" demanded Ryl. She normally would not have minded the dark if her family was with her, but their recent reduction in numbers caused her to doubt herself.

Nyx calmly pulled Ryl's face toward his own and leaned his forehead into hers, as Parsifal continued on. After a few moments of gentle chiming, she settled back down and hugged around her sister's waist.

"Nyx will fix it." She stated simply without further comment.

Safara was not so sure, but as the small creature had not let them down in the past days, there was little reason for doubt. She simply could not understand how her shy sister had taken so thoroughly to the faerydae. They communicated easily without speaking. Ryl said pictures would pop into her head unbidden. Nyx seemed to receive the same in return, but Safara only ever heard the tinkling sound he made. She mildly resented that he did not seem interested in talking to her. If

Nyx noticed her injured feelings, he did not seem to care. She idly ran her hand along the wall tracing the veins absently. She felt the echo of the Song in the tunnel. Whether the walls were still echoing with the sounds that made it or if she was feeling residual maintenance was impossible to tell. But the Song was present nonetheless and she felt comforted whenever she could sense it.

After a time, they came to a cavern. The smooth walls dropped away on either side and the thin light dispersed less than a cart length to either side of the path entrance before it was swallowed. A small oval at the other end seemed to be the way out, but the light was fading fast. Water plinked and plopped from menacing stalactites into fathomless pools below. Mounded pillars formed at irregular intervals where stalagmites had joined with their siblings above. From what was visible, the path crested just before them and then plunged into the darkness somehow wending its way to the fading pin-prick of light.

Nyx took Ryl's upset face as his cue to fix the problem. He did not mind helping the older girl or even the horse by association, but Ryl needed light. With a small shake of his wings, Nyx flew to the ceiling of the grotto. He found a crystal deposit that seemed to follow their general path and focused on imbuing his light melody into it. After several minutes, the structure of the crystal seemed to glow faintly and grow brighter as his melody boosted its refractive properties. Light spilled across the cave ceiling, spider webbing out from his location as the changes to its structure passed along from one node to the next. Red, pink, white, yellow, green, and blue light shone all about. The space which recently seemed like a threatening nightmare was turned into a rainbow wonderland complete with rippling puddles.

Unknown to most, the Faerydae were master manipulators of the Song, but they were strongest with light because they loved the sun and coveted its warmth and how it made their plants grow. This special connection to light was granted to them by Stahd. Other races had affinities for their own elements, but they also shared those abilities with one another to a lesser degree. Light belonged exclusively to the Faerydae and it was not a fact that they advertised.

"Nyx! You fixeded it! You did!" Ryl cackled below as she slid off of Parsifal and spun around truly smiling for the first time since leaving the homestead. Safara slowly looked around before dismounting. The light was strong enough to see all corners of the cave, but was not so bright as to hurt their eyes. The different veins cracked along the ceiling shining brighter at intersections and fading out as each narrowed down to a point.

"Thank you," she breathed in awe as Nyx came tinkling back toward their group. He nodded his head in acknowledgement and took his customary spot on Ryl's shoulder lightly. Even Parsifal nickered his approval, as his worry for the girls' safety ebbed a fraction. They made their way along the path to a niche set into the bottom of a large column. It appeared that some previous traveler had carved out a space big enough to fit them all. Additionally, a bit of wood had been stacked to one side. Safara found it around the side of the column and hauled it around for Nyx to light. With light, warmth, and comfortable dryness, Ryl and Safara curled up into Parsifal's side and quickly went to sleep. The faerydae and horse took turns at the watch until both children woke up naturally.

The next day was spent almost entirely in the tunnel passage lit by natural light and the fading echoes of Nyx's song. The group passed through several more caverns, but none as grand as the first. By evening, they were through the other entrance of the mountains and they camped a short distance from the road leading down the other side. The switch back trail on the western side of the mountain was almost twice as high as the previous. In the morning, they started the descent as soon as the sun came up.

The land on the western side of the Spina Ardus sunk away from the mountain pass into the Great Marsh. The marsh was generally impassible except to locals, and most travelers were smart to skirt the edges and not trust any solid footing that seemed available. Spurts of mist indicated the formation of a new sink hole every day or so. After which, the surrounding formerly solid ground would either disappear suddenly or slowly abandon its holdings to suffocate in the mire below. The land smelled of decay and death. However every few years, Vallis Lake across the Long Road would overflow and steal the rich muck of the bog for the farmland in the surrounding areas. Farmers in the area were equal parts fearful of the Great Marsh and worshipfully thankful for its presence. Hearers in the area were primarily used to predict flooding and enjoyed moderate success as weather beacons. As a precaution, most farmsteads were built on stilts to sit above the noxious waters. The animals were allowed to freely roam in the hopes that they would out run the flood waters. As additional protection against an unexpected flood, barns were elevated on pontoons and could be poled to find pastures.

As the girls came down the mountain, a geyser of murky water shot into the air pushing a batch of foul air in their direction. A small island covered in grass and one scrubby bush was quickly sucked in. Birds shot out of the bush in all directions screaming their displeasure at being disturbed so violently.

"At's so nasty!" Ryl complained, holding her nose and waving her other hand in front of her face to dispel the smell. Her gestures were futile, as the air was thick with the reek of compost. Everyone else agreed and both girls took to hiding their faces inside of their shirts for the rest of the trip down the mountain. The odor at the bottom of the range was not any better and they gradually worked their way around the north end of the bog. None of the party was willing to rest for the night until they cleared it completely and the tang of salty sea air greeted them. That night they rested beneath the stars within a mile of the beach their father had intended to visit with them. The air was warm near the coast in the summer and the waves gently rolled in the distance.

As day broke, they were almost caught by local fishermen on their way to market in Syreni with their catch. Parsifal awoke to the danger of discovery first. He had slept with his saddle on, as the children were too tired to remove it. He quickly woke both girls and Nyx with a shake of his head and quiet whicker. When Ryl began to complain at being woken, Nyx quickly quieted her as he assessed the approaching group. While the men seemed innocuous, the Faerydae was uneasy. His instincts were good, as Hearing children were especially valuable on the slave market. It was common knowledge that some were even sold by their parents. The liability of keeping such a child was just too high outside of The Band. Identified children were either taken to the school for protection or used for any purpose the owner could imagine. Both girls were now in danger, as they obviously had no parents present. Even if they were not Hearers, child labor was not illegal and they could be forcefully adopted and kept indefinitely.

Silently, Safara lifted Ryl onto Parsifal's back and then clambered up herself. Once the group of men was past, Parsifal stood carefully and began to make his way out of the brush. Cover was scarce this close to the sea, and the next stand of trees along the road might as well have been miles away. Nyx chimed at Ryl quietly and then took off in a streak for the men. The black faerydae clanged deafeningly at them and then flew off in the opposite direction purposefully leaving a thick trail of silvery-grey smoke in his wake. All five gave a shout and dropped their loads to pursue the tiny creature with their nets and hooks. As soon as they were away, Parsifal thundered down the road toward the next patch of cover.

After leading the fishermen back into the bog, Nyx took advantage of the fog that clung to the air and waited almost an hour for them to become thoroughly lost looking for him. He would tinkle just past their range of vision and then fly up and over the group to repeat the process on the other side. The grumbling group eventually tired of the chase and angrily headed back to their nets. Nyx gave the group a wide berth and headed straight back to his group silently. He soared as high as he dared to escape detection from below. Anyone watching would mistake him for a bird as he flew along.

"Sank you both!" Ryl hiccupped as she tried to calm herself. Nyx snuggled comfortingly into her neck. Safara held her tight around the waist and shuddered a breath. Neither were feeling well and although it was barely passed noon, they were exhausted.

"Can we stop?" asked Safara. "I think I am going to be sick." Parsifal stopped at the next group of trees which was near a small stream heading out to the sea. Safara lurched off his back and promptly threw up in a bush. She rolled to her side and stared at the running water. The sound calmed her enough that she fell asleep almost immediately. Ryl curled up next to her and exhaustedly joined her. Neither Parsifal nor Nyx had the heart to wake them.

By nightfall, both girls were awake and had moved past the initial shock of their earlier brush with capture. As a group, they agreed to angle northwest until they reached The Band and follow it until they reached its solitary gate. Guard posts were dotted along the top of the wall every quarter of a mile and some would be occupied. Should trouble arise, Sonaran guards would lend aid to any troubled traveler. Some of the guards were even minor or mid level vocalists and canticles. Fortunately, the moon rose high and full in the clear night sky. The scrubby trees cast sharp skeletal shadows against the drifting dunes. No one felt inclined to talk and both children dozed occasionally. The lapping waves lulled them to sleep, drowning out their nightmares with oblivion. Hour after hour, they trudged north. Parsifal never faltered with his precious burdens. He thought about the loss of Jael and her constant presence in his life. Aries made her happy and in turn that made Parsifal happy. His hooves moved forward; sad, yet confident in the knowledge that he was doing as she wanted. His friend knew her children's needs. In many ways, Parsifal considered them his own foals. He watched them take their first steps and played with them in the yard. No harm would ever come to his girls. That thought made him think about Iyna, the silver haired imp. She was pure sunshine and happiness. Ryl was more serious and prone to contemplation, while Iyna was impulsive and playful. The twins balanced each other and supplied what the other intrinsically lacked. A mournful noise escaped Parsifal's lips, waking Nyx, who had been sleeping between his ears. With a small sympathetic pat, Nyx comforted his fellow guardian. It was something and, oddly, Parsifal was glad to not be alone in caring for the girls. He nickered softly in response. Nyx leaped lightly from his perch and floated peacefully beside the horse. Both could just now see The Band looming on the horizon.

The imposing structure soared just over one hundred feet in the air. The flat, grey façade looked deceptively close. From previous trips, Parsifal knew to check the urge to increase his pace. They would not reach the base until after sunrise and wasting all of his energy racing to a solid wall was ridiculous. However, both guardians felt relieved that their goal was in sight.

The history of The Band and Sonaris were deeply intertwined. One would not exist without the other. The same Chorale that created Sonaris erected the wall almost immediately after finishing the school. The location was chosen specifically at the foot of the peninsula containing Sonaris and all of its supporting farms and industry. The base blocks of the wall were twenty feet wide and over ten feet tall. While there were some corridors and passages within the wall itself, most sections were completely solid. Stairs to access the cartway on top were built against the inner side of the wall and served as buttresses. Each successive block was slightly narrower at the top than the base. While the base of the structure was close to thirty feet deep, the top was half that. A cartway ran along the top containing guard posts, which rested on narrow stone pillars above it. The posts could only be accessed by ladders on the inner side of the wall. Reaching the post required the guard to swing herself out over the hundred foot drop and pull up until a foothold could be found. The travel system was an addition to The Band and the only major change made to its function since its inception aside from general maintenance. As a gift during the 5th Cycle, the dwarves used their affinity for earth and stone, cleverly improving functionality and design. The engineers and Users modified the top of the wall to function as a chute for large transporters similar to a minecart and rails. However, the system drew energy from the Song within the stone, not gravity or ropes and pulleys. These cart-devices echoed the Song within The Band itself back into the stone, thus strengthening the structure and allowing the carts to flow along the top between guard posts at regular intervals. The distance between the east and west ends could be traveled in less than two hours.

Parsifal shook his mane gently to wake his sleeping passengers, as the sun rose over the eastern horizon. He was exhausted and needed a rest. At the next grouping of trees, the quartet stopped for a break and he quickly fell asleep for a few hours joined by the girls, as Nyx stood watch. The early light washed the smooth façade in the distance with an array of gold, purple, and pink. The cheerily dyed structure reminded Nyx of a faerydae cake, which made him hungry. He busied himself finding any and all edible food within a stone's throw of the camp, making a small offering for his compatriots on a couple of leaves. Upon waking, everyone had their fill of the berries and chewy root vegetation he gathered. Feeling less worried than the day before, the group started off by midmorning and was in the shadow of The Band before noon. They attempted to gain someone's attention at each guard tower, but according to Nyx they were all unoccupied.

About halfway between the eastern edge of The Band and the Gate, Nyx found a pair of guardsmen just arriving for their weeklong duty. With a loud, angry jangle, Nyx got their attention and pointed to the small group on the ground. The guard nearly fell leaning out his window. He was barely able to make out the forms of both girls, who waved frantically at him, and a weary horse. The guard quickly sent his partner back to the gate with the message that there were unaccompanied children. He waved back at the children and started walking along the top of the cartway as a look out and guide. Within a few hours, a large contingent from the gate arrived to escort the tired group inside.

* * *

Captain Palmer quietly eased the chamber door shut, leaving the girls to sleep as long as they would. He leaned against the outside of the door and scrubbed a large, dark hand across his stubbled beard. Both children were painfully thin and their horse was almost ready to drop where he stood. The older one, Safara, gave their names and faintly requested some water. The little one, Ryl, started crying and asked to be picked up by Jameson, the guardswoman nearest to her, promptly passing out as soon as she was comfortable. *Miraculous*, he thought. *These girls are blessed to have survived!* He silently thanked Stahd for his protection and quickly made his way back to the hub of the gate house after a quick word to the guard in the hall.

"Make sure they aren't disturbed and send someone to see to baths and new clothes. I will request a light supper be sent. I am to be informed the moment they are awake. Keep Jameson close. The youngest seemed reassured by her on the trip back."

Palmer was not a man easily swayed by emotion, but

anyone with a beating heart would feel for these children. He repeated the scrubbing motion across his chin once he was out of the guard's sight and allowed himself to be upset for several moments, blinking back tears from his mahogany eyes. Eventually squaring his shoulders, he stepped into the room.

"Has word been sent to Master Parke at Sonaris? He is needed urgently."

"Yes, sir. The dispatch was sent by raven within minutes of your arrival. No details were sent other than the sudden appearance of two children riding a horse with a Sonaran brand on his side. I would expect his arrival before the evening meal." The entire room snapped to attention when the Captain entered. The room was the largest built into the fortress, while not huge it contained enough room for several desks and a flat central table used for meetings. Currently, a map of Telaria occupied the tabletop with a handful of orange pins in it, which indicated possible sycop sightings. There were far too many for Palmer's comfort this early in a cycle.

"Thank you. I am to be informed the minute we have word on his arrival. The raven will return with an approximate arrival time. Meanwhile, please set up for a long night. Whatever these children portend, good or bad, we will be ready. I will be in the records room." At his exit, the room exploded into controlled motion.

The narrow corridor was lit with torches along both walls and the first door on the left led to the records room. Palmer quickly lit the lantern he knew would be just inside the door. Musty and dim, the room smelled of books, ink, and leather. Copies of documents deemed necessary to the defense of The Band were kept here, but that was not his goal. The captain pulled out the bottom drawer of a cabinet in the corner and removed a leather binder. He dropped it on the table and turned up the lantern, as he shuffled through the papers. Many were his own personal notes on missing persons or Hearers that were known to be kidnapped and enslaved. Something about the horse was familiar. Years ago, when he was a lieutenant, he remembered a horse being stolen by two students fleeing the school. At the bottom of the stack he found the entry he was looking for:

"Cycle 6, Year 86, 3rd day of Planting

The status of The Band remains constant. The threat level is rising and more sycops are sighted every day. The end of the Cycle is near. It will not be tomorrow, but we have years, not decades left before a full scale confrontation is inevitable. The school assures us that there is a bondpair strong enough to push Rasulo back into a weakened state, if not destroy him for good. Welcome news indeed..."

After this beginning, much of the page was illegible due to a large ink blot, as though the quill was thrown down in haste and left to empty as it would across the surface of the paper. The entry picked up on the page underneath.

"...we were all summoned to the edge of The Band. Just as the Gate was opening for the day, a large stack of hay near the stables caught fire and acrid, black smoke filled the entrance. Any able vocalist not choking on the smoke quickly called water onto the blaze before it caught the nearby buildings. Smoke was replaced by steam, but it was too late. From my post atop the wall, I saw an enormous silver-grey stallion burst through the gates and make its way east toward the mountains. I watched the cloud of dust until it settled, but the horse never slowed and the passengers never looked back. Shortly after the fire was settled, a raven arrived from Sonaris. The chosen bondpair have fled and we are without a way forward. Stahd's Wrath upon them both for abandoning us all!"

Palmer shuffled through the binder for any additional information, but that appeared to be the only pertinent entry. No bondpair had ever fled before or since, and horses with the Sonaran brand were carefully raised and quartered. Few had ever gone missing, much less one with such remarkable coloring and the intelligence that usually came from a prolonged familiar relationship. He seemed to know that the guards could be trusted with his wards and although he would not be led by his bridle, he did follow along without prompting. The Faerydae was another surprise. Had anyone told a member of the guard they would ever see a Faerydae outside of a book or painting, they would have been laughed out of the gate house. Few ever saw the creatures and no one saw them up close for longer than the blink of an eye. Yet the tiny creature remained with the youngest girl suspiciously eyeing Jameson for the entire return. He tinkled angrily every time an adjustment was made to how the child was held. Clearly these children were without parents, but they were by no means unprotected. Carefully reviewing the entry again, Palmer restored the binder to its place at the bottom of the cabinet and made a mental note of its location. After snuffing the lantern, he proceeded to the stable to check on what he expected would be the most reasonable of his guests.

"Well met, Sonaran mount," he gently greeted the horse. Even in his exhausted state, Palmer could tell that this horse was even more magnificent than he remembered. He approached the horse's stall slowly with his hands out and offered him an apple. After some thought, Parsifal eased over and took the fruit slowly, never breaking eye contact. Palmer nodded and slowly blinked and looked away. He raised a hand and scratched the side of the horse's neck gently. He whispered calming words and slowly entered the stall. After checking the horse over for injuries, he called for water and led the tired mount out of the stall to be groomed. Over the next few hours, Palmer calmly washed and groomed the tired beast. He cleaned and bound each scratch. Every burr was removed from the lovely grey mane and tail. The entire time he alternated between a soothing mantra and humming. Parsifal seemed to appreciate the gesture and allowed the captain to work without shying away.

In the middle of the session, Palmer was briefly interrupted with a message that school representatives would be at the gatehouse by early evening. He thanked the lieutenant for the information and went back to his work having noticed that his charge flicked his ears in interest when Master Parke's name was mentioned. Casually working the names of several masters of the school into the one sided flow of conversation, only Parke and Deckard seemed to elicit any sort of reaction from the horse. Not negative, not positive, just acknowledgement. Palmer continued to groom the horse until his coat was shiny and smooth. Appreciatively, Parsifal settled in for a long rest, while Palmer gathered his lieutenants to wait for Master Parke.

* * *

"Hail and well met, Captain Palmer!" Master Parke's eyes warmed with a greeting although his illusive smile remained hidden.

"And also you, Master Parke." Palmer returned the traditional greeting with the current head of the Sonaran school.

"Your summons seemed urgent. I gather there has not been an attack on The Band or a sighting of sycops?"

"No, we have somewhat of a mystery on our hands." Palmer began speaking even as he led the way to the stable. "Several hours ago, a guard arrived on the tram babbling about children on a horse outside of The Band. I led a group to investigate, half expecting some kind of ruse or trouble. What we found were two young girls riding on a Sonaran horse. The oldest is about eight and her sister is five. Their names are Safara and Ryl. That is all we got out of them before they collapsed with exhaustion. They were painfully thin and extremely skittish. The horse's condition was better, but you could tell they have been traveling for days or possibly weeks. The brand on the horse is why I sent for you. I searched my old records and I believe it was the one that carried away the bondpair that fled years ago."

At this pronouncement, Parke stopped and swung his head to make direct eye contact with Palmer. His every expression and movement betrayed his surprise and a hint of regret. "Was there any sign of the parents?"

"No, sir. The children were very much alone other than the horse and faerydae. Both girls are resting. I left explicit instructions that they were not to be woken and the guards in that hall are to fetch me as soon as they are awake, fed, and changed. One of the girls asked a guardswoman to carry her on the way back, so Jameson is on their detail until further assessments can be made. The horse is formidably intelligent. He seemed to recognize your name and Master Deckard's while I was grooming him."

With that, they reached the stable and pushed the door open. Parke did not need the mount to be pointed out to him. "Parsifal, you are welcome, old friend." Parke extended a hand and offered a carrot from a barrel at the entrance. Parsifal whinnied politely in return, but did not move to take the carrot. He shook his silvery mane and lightly pawed at the ground with his front hoof. "I know you dislike me for the role I played in your friend's training, but you must understand, she was our best hope despite her fears. Aries, too." Parke paused for a moment, turned to the side, and broke eye contact with the horse. "Where is she, Parsifal? Where are they both?"

A mournful whinny was his reply. Unable to process the loss of Jael, Aries, and Iyna on the journey, Parsifal was now feeling the full impact of their loss. He stamped his hooves and butted against the sides of his stall, eyes rolling back in his head. Parke reached out a hand humming the notes to Jael's favorite melody. She constantly hummed it when she was thinking or just puttering around. It was such a part of who she was that she unconsciously sent it out around her. The melody was simple and sweet. It did not do much but enhance the colors around her and make the breeze smell sweeter, but it was HER. It was hugs and smiles and kind assurances. The essence of what made her Jael. Parsifal stopped and listened, his chest heaving. He took a few steps and met Parke's hand just over the railing to the stall and allowed the sound to wash over him.

From across the stable, Palmer saw the entire interaction and witnessed the silent tears tracking down Parke's cheeks as he comforted the horse. Feeling like an interloper, he quietly left the stable to wait outside. Several minutes later, Master Parke emerged and stated that Parsifal was sleeping and asked that he not be woken unless the children asked to see him. His calm demeanor was belied by his red rimmed eyes. Both trekked back to the gate house side by side.

"From what I saw, I take it you know this horse and his mistress?" Palmer began slowly.

"Yes, I did." Master Parke supplied, looking decades older than earlier, weighed down by grief. "Jael and her bondmate, Aries, were my students in the last cycle. She was a formidable vocalist. The most powerful we had ever trained. Reminded me of my mother, actually." Parke almost quirked a smile at the thought. "Jael came to us as a child and she was trained through the disciplines and passed her acolyte test at the top of her class without even trying. But she lacked confidence in her abilities. It was as though they came so easily to her that she could not accept how unique she was. Aries came to us at almost sixteen. He was old enough that we almost didn't train him, but as a canticle, he was just too valuable to ignore. They bonded almost as soon as we tested them together. Instead of increasing her confidence, the presence of a bond seemed to make Jael more fearful. She feared losing her mate and her protective nature surfaced.

Just before we could sense the next cycle end, Jael convinced Aries to flee. She knew they would be the ones to face Rasulo and it was too much for her. The fast pace of the current cycle is a direct result. Scoria and Fairn were lucky to stop Rasulo and end the last cycle. But he has arisen faster, as he was barely contained and managed to retain a fair amount of his power." Parke glanced back at the stable and continued.

"Now to Parsifal. He was given to Jael as a foal after she passed her acolyte test. It is common for students to keep familiars, but she had never searched for one. When that horse was born, she was in the stable and his first steps were away from his mother and toward Jael. Their friendship was deep and trusting. Jael didn't even have to break him to a saddle. He just accepted that she belonged with him. Of course, he didn't take to Aries until after Jael accepted him as her bondmate. Once he accepted his mistress' mate, he treated Aries much the same. He herded them everywhere and checked in on them constantly. I can only imagine how he treats Jael's children." Parke let out a brief chuff. "I would hazard you had a hard time putting the children in a room he couldn't access."

"You are right there. The horse, I mean Parsifal, only let us put them in a room once the older girl and the faerydae reassured him. She was asleep on her feet, but stopped to give him a pat and send him to the stables. He was...reluctant."

"Mayhap he will find rest now. He looks like he has been going for days or weeks. I doubt we will ever know for sure where those two managed to hide away. The oldest girl likely won't know much and I would feel terrible questioning her in any event." Master Parke stopped in his tracks and turned to face the Captain. "Did you say faerydae?" His wide eyes betrayed his disbelief.

"Oddest thing ever. The younger girl has a black Faerydae that follows her everywhere and will only communicate with her or, occasionally, the horse. When he talks, it sounds like water or bells. She answers verbally, but they do a lot of staring at each other. He has no interest in the older girl. I don't think he will agree to be separated from his charge. The little one called him 'Nyx' at one point and he rode on her shoulder."

"No one has seen a faerydae in a hundred years. They don't like any kind of humans, dwarves, or elves. Not to mention the Mer would rarely have an opportunity to interact. We will have to see what Lucia thinks. She has made a study of the creatures as a hobby. I honestly never thought it would be useful. She will be insufferable about it."

At the gatehouse, the pair was quietly approached by a guardsman and informed that the children were awake, clean, and eating a substantial meal. The older girl had her long brown hair pulled back in a loose tail at the base of her neck. She watched the two men enter with wary, red-rimmed, hazel eyes. Her younger sister had her blue-black hair neatly braided and the dark eyes darted about the room taking in every detail. The dusky Faerydae sat beside her plate and prodded her to eat with an urgent tinkle. She snapped her eyes to him and he patted her arm while pushing some fruit toward her.

"Hullo, ladies. My name is Parke. I knew your parents. In fact, I was their teacher. May I have your names?" Parke used his 'welcome-to-the-first-day-of-class' voice in an attempt to re-assure them.

"Safara," stated the flat voice, as she pointed at herself. She briefly gestured at her sister, "This is Ryl. We lost Mama, Papa, and Iyna." Her voice had increased in pitch as she spoke and the candles on the table sputtered and flared up. The four nearest her burnt through completely. Parke quickly doused the table under the candles with water. Ryl stared at her sister indicating that this was not a regular occurrence.

"I am deeply sorry for your loss." He stated uneasily, awkward in the face of their grief.

Palmer quietly replaced the other candles with enclosed lanterns for the time being and indicated that Jameson should move to comfort the girls with a confused jerk of his head. Jameson slightly rolled her eyes at him, as she already had Ryl practically in her lap. She compromised by shifting Ryl across her lap and cuddled a child to either side. Both girls folded into her sides and buried their faces against her tunic.

"I would like for both of you to come and live at the school your parents attended. We have classes for children of all ages and you will both find friends in your classes and be able to spend as much time together as you need. Many of the people at Sonaris knew your parents and will be glad you are with us." Master Parke spoke encouragingly and Safara began to peek out from Jameson's side.

"Ryl stays with me and Parsifal." It was a statement and not a question.

Parke's heart broke as he saw her father's face staring out at him. Just as determined as Aries had ever been, but with a hint of Jael's reluctance. "Yes, child. Sisters should stay together, just as brothers should. My younger brother, Deckard, is also at the school. We have never been apart for more than a few days and I would wish that for you and your sister, as well."

"Sisters," corrected Ryl so quietly that they almost missed it. "I has sisters, Fara and Iyna. But Iyna got eaten by a bush and then gone. I shouldn't have left to tell Mama. That's when I lost all of them." The child began to cry again and Fara moved to her sister with Nyx chiming in gently. Clearly, neither girl was ready to say more.

Parke moved directly across the table from the girls and leaned across to place a gentle hand on each of their arms humming the same tune for them that he had for Parsifal. Both girls relaxed, but still held on to each other while looking at him in disbelief.

"We will have to get you to the school where you can see where your dear Mama grew up and met your Papa. We will leave in the morning once Parsifal is more rested. He has just fallen asleep." His eyes crinkled reassuringly and he left to oversee preparations for the morning.

❋ ❋ ❋

Morning dawned swiftly with a misty haze hanging over the guard tower yard. Master Parke had requested that Jameson be reassigned to the school by Captain Palmer, which was quickly approved. The girls were still painfully thin, but they looked somewhat rested and Parsifal was relieved to see them again. Safara patted his neck and Ryl crowded next to his legs behind her sister. Both were relieved to complete the last leg of their journey and rest. Neither girl was excited about starting schooling, but they were grateful to know where they were going and that they would be cared for. Nyx was briefly introduced to Master Parke, but showed no interest in furthering the relationship once he determined that the older man was not a threat to his girl. The trip was several hours across the farmland that dotted the peninsula from The Band to Sonaris. Nyx zipped about bringing Ryl bits of flowers and grass to look at. He occasionally relaxed in his old spot between Parsifal's ears. During a rest, Parke pointed out the distant shining spires of the school to them. Eight tall silver towers thrust into the morning light. The walls caught the light and flung it back in all directions. Each tower was set equidistant from the next in a circle forming the points of an octagon. The towers differed in height, width, and function. The northern and southern most towers were the tallest with the east and west towers being the shortest. The towers in between were of a middling height, so that the line seemed to scallop down from the points. Running clockwise from the north, the towers alternated between practical studies buildings and residential: Linguistics, Neophyte's

Tower, Sonics, Instructors' Tower, Chorale, Stables, Focus, and Acolyte's Tower.

Upon arrival, Parsifal was assigned his old stall and paddock. He seemed at home, but wary. Several of the horses in surrounding stalls were friends and despite his sadness, he was comforted by his old herd. Safara held Ryl's hand and watched as he settled back in. Nyx moved inside the pack to give them some privacy. Both girls moved to stroke his side and eventually allowed themselves to be led away by Master Parke, who seemed in no rush and willing to let them move at their own pace. Jameson followed after stopping to have a word with the Stable Master about Parsifal's recent ordeal. The excitement of a new place helped push the sadness aside for a time. They moved out of the stables tower and along a direct path to the Neophyte's dorm. Each tower had a direct path to all of the others forming a complicated star pattern of pavement within the octagon containing the towers. This star, they would come to learn, was the school crest and was affixed above all the entrances to each tower.

"Your rooms will be in this tower. Yours' as well, Jameson," said Master Parke as the guardswoman joined them. He indicated the middle height building in front of them with a flora and fauna theme etched into the outer façade. Animals and plants of all kinds wound their way up the building to its flat roof. Windows and balconies poked out at regular intervals and several held students that were talking or playing. A ripple of water appeared overhead in the form of a small wren. Just as they walked underneath, its form fell apart, soaking three of them and barely missing Master Parke who had managed to blow away the water above him with a burst of song. Nyx shot out from the pack and clanged his fury at their wetting.

"Terris!" he shouted, eyeing a boy of around twelve years old a few balconies up from the first floor. A wild mop of brown hair appeared over the railing followed by large blue eyes and a lopsided grin.

"Hullo, Dad!" The voice did not sound at all contrite. "I didn't see you there. Did you like my bird?"

"Bad form to conveniently lose control just over our heads, son. Come down and apologize to our newest students and Guardswoman Jameson. Safara, Ryl, I am so sorry for this." He tried his best to dry their faces with his cloak, only to have Nyx bat his hands away and wipe the largest splatters away with his wings. Both girls were soaked and grumpy. Ryl sniffed back a tear. Safara was in no mood to hear an apology. When the door opened and Terris loped out, she did not let him get a word out.

In a quiet, furious voice, Safara moved toe-to-toe and whispered, "That was not nice. My sister did nothing to deserve your bullying and we don't need your apology either." She gently took her sister's hand and purposefully pushed past the penitent boy. Jameson followed the girls inside with a brief, but hard stare at the boy. Nyx hung back and pinched Terris' ear hard causing him to yelp and jump away.

"Good for you, Safara." Jameson quietly encouraged her. "Protect what needs it and forget about what doesn't."

Master Parke quickly followed and told his son they would talk later and to go back to his room immediately. Terris had the good grace to look ashamed and knew his punishment would not be light. He sighed, gave the angry girl a chance to move through the entrance before he went to his room to wait.

The girls were brought to a pair of connecting rooms on the outer side of the tower. They were about three quarters of the way up the tower from the ground and the ocean spread out to the east. Each room contained a wardrobe, desk, bookshelf, and poster bed. A balcony was off of Safara's room where a large sea turtle spread across the exterior wall next to the door. The room was decorated with sea creatures and all of the fabrics were blue and green including a large plush rug on the floor. Ryl's room had a spacious window seat with a bookshelf built in on one end. The thick curtains could be pulled shut to completely separate the seat from the room. The casing around the window was covered in flowering vines and butterflies. The carvings from the outside crossed behind the glass and crept into the room's wood trim. The flowers were yellow and pink and the butterflies were vibrant orange and blue. The rug and bed hangings mimicked the trim and made for a happy, peaceful space. Taking a wedge out of each room, there was a shared bathroom with its own window facing the sea. It contained a commode and large copper tub for bathing. Neither child had ever seen such a place and they were silent for a moment before running all over the rooms calling out their new discoveries and rushing to see what the other was doing. Master Parke left for a meeting after a few minutes and informed the girls he would see them for dinner. Jameson's room was down the hall a couple of doors. She left to change after finding towels and clothing for each girl in their rooms. Once they were dry again, Safara and Ryl climbed into one of the beds and slept. Nyx kept up a gentle chiming noise until both were asleep and then scoped out his own hideaway in Ryl's room, high on a bookshelf inside a flower shaped vase.

Hours later, Jameson gently knocked on the door. She entered when there was no answer and found Ryl still asleep on the bed. Safara had relocated to the balcony and was curled up in a chair staring toward the sea. The eastern view did not reveal the full force of the sunset, but the approach of night was like a warm blanket slowly being pulled over the ocean and landscape. The distant slap of waves against the cliffs was hypnotic and for the first time since their meeting, Safara looked peaceful.

"It's almost time for dinner, little one." Jameson called from the door in a hushed voice. "I will wake and dress your sister, but we should head down soon."

Safara faintly grunted an acknowledgement. She slowly moved inside the room and pulled the door closed. Dim lanterns illuminated the room and helped dispel the long shadows created by the window.

"How long will we stay here?" she asked in a normal voice.

"I would imagine until you complete your training at the school. I loved living here during school and consider Sonaris my home. It is odd at first, but you will enjoy learning new things and making new friends. This place will be your home and the students and staff here will be your family." Jameson answered in a reassuring voice as she maneuvered a sleepy 5 year-old into a new tunic and leggings. Ryl could barely stand and was basically folded over Jameson's lap trying to wake up. "Come on, jelly-legs. Stand up for me. There's a girl. Now, let's get you two some dinner and we can worry about classes in the morning."

The trio headed for the stairs and soon joined the rest of the Neophyte's dorm in the common rooms at the base of the tower. Both girls were a little overwhelmed, as they had never seen so many children in all their lives. The room was long and low with arched beams that met in a point at the ceiling. Tables of all shapes and sizes scattered about the room mixed with chairs and comfortable sofas. Fireplaces were set into the walls at regular intervals each with a different theme based on the basic elements: fire, water, wind, and earth. Children milled around. Some ate and others studied, still others played games and chased each other around. At precisely 6 o'clock a horn sounded and all the children quieted. Master Parke came through the door with another man around his age. Both had similar height and build, but Master Parke had black hair and the other man had tightly curled reddish hair and freckles. Their expressions could not have been more different, but they possessed the same brown, almond shaped eyes and golden brown skin. Master Parke told the children to settle and find seats at a table. Then he gestured to the other man, his brother, and said, "Might as well start, Deckard. They won't ever be quieter than this."

The other man, Deckard, smiled widely and started a praise to Stahd, the Angel of the Heavens. "Stahd, defend and guide us. Show us how to best heal and protect this land. Hearers all and Singers few, we listen for echoes of you." He ended with a quick flourish that flared all the fireplaces and lanterns to full burn. The meal arrived quickly. It was simple, but plentiful. Deckard's face lit with a kind smile when he found Safara and Ryl in the crowd. He made his way over and sat with them, quietly introducing them to the other students at the table. There was a young Mer girl named Ayo who was also eight and just starting at the school. Her long blue hair had tones of green and brown mixed in. It almost floated around her shoulders, as though it forgot that she was no longer in water. Ayo was slightly shorter than Safara and spoke in a thin, reedy voice.

"I saw you come in. I'm sorry about your wetting. I tried to catch the water, but I'm not very good yet. Next time, I'll keep you dry. Water likes me." She laughed a little as though her joke was quite funny. Safara let out a slight giggle and decided she liked this girl.

"I don't know what likes me, but that water just made me mad. That boy was rude." Safara pulled a face and set her new friends laughing as she caught Terris watching them from across the room.

"Yes, I heard about my nephew's escapade. I am sorry. He will be on his best behavior, but I have a feeling he was trying to show off for his father and the new students. Didn't go as he planned." Deckard's laugh boomed across the table and earned him a betrayed look from Terris. The uncle just laughed harder and saluted his nephew with his water glass. "Don't hold it against him; he can be quite thoughtful when he tries."

Safara had already decided that she liked this new person

and agreed to move on from the incident, although she secretly knew she could not forget the crushed look on Ryl's face and determined to avoid the boy when possible.

* * *

Over the next few days, Ryl and Safara found a rhythm. Their sadness slowly gave way to acceptance and they both focused on making friends and a home in Sonaris. Safara could be found with Ayo more often than not, as all of their classes and free periods were together. Ryl was with them as much as possible, but eventually she too found friends closer to her age.

After a month or so, Safara found her pack under the bed and realized it was not completely empty. In one small side pocket, she found three leather necklaces: one for her and one for each of the twins. They were leather with the most beautiful beading. Each girl's name was embroidered with a different motif. Safara's had red fire berries and the colors of the sunset. Ryl's had lovely violets and lilies of the valley. Finally, Iyna's had calming shades of blue in a wave pattern. Each was perfect for the intended recipient. Safara remembered this was the pack her father took on his last trip to the coast and decided he must have forgotten about them. She hugged her necklace tight and felt loved, as though her father approved of their new home.

At the bottom of the pack, she found her mother's journal. It had been beaten around and a few pages were water damaged. Safara started to read the first few entries, but soon gave up as she did not know the people it was talking about or why her mother seemed to care so much about them. She sensibly took the journal to her next class in Sonics and gave it to Master Deckard. He asked permission to read the journal and promised to keep it safe for the sisters until they were older. Safara quickly agreed and took her seat by Ayo. Classes were small with no more than ten or so students sitting in a half circle around the room. Master Deckard moved to the lectern at the front of the room.

"Good morning, all! We have now reached a point in your training where we need to delve into the topic of Sonics. All of you can hear the Song; Sonics will help you learn to manipulate it. If you can find your way to the part of the Song that is influencing specific materials close by, you can modify that portion of the Song to your purpose. Many Hearers and Users show an affinity to different elements in particular based on their personality or their style of melody. The basic elements Earth, Fire, Air, and Water are the easiest to learn initially. For example, I have noticed that Ayo, unsurprisingly, has an affinity for water. Water responds to her better than any other element. I, personally, prefer wind, but can with difficulty, work with water. Still other Users can use plants, animals, or shadows. It all goes back to what portions of the Song you hear best and where you can insert yourself. It is rare for a student to show promise in more than a few portions of the Song, but just because you cannot manipulate a portion of it does not mean you cannot learn to hear it. My mother was a talented Canticle who worked best with wind and the laws of nature. She could manipulate not only how plants grew, but affect how a rock fell, or how much an object weighed. My father was her pairbonded Vocalist. He was a fire and earth specialist. When the two of them worked together, my father would form a construct out of earth or fire and my mother would refine it. The façades on each of the towers reflect their work. It was how they practiced together. The earth and sand melted by fire prepared for work by my father, but the patterns and motifs were created by my mother's imagination and manipulated into their shapes by her guidance." Here Deckard paused for a moment and moved from behind the lectern.

"All Users can influence the Song with varying degrees of success, you see. For example, I have never in all my life met a User as skilled with fire as Safara's mother, Jael. She could burn a hole through a metal plate, just like a cannon shot from one hundred feet away,\ with one peep of song. Absolutely terrifying. On her own she was a force, but once she bonded her potential grew exponentially. We are stronger as a team, when we work together. Whether that is through a pair bond or a chorale is immaterial; the rule remains the same. Songsmithing also involves weaving your song with others'. When you combine with a shared focus almost anything is possible. This school was built by the first Sonaran Chorale and it has endured for hundreds of years and through six cycles. When Jael bonded with Aries, her firepower was channeled and focused. She could use her fire for blacksmithing or in one incident, a firebreak that saved a farming village from a wildfire." Safara was intent on every word of the class, especially the portions that focused on her parents. Of course she knew they could use the Song, but they rarely spoke of their time at the school or what life was like before they created the homestead. It made her wonder why they left at all, but the topic shifted and moved on without answering that question.

"Pair bonding happens between a Vocalist and a Canticle. This is a match made for life. If you are blessed with one, you will never have another. It is the most sacred and rare bond we have. It can happen between any two people, although it is most common between romantic pairs. But in the case of some, it is a sibling or close friend. In one case, a pairbond was forced and it has endured, but this was an extreme circumstance and that is not a route I would recommend. As Canticles are rare, it is unusual for them to be unpaired. The school will test pairs together to see if a bond is viable, but usually the process happens on its own. My parents were a bonded pair, but neither my brother nor myself have ever bonded with a Canticle. We can work with a chorus or individually with a Canticle, but without the bond, the corroboration will never be the great work it could be. Now we are going to test different elements with each of you and see which respond best. This is not a definitive test and you could show promise in any area. The best person to determine your abilities is you. Now split into pairs and each take a tray from the table by the window. Each of the four main elements is represented. See what you can do and above all LISTEN."

All of the students split into pairs, Ayo and Safara grabbed the tray nearest them and headed to the back of the room and huddled into a niche. On the tray was a small bowl of water, another of dirt, a pinwheel, and two candles.

"Do you want me to go first?" Ayo asked, picking up the bowl of water while Safara lit the thin tapered candle.

"Sure. I like seeing you play with water," Safara agreed.

Ayo let out a light sigh of music and pulled a stream of water up out of the glass and into the palm of her hand. With a slight change to her tone, the water contracted into a small swirling ball. She rolled it back and forth across her palm. When she stopped her song, the water splattered against the tray.

"You try," she encouraged.

Safara tried to emulate Ayo's tone and rhythm, but it felt off. The water remaining in the cup did not move.

"Listen!" came the reminder from the front of the room. She tried again. This time she felt a small tug in her lower register. She let out a low, deep tone and the candle flared up almost a foot and burned out the wick. Ayo leapt back barely keeping her eyebrows from being singed.

"I think you heard the fire, not water, Fara. Maybe we should leave that other candle alone for now."

Safara quietly apologized and agreed. She tried again with the water. Now that the flame was out she heard a lighter tone and reached out to it with a small peep. The bowl of dirt turned on it's side and clattered to the floor leaving the girls and cushions covered in sand and tiny rocks.

"Not that either!" Safara grunted. She wanted to be able to make pretty shapes with water as Ayo did, but apparently the water would not talk to her. With her next try she managed to turn the head of the pinwheel held on the tray. It whirled round and round, but the closest she came with water was making the surface ripple, which may or may not have been her breath. For her part, Ayo could also manipulate wind, but fire and earth did not respond to her either.

By the end of class, both girls were exhausted. Master Deckard commended all the students on their results and carefully recorded each success and to what extent they were able to control each of the basic elements. Safara was at the top of the class with some success in three of the four options, but the teacher was quick to remind all of them that there were more elements than just those four as possibilities. The students were too tired to say much to each other and all headed to the dorm for a nap before dinner.

Each day blended into the other in a maddening succession of busy days and restful nights. Both Safara and Ryl learned to hone their skills with the Song. Ryl had a marked aptitude for wind and light manipulation. Her predisposition was attributed to the Faerydae or possibly what attracted Nyx to her in the first place. The ability was unknown outside of the faerydae. Safara developed additional affinities for flora and fauna. Occasionally, Terris would wake up to a bed filled with acorns, although Sonaris had no oak trees. As her proficiency with fauna grew, Safara asked a squirrel to bring her a seed from one of the trees outside of The Band and she periodically influenced the small, potted tree to produce acorns, which her squirrels then deposited as directed. Terris understood the message. Although he was annoyed, he and Safara maintained a truce.

With time, the ache of missing loved ones lost its immediate edge, but the weight of their loss, especially Iyna was not something ever forgotten. On calm nights, Ryl would wake to feel a tremor on the wind. It was a soft disturbance, more a feeling than a sound, delicate and somehow reassuring. She knew that Iyna was out in the world. However, when she sent back a pulse along the connection, it immediately disconnected and she felt alone again. After a few months the feeling would return, suddenly and increasingly concentrated as though seeking her specifically. This pattern continued for years and Ryl faithfully reported each incident to Jameson, who had a semi-permanent post with the girls, and Master Lucia, who taught Focus. For her part, Lucia agreed with Ryl and searched for a pattern to determine if they could predict a contact, as a more experienced Hearer might be able to uncover better information.

CHAPTER 3

The carriage rocketed to Mount Profana at a decent clip along the cliff edge of Fel Loch. The term "road" was generous for the state of the area, but it was the quickest route around the mountains. Any other path would take the party too close to cities, farms, or trading centers. A herd of sycops moving through any territory would be noticed and reported to Sonaris for tracking. And no carriage, no matter who it carried could make it through the Spina Ardus. The surrounding forest was unusually quiet. Bird calls rang out in the approaching area only to fall silent as the carriage advanced. The limestone cliff above the loch angled downhill toward the delta of the River Fel. Mount Profana sat just to the south on the eastern side of the river. It was the tallest mountain in the Spina Ardus and stood off by itself.

Rasulo maintained his stronghold within the mine-riddled caves of the mountain. Traditionally, it provided cover as he raised his armies and recovered from the previous cycle. During the last conflict, Fairn and Scoria confronted him at the entrance to the warren, pulling the heart of the mountain around him, encasing him in rock and lava. While their desperate gambit worked, it failed to weaken him as much as in previous cycles. Rasulo was able to withstand the heat and pressure of his prison for several years before breaking out. Unfortunately, he managed to retain his physical body. He was gathering what he could of his scattered sycop forces back to the mountain and stumbling upon the homestead was a bonus for the trip. Any Users Rasulo encountered were conscripted into his service reconstructing his fortress and armies.

Rasulo twisted a grimace at the small, pale figure still asleep on the bench across from him. He could tell she was a vocalist, not the canticle he wanted, but talent was talent. He kept her asleep artificially. While not currently strong enough to present a challenge for any competent User, he was creative and she was a child. Had the mother only known how weak he was, she would have easily overpowered his defenses, resetting the cycle. Luckily, she had managed to do his job for him.

Days later, they came to the base of the mountain and started their mile long ascent to the entrance. The cave was wide and deep enough to hold several carts, carriages, and a stable area. The ochre walls were rough and dimly lit. Sycop guards moved to their positions around the room, as several other minions started unpacking boxes and removing several large duffels that hung on the outside of the carriage. Most were filled with artifacts, books, and supplies for the living quarters. But as the slaves reached for the last and heaviest, Rasulo ordered them back.

"Do not touch it. That is mine," he shouted. "You two!" He motioned to a couple of sycops standing near the door to the storage areas. "Take this sack carefully and put it in an empty cell. Do not open it. I will know if you do." As the guards hefted the bag down and carried it between them, the closely tied mouth opened slightly and left a dusting of ash on the ground. "I said carefully, you imbeciles! Pick it up."

With the residual effects of the sleep song fading, Iyna began to move and rolled off the bench with a loud thunk. She awoke confused to a strange man looking down at her. Weak with hunger and desperately thirsty, the girl screamed and called for her parents and sisters.

"Who do you call for, child? There is no one here but us and my minions." Rasulo attempted to be reassuring.

Iyna's cries continued unabated. "Momma! Papa! Ryl! Fara!" She screamed their names over and over with tears spilling down her cheeks until she made herself sick. Tumbling out of the coach, she tried to run for the mouth of the cave, but was stopped by a sycop trooper. His ugly, chalky face scared her as much as the absence of her family. She backed away into Rasulo's legs. He took her by the arm and guided her roughly up some stairs set into the wall of the cave. After several dank hallways and more stairs, he opened a heavy, wooden door and indicated that she should enter. An elderly dwarf and a young mer were the only occupants.

"This is the newest member of my collection. You may want to feed it before it passes out again." Rasulo shoved the reluctant child into the room and the mer darted forward to catch her before she hit her head on the edge of a bench. "She starts training tomorrow."

Iyna instinctually huddled behind the two new adults. Both were standing between her and their captor as the door slammed shut and the lock slid home. The room was dark, save a small window set high in the wall which allowed in some light, but did not offer a view. Torches were mounted on the wall, but neither was lit as it was late afternoon. The tan stone walls of the room were smooth. In contrast, the ceiling was covered in the original stalactites of the cavern from which the room was created. The room contained a rough table and several wooden benches and bed nooks lined the wall across from the door. Someone had set hand and foot holds into the wall below the high window.

The mer was a teenage girl, no more than fifteen years old. She was tall and slender with yellowy-green hair haphazardly pulled up in a top knot. She gently picked up Iyna and held her as she cried. The other occupant of the room was an elderly male dwarf. His long grey beard was braided carefully, but the rest of his hair was trimmed short along his skull. This revealed a collection of dark tattoos across his skull, down the back of his neck, and across his arms. He moved quickly to a cupboard gathering bread and water for the distraught child.

"There, there, sweet girl. We are here. It will be okay, fish." The mer, Samal, repeated herself over and over as she cuddled the child close rocking back and forth. She did not try to stop the tears or sadness, as her people believed that grief should be accepted if it is to be overcome. Once Iyna had subsided into hiccups and shuddering sighs, Samal introduced herself and Darek. The dwarf bowed in acknowledgement, but offered no interference with how Samal chose to treat the child.

"I'm Iyna," the small voice answered. Her white hair hung in her face and she was smudged with dirt and soot from head to toe. Her large light eyes were red rimmed and swollen. She asked for her parents again and then looked away to the window when both replied that they did not know anyone in the compound who had a child. After a time, Iyna was encouraged to eat and then coaxed into bed. She refused to sleep alone saying Ryl should be with her. She finally lay down once Samal offered to share a bed nook with her.

❈ ❈ ❈

Morning came early for them all. The night had been long and fretful. Iyna awoke every hour or so calling for her parents and sisters. At sunrise, a small shunt was opened and several gallons of water came sluicing down into a trench. Darek refilled the water pitchers and stowed them. He then pulled the curtain shut on his bed and gave both Samal and Iyna some privacy to wash. It took a while to get Iyna's hair anywhere close to clean, but in the end she was at least presentable with her hair combed and braided down her back. All three had the remainder of the bread from the day before as breakfast.

Just as they were finishing, the cell door crashed open and

three large sycops entered. Each guard took the arm of a different prisoner and hauled them off in different directions. Darek was led to a mine at the bottom of the complex and made to use his song to find coal and ore for the foundries. Samal was taken outside to the mills and she used water to increase the speed of the current. One of the mills was for grain and the other lumber. By the end of the day, both were generally too exhausted to even think about anything other than rest. Not to mention that constant use was wearing on their voices and focus was difficult over long periods of time.

Iyna was taken to a reception area and made to wait. After some time, Rasulo arrived and began to question her. But Iyna was in no mood to answer questions from the mean man, who threw her around the day before. In truth, she was terrified. He was old, but his age was more of an impression than actually shown. He just seemed changeless like the boulders near her house in the woods. His hair was long and lank. It hung down his back and did not look like he tended to it at all. Almost like it was forgotten. His robes were different than yesterday, now a deep red and belted at the waist with a gold cord. They also seemed ancient, but were pristine. No holes, tears, or worn spots to be seen. They were iridescent and shimmered as he walked. His eyes were disturbingly black with no differentiation between iris and pupil. It was impossible to look him directly in the eye, as one felt like the floor would open up and suck the entire world into the void. She shivered and hid behind a chair.

"That chair will not save you, child." Rasulo's voice rasped across the room and Iyna was compelled to move closer. "You intrigue me. Your mother burnt herself to a crisp to keep you whole and well despite knowing I was the one who killed your father. What makes you worth that?"

At this pronouncement, Iyna began to wail and call for her parents again. She was sick to her stomach and her head hurt, but she felt a tug like she had with the berry bush. Leaning into that portion of the song, she screamed. For a moment, nothing happened. Then with sudden force the stone floor was forced up and a wall emerged between Iyna and her captor. With a quick push of song, Rasulo swept the stone to the side and picked his way across the ruined tiles of the floor. He bent down in front of the exhausted and terrified child.

"That is it," he said with a satisfied expression. "Your mother knew what you were and you definitely have value to me. You will be trained and we will see what uses can be made of you. The mer and the dwarf both have affinities, but neither approaches this amount of raw power. We will test your affinities and train you as a vocalist. You lack the flair of a canticle, which is a pity, as I have never owned one." He shrugged off the thought and signaled the guard to take her away. "Take her to Faustus. He will start her training today. I want a full report on her affinities by the end of the week."

The lieutenant took her down the hall to a decidedly unimpressive room containing a table, two chairs, and a sideboard. The window faced due east and let in the midday light. A cruel, young man sat at the table pouring over a map. He looked annoyed and angry at the interruption to his studies.

"Another?" he whined at the guard, who only shrugged and harshly deposited Iyna into the wooden chair on the other side of the table.

"The Angelic wants reports on this one, all of her affinities by the end of the week," came the disinterested reply. He moved to the door and waited just outside.

"An assessment, it is then." Faustus leaned intimidatingly across the table and eyeing the tiny girl as though she were a worm or beetle pinned to a card. Iyna shrank back, but kept her eyes on this most recent unknown.

"Well, we should get this over with. Take a drink of water

and tell me what you have done to make the Master so interested in you." He indicated a tumbler of clear water sitting at the far end of the table. Iyna was unsure, but she reached forward and did as she was told.

"I was stuck in a berry bush. Ryl was on the other side; then I goed to sleep. When I woke up, no mama, or papa, or Ryl, or Fara." At this her lip started to tremble and a large tear ran down her round cheeks.

"None of that!" Faustus brought his hand down on the table with a thud. Iyna jumped in her seat and tried to stop crying. The more she tried, the harder the tears came.

"I-I-I wwwwaked up here and the mean man hurted my arm. I don't like him. So I built a wall this morning, but he knocked it away and made me come here." By this time, Iyna was equal parts angry and upset. This time she easily felt the song that built the wall and reached for it again.

"None of that!" Faustus yelled again. He threw himself across the table and clapped his hand roughly over her mouth. "We are going to see what abilities you have without attacking me, you termagant. I will have you muzzled if you try anything like that; besides, you are too young to be able to focus your affinities in any meaningful way. I will remove my hand and you will behave." Iyna's eyes were huge as she slowly nodded her head.

Faustus moved quickly to the side board and gathered several items on a tray. He plunked it down on the table in front of the wide-eyed girl and began shoving items in her face and telling her to sing. All bindings and auditory distractions had been removed from the training rooms to enable practice in any area. The rooms were high enough on the side of the mountain that the missing defence of the mountain's binding was not an issue. For the next several hours, he tested Iyna for all known affinities. Aside from earth and flora, she showed competence in fire and sound.

Sound was a strange affinity. When matched against another User, it could create a counterpoint to another melody and cancel it out. It required extreme focus and even those few who had the ability often could not manage to master the technique. To maintain a counterpoint with sound the User must have knowledge of the portion of the Song being called and the intended use of the melody developed. Outside of clairvoyance, the only way to use Sound was to be familiar with your opponent and their style. It was not a talent most invested their time into because of the obvious constraints. But Faustus knew his Master and his desire to possess the unique. Rasulo would find a way to use Iyna and her stable of talents for his purposes.

❋ ❋ ❋

Weeks blurred into months as Iyna studied with Faustus. Occasionally, there were whispers of new talent in the compound, but the child never saw them. Samal and Darek continued to be overworked. Neither was considered talented enough to receive extra training, so they were kept at their original tasks like oxen at a plow. Iyna grew protective of her new family and attempted to sneak them extra food and water, which was always available on the sideboard in the classroom. Many times she was caught, but she was resourceful and learned the patterns of the guards and Faustus to her benefit. Occasionally, Rasulo would participate in her training or perform an assessment. These sessions were always tense and Iyna hated the sight of the "crinkly, mean man" as she referred to him.

On warm days, Iyna was blindfolded and led out of the compound and off the mountain. Her affinity to flora could not be practiced without plants. Thus, she was taken to the forest to work with the added benefit of spending time outside and away from the dust and dirt of the constant construction inside the tunnels and halls. In the forest, Faustus carefully watched the girl, but generally let her have more freedom. She spent hours climbing trees, wading in the river, and interacting with the plants around her. Only in the forest did she find any peace. The plant life around Mount Profana was limited, but with Iyna's encouragement over time, the forest expanded slowly up the slopes. She encouraged trees to grow and ground cover to spread. Animal life did not venture closer. No matter how attractive the sides of the mountain became, no animals were foolish enough to voluntarily approach.

She often thought of her family and sometimes would send pulses of Sound out to Ryl wherever she was, hoping to feel a pulse back. Every time she attempted that sort of communication, Faustus was quick to interrupt her and immediately take her back to her cell. He felt it impossible that she would ever reach anyone, as she was too young to know anyone else's melodies or rhythms. But he still did not like her trying.

* * *

On a temperate spring day five years after her capture, Iyna was taken to the woods for a normal training day. A complement of sycop troops kept a loose ring around the girl about a hundred paces out from the center of a glade where Faustus was putting her through her paces. Today's test was to combine two plants and create a new species. The past two assignments with this ability were abject failures. The sludgy hunks of the previous attempts were still steaming nearby despite the rain the previous day.

"None of that!" Faustus yelled pointing at the black pile. "You need to focus. Your ability to control what you produce is a direct correlation to your focus. Without focus, you will fail every time."

"I can't focus with you constantly yelling in my face!" Iyna responded tartly. She was more than an arm's length away and did not fear an immediate physical reprisal for her outburst.

"In battle, you have no choice but to push out the distractions. You lose focus; you die, child." The response was bitter, as though he had personal experience with those losses. "Chaos exists to distract. Those who learn to push through will always be victorious. Again." He pointed at the two objects in her hand.

Iyna bent and planted both in the same shallow indentation at her feet. She then lightly covered them with dirt and began her melody. Her tune felt in the dirt and slowly melded the plants together as they pushed through the dirt. One was an acorn and the other a tulip bulb. As the oak tree grew, its bark took on a distinctive green hue and orange tulips sprouted all over its branches. The bell heads turned upside down as the tree rose from the earth. The flowers bowing toward the ground as though acknowledging the fledgling vocalist standing below. Briefly losing her melody, Iyna let out her first genuine laugh in ages. Oak leaves spread in all directions stretching to capture the sun. She clapped her hands in glee and danced beneath her tree as the trunk thickened and the canopy increased. She pressed her hand to the smooth, celery colored stalk and felt her song echoing within. Ripples of sound reverberated against her palm reassuringly. Iyna laughed again and allowed herself a brief twirl below the branches before gently ending her melody. As the fauna melody ended, the tree's growth arrested and resumed a normal pattern.

"Well enough for now. We will have to see if this combination is successful and lasts the week," said Faustus with a sneer. "Next time you will have to produce the same result while the sycops spar all around you. Back to the caves for you." The tutor indicated that Iyna had better move or she would be forced to do so. With a long look over her shoulder, the girl moved back along the trail to the compound.

Samal and Darek were just returning from their assignments for the day. Both looked exhausted as normal and their voices were quiet from overuse. Iyna used her song to make a fuelless fire under a pot. Once the water was boiling, she made tea for both of her friends and generally helped as best she could to ease their discomfort.

"I can't take this much more. Watching you both work yourselves mute for a monster. Why can't we just escape? Darek and I can tunnel through the stone to the outside and we can escape tonight." Iyna paced back and forth below the tiny window restlessly.

"Ach, child. It wouldn't work. Lovely thought, though it is. We are well and good trapped in this labyrinth." Darek indicated that she should seat herself. "That witch of an Angelic has us all caught proper. No one gets out. At least half of the Users in here can work with earth, so no use keeping us in cells made of dirt and rock for all this compound looks like it. He picks Profana for a reason. The rocks aren't right here. Work in the mines is hard, but we aren't moving the earth. We are summoning out ore and resources with our affinity. The earth here is heavy, cursed, if you ask me. You may be able to remove the layer of flooring, but the earth and rock below it is nothing we can manipulate." He took a moment to wet his mouth with the tea, buying himself a moment to think before he decided to reveal what he knew. Samal nodded her encouragement knowing Iyna was old enough to know just how bad it was. He sighed and reluctantly continued, careful to make eye contact and keep his voice steady.

"The truth is some Users have been here so long that they can't leave. Whatever binding is in this earth is toxic, poison, addictive. Those who work in the rock and mines have it worst. I have spent the last eight years in this mine. Slaving for a cause I hate and now I can't leave. When a User loses their voice completely, the sycops take them out of the mine and drag them away from the mountain. The farther they get the more the User fights, but not to get away. To get back. We are so addicted that we crave this hell. The binding warps our song, steals it, and leaves nothing but a mindless addiction in its place. I am sane enough as long as I have a constant supply of whatever the earth binding is, but I cannot leave. Samal is better off. She works outside in the wind and sun. I promise you two that we will figure some way out for you to get away. I am an old man and could not keep up, but we will sort something out."

When Iyna realized Darek's implication, she almost started to cry, but steeled herself and opted to lean across the table and take his hand. "We will all go," she stated fiercely. "There has to be a way to break this binding and I will find it. I will learn what I can from Faustus without being direct."

"Fish, do not be disappointed if it doesn't work," Samal started. She took Iyna's free hand and gave it a gentle squeeze. "We have been trying to find a way out since before you were brought here. Despite our limited contact with the others, we still pool our knowledge. The binding is ancient. Rasulo likely put it in place before the start of the cycles. There is no other reason why he would consistently make his base in the same location. From the bodies found in the mines and tunnels, we suspect he has been capturing and slaving Users for centuries. He is looking for something. We do not know what, but he is not moving on until he finds it. If he is here, none of us are going anywhere. His power grows every day and he keeps us segregated, tired, and afraid. I'm surprised he has left the three of us together for so long. Most are kept in pairs and those are rotated every year. They try to make the pairings unusual to ensure we inmates feel as lonely as possible." She shrugged at Darek. "I know it was a long time before I felt anywhere close to comfortable with a dwarf as a roommate. Aside from a common language, we are very different." Here she smiled. "But that is for the best. Unity, despite our differences, will be our best tool for maintaining ourselves and our sanity. Your strengths compliment my weaknesses and we became a family. I agree with Iyna; we will gather what information we can and all of us will make the attempt."

"I will attempt anything to be free of this place, but past failures make my success unlikely, just so we are all on the same page. Hope is a powerful motivator, but neither of you are to regret me if this turns out badly." Darek reached out to squeeze each of their hands and then stood to signal an end to the conversation. He climbed into his bed nook and closed the curtains just as he did every night leaving both Samal and Iyna a measure of privacy to get ready for bed.

Days later, Iyna was taken back out to the forest to continue training and to check the state of her tulip tree, as she called it. The tree was doing well and had maintained its form. Additionally, it attracted bees and other insects to the area as an interesting development. The bees flitted around the fist sized tulips pollinating as they went. Butterflies sunned themselves on the branches and dragonflies shot back and forth between the tree and the river not a stone's throw away. A fish jumped out of the water snapping unsuccessfully at one of the dragonflies narrowly missing its chance at lunch.

Iyna thoroughly inspected the tree with the guards and Faustus standing off to the side. No decay spots were visible on the smooth trunk. A pattern similar to bark decorated the exterior of the tree, but it was glossy and supple like a tulip stalk. Pressing her hand firmly against the pseudo-stem, she felt her tune, rather than heard it. The echo was still present deep within the plant flowing through its channels, leaves, and flowers. She bent and performed the same assessment on the ground around the tree. The echo was more faint, but still present. Whatever her song did for the tree, it had spread to the immediate area. As she fanned out around the glade, it appeared that the effect lasted for around a forty foot radius around the tree. That circle was the only area that attracted the insects. Once the echo faded, the bugs moved no further. She kept her observations to herself and warily watched Faustus complete his circuit around the tree.

"I think it took, sir." She offered quietly.

"Perhaps," he said distractedly. "Time will tell if this combination is successful. While this was a useful demonstration of your abilities, there is no practical application for this tree. If it survives the year, I will recommend Rasulo come out to assess. Who knows what combinations are possible if you can combine a seed and bulb?" This last he said more to himself than his audience. He shook his head and brought his thoughts back to the present and looked Iyna in the eye. "Maybe you aren't completely without use. See if you can do it again." He threw another acorn and bulb at her feet. "Get started."

True to his word the week before, the sycops took up positions around the glade and started a skirmish. Boots crushing the plant life and tearing into the dirt below. The sunny glade quickly lost its appeal in the angry melee. Actual sycop training was hard to watch. Their society placed a very low value on life. If a grown sycop was unable to fight or defend themselves, the others would not offer assistance or help. Training was no different. Sparring matches ended at first blood only because Rasulo forbade them from killing each other. They would prefer to kill or be killed even in training. Their only concession to training was that the weaker or lower rank must offer the challenge. The more formidable the sycop the more challengers they have. The most battle hardened eventually cannot offer challenges any more, only accept them, until the inevitable day they fail.

Iyna quickly bent and covered her acorn and bulb with dirt. Two sycops charged each other swinging their weapons wildly. She barely tumbled out of the way in time. Within seconds the glade erupted into mass chaos, trampling feet, flailing weapons, and battle calls from all sides. The young girl was terrified and backed up until she hit her tree. Although not a target, the noise was deafening and she could not hear any remnant of the Song, neither flora nor other strain. Her breath came in short gasps as the fighting continued. She closed her eyes and tried to concentrate, but every time she heard a note of the melody she wanted either a sword arced over her head or a scream let loose in her ear. She sank to the ground against the trunk of the tree and pulled her knees up to cover her face.

"Focus, girl!" Faustus shouted over the din. He used wind to lift himself over the group. *Whack!* Iyna felt a sting on her cheek near her ear. She raised her hand and wiped blood away. Faustus pelted her with stones from above and shouted at her to move on with the exercise. "They have been instructed not to hurt you…this time." Iyna rolled her eyes. She had never seen the tutor enjoying himself so much. He kept himself well above the melee and watched as she struggled.

She got on her hands and knees and crawled back out toward the spot. The pile of dirt was trampled flat. Crawling with her hands against the ground, she could feel her melody from the day before reverberating. A small plant speared its way out of the ground where she had buried the seeds. Hands firmly in the dirt she amplified the echoes and focused them on the plant pushing through. It began to grow, slowly at first but gaining speed as her confidence increased. *Whack! Ping!* Pebbles from above smacked her in the face and the back of the head. She ignored them. Once the tree had more height, she could use it to block out her bullying tutor. She dodged a sparring pair as a sword came dangerously close to her shoulder. The pair began wrestling and she almost lost the melody as they came rolling past. The one on the bottom misjudged his aim and punched her in the thigh. Iyna screamed and covered her leg, yelping in pain. She gritted her teeth and refocused. The tulips on this tree were pink and stripped from the end of each petal to the center with yellow. Despite the battle, the bees quickly moved on to this tree, as well. For the next ten minutes, she sang and dodged until it was a similar size to the other. Gradually, she pulled her melody back and stopped. She was a sweaty, dirty mess from the effort. Her leg was sore and useless as she pulled herself above the fray and into the branches above. Breathing heavily, she willed herself to calm down as she watched the fighting and tried to detach. When it was over, she lowered herself gingerly to the ground and waited for Faustus to approach.

"This one took longer," came the snide, expected remark accompanied by a smarting slap to the back of her head. "You need to LISTEN." He leaned menacingly over her and yelled. "Nothing matters but the Song. Find it. Focus it. Use it. Hesitation is your worst enemy. Just start and the Song will guide you. Get back to the compound." He nodded to a sycop standing to the side. The guard grabbed her shoulder in his meaty paw and shoved her toward the warren entrance. She stumbled and cried out as her leg gave way. He picked her up and threw her over his shoulder without breaking stride. Iyna rubbed her leg and did her best to keep quiet. Sycops resented the Users in the compound both for their speech and affinities. Her leg jostled back and forth hitting the against her ride's armor. She muffled a whimper and tears pricked in her eyes. She looked back at her twin trees and thought of her sister. Ryl was alive. She knew it, could feel it. Although her calls were not answered, they had reached her sister. Iyna could tell that much. Until they could escape, she would focus on her lessons and learn everything she could about Profana. She had to believe an opportunity would present itself.

✳ ✳ ✳

He swept down the fortress stairs in a flurry of robes and winking shadows. The torch held carelessly in his hand. Most of the inhabitants were asleep or stationed at their posts for the night. The watch sounded off in the levels above, each returning their call to the watch leader. In a few minutes a patrol would round the corner ahead and sweep this section. Using careful timing and silent feet, Rasulo moved deeper and into the cellars and dungeons of Profana. Easing into the empty room, he quickly hefted the large sack off of the table at the side of the room. Layers of thick dust fell off in clumps and clung to his robes and shoes as he moved back toward the door. A mote of light appeared around the corner as he darted across the hall and down yet another set of stairs bowed under the weight of his burden. The musty storage area at the bottom was practically empty other than a few barrels and other rubbish. A rat skittered across the floor and burrowed into the wall. Even he had not been in this particular section of the mountain for over a century. But he knew all the ways and passages around his home of almost a millennium and this was the quietest section of the compound.

He moved to the far wall and felt for the twisted, cruel Song of the mountain. His binding was heavy and malicious. It did not give up that which it held within its boundaries. He matched the binding note for note piercing its wall and then created a new corridor, the entrance hidden behind a false wall. This new space angled down and curved around to reduce line of sight. At the bottom he created a vault with a high ceiling. He carefully pulled a boulder out of the wall and placed it to one side to block the entrance when needed. Inside the room, a large pedestal erupted from the ground and he hefted his burden onto it. Dust and ash scattered in all directions upon contact. The torch found a home in a sconce on the wall. Ending his work, he pulled the mountain binding down and sealed the fissure he created around the new section.

Determinedly, he began unpacking the prized husk within, careful not to remove more of the top ash layer than was absolutely necessary. The lump was fused tightly together. Any observer would not have been able to guess the origin of the charcoal. Indeed had Rasulo not known himself he would never have been able to guess. Using his Song to soften the lump, he began to straighten sections and lay them out in their original form. The outer shell was hard, grey, and sooty. For hours he transformed and laid out his project; this artifact was the key.

He cackled quietly to himself as he went on humming to maintain his tune. *"Sheer brilliance and complete surprise,"* he mused to himself with a wicked smirk. This was what he needed to break the cycles and move on to a new and better order, his Order. He just needed to get it working again.

❋ ❋ ❋

Sunrise came to Profana just as on any other morning. The early morning light broke unenthusiastically against the rough brown stone and dirt of the mountain. Just beyond the morning rays, a shadow rustled through the darkness searching for a place to hide against the growing light. A tail whipped around the corner of a rock and a hint of whiskers appeared on the other side. She did not like this area of the mountains and wished to be away from the heaviness that warped the Song, pulling it to the center of the mountain. With a hiss, she darted between long shadows created by the rising sun and picked a way down the slope. At the bottom, two flowering trees appeared one pink and the other orange. Here was something to investigate. Cautiously, she approached and scented the air. It was different, fresher without the warp felt farther up the mountain side. As she set a foot near the twin trees, she felt a change in the Song, an echo of life and hope. The air and insects felt it too as they suddenly became lively.

Celeste neared the closest tree, the one with the pink flowers and rubbed her chin against its smooth trunk. With a leap, she jumped to the first branch and prowled her way around the branches feeling for the Song that established and maintained this curiosity. She batted lazily at a tulip and chuffed happily as it swung back toward her face. As the sun rose, she curled up into a ball high in the branches to wait for darkness.

Hours later, Faustus sent Iyna to the trees for an assessment. Both trees had withstood a full season of growth and the petals on the flowers were just starting to turn for the summer. As she approached the area, Iyna felt like something was different. Her trees seemed the same and the echo of her melody was still audible, but she felt less vulnerable than she had on her walk down the mountain side. With a happy chirp, she began to climb up the orange tree before the guards noticed what she was doing. They moved below the tree to make sure she could not get away, but otherwise left her to her own devices and eventually moved back to the perimeter. Sighing with happiness, the young girl leaned against her tree and let out a little trill of song aimed at the nearest tulip head and turned it purple. She continued playing with the color of that flower curious to see just how many changes she could make.

She felt the branches above her move suddenly and without wind to push them. Curious she looked up and saw two large yellow eyes peering out at her through the foliage. The vertical pupil slits gave them away as cat eyes, but no fur or face was visible other than a faint impression of movement. Iyna did not whimper or feel afraid, as this was the presence that made her feel less alone. The greenery moved slightly and wave of silver and gold appeared and moved down the head and body of the cat revealing it from tip to tail. Deep purring noises emanated from the cat's body as it edged closer to the child. When it was close enough to touch, it butted her hand with its forehead and let out a faint meow.

"Silly kitty," laughed Iyna as she petted the strange beast. The cat was easily the same size as she. It's fur was a mix of tawny gold and sparkling silver that reflected the few rays of sun that penetrated the canopy and flung them all about the bower. It had large, intelligent eyes momentarily closed as it enjoyed the light stroking along its head and upper back. "How did you come to be here?" A flick of the tail was her only answer, but Iyna did not mind. "You are so pretty. Look at your colors! I wonder what kind of cat you are, not a lion or a leopard certainly."

In fact, Celeste was a shadow lynx, a rare species of cat that generally lived high in the Spina Ardus. Occasionally, they were seen in lower altitudes during the winter, but she had ranged far during the cold season and was only now making her way back to her territory. Normally, the reclusive animals were shy around humans or other creatures, but the echoing song had a strong attraction for her. She spent the better part of the morning lazing about the branches feeling the soothing buzz deep within. Shadow Lynx fur was especially prized for its refractive properties, which the cats used to camouflage themselves against their predators or aid them when hunting their prey. The silver and gold colors were controlled by the cat and they could fade or appear at will.

Iyna reached out a tentative hand just as she used to do with the cats at the homestead long ago. A vague memory of Aries teaching her how to make friends with the barn cats flitted around her mind. Her father's laugh came from behind her, as he held her wrist, hand palm down to allow the pure white kitten to scent her fingers. She remembered giggling when the kitten bent its head in a demand for a petting. She smiled in recollection. The lynx was easily the size of a goat, but it acted much the same as the kitten. First scenting her fingers and then immediately requesting her affection. Within minutes, the cat was partially in the young girl's lap purring loudly and being given all of the attention it could desire. But the happy interlude could not last forever, as it was a training day. Celeste's tufted ears jerked forward the moment Faustus entered the perimeter. She hissed slightly and faded her colors until only her eyes were showing. Iyna shoved her back along the branch and hastily began to climb down, not wanting the tutor to discover her new friend. The girl knew she would not be permitted to keep her friend; indeed, she would never have wanted to subject the cat to life in the compound.

As she reached the ground, Faustus grabbed her forcefully by the arm and hauled her out into the open. Iyna felt rather than heard Celeste's protests at this treatment. She shot a rueful look over her shoulder with a quick shake of her head, hoping the lynx would remain where she was. Celeste opted to follow only part of the silent message. She remained hidden, but she descended the tree and followed.

"You are to remain where I can see you, girl." Faustus spat at Iyna in frustration. "I have little enough desire for these training sessions. The last thing I want is to waste my time chasing your skinny tail around the forest. The faster you listen the less time I have to put up with you and can put you back in your box where you belong." He paused to collect himself and began again in a calmer voice. "Today we are going to work on your earth talent. As you know, the soil of Profana is not conducive to manipulation with normal earth song and the training rooms are too small for this exercise. The root melody of the ground has been changed by the Master himself, so we must travel here to find untainted earth."

He caught himself rambling and quickly returned to the topic at hand. "Earth is one of the four basic affinities. It is closely tied to flora and fauna, as well. You demonstrated a strong link to this kind of melody on your first day in the compound, but we have not explored it much since, as the Master sees it as pedantic and common. However, earth is powerful. It is the most enduring of the elements and can be used in many applications from construction to battle and even healing. It is thought that the dwarves have the greatest affinity for the earth as they were formed directly from it by the Angelic choir. My research has borne that out as an accepted fact, but humans also possess a strong bent in that direction. Personality also plays a role in what elements an individual can manipulate. Those who can use earth tend to be loyal and strong. Fire Users are passionate and protective. Water shows flexibility and thoughtfulness. Wind manipulators tend to be broadminded and temperate. However as your personality traits play into which abilities you can access, they will also influence your style of use. Some vocalists have a great lung capacity and will simply bowl their opponents over through sheer strength, hoping the longevity of their breath support will allow an attack to penetrate when the other takes a new breath. This approach can work, but it is banal and easily deflected. Overwhelming volume is also a popular attack. You will be better than that."

"Focus is where the true artist puts their trust. Know your preferred style and how you best manipulate the element you have chosen to find chinks in a wall of sound. Learn to produce a melody, but also listen to those around you. For example, if they strike out with fire, but their vibrato is sloppy, you can hit back with a quick burst of water or wind using a toned vibrato that slips through their wave and extinguishes it at the source. It is difficult to do, as sustained output is not always possible. Your voice will tire easily and prolonged use without proper technique will do lasting, unalterable damage. It is much better to lash out fast and stave off a protracted fight. Now we will begin some exercises. For this first, you are to summon a single stone to lift off the ground and hover at your eye level. The size of the stone is irrelevant at first, but for the second exercise it will need to be smaller than a walnut, so keep that in mind. Feel for the stone you picked and call to its essence. It will respond to you."

Iyna reached with a soft, but sonorous tone for a small blue rock the size of a snail's shell near her feet. She focused all she had at it and was grateful when it started to lift in response to her summons. She increased her volume and immediately regretted it, as the pebble shot into the air and straight into her forehead pinging away and landing back at her feet in the grass. Faustus laughed wickedly and kept her at this task for the rest of the afternoon until she could reliably lift any of the stones in the area and hold them at eye level for a full breath. The entire time Iyna could feel Celeste watching her from her perch in the tree to which she had returned when Faustus started his lecture. The lynx barely moved other than the occasional twitch of her tail and ears. Iyna could not see the cat, but could feel her basic, instinctual drives.

Iyna and the tutor returned with their guard to the glade every day for months to practice earth and eventually fire manipulation, as Faustus refused to share his practice space in the compound with a child. Rasulo left them alone for training as long as Iyna's progress continued. Every day, the lynx appeared in the trees and even during winter, Celeste stayed and observed training. Months stretched into years as the bond grew steadily between the two. They rarely acknowledged each other as they almost always had company, but both derived comfort from the connection.

CHAPTER 4

In the beginning, the Radix Cordam began the Song. Every living thing in the world and of the world was conceived in its intricate melody and burgeoning harmonies. The Pond was the nexus of his work, echoing and amplifying the intent and force of his will over time and space. Oceans spread and mountains rose. For a small eternity, he worked alone and laid a firm foundation for all that he imagined this world would be. Note after note reverberated around him, all in set patterns that he dictated.

But as time went on, he became lonely and desired others to aid in his grand work. He turned to the river that flowed from the Pond and introduced a new melody while focusing on the rocks, logs, and sand of the river bank. Vaguely humanoid forms shaped and arose from the natural objects scattered about; dozens upon dozens shot up. Different textures, colors, heights, and shapes melded together as they all took a collective first breath. He smiled and they all smiled back.

"My children, I have made this world for us to explore, define, and mold as we see fit. Each of you will be imbued with a measure of my creativity and abilities. Go out into this world and add to my Song. Make every forest, field, and flower a work of art for the people I will create for it." His voice boomed across the crowd as he walked among them, noting every face and personality. Some were merry and bounced with excitement. Others were serious and thoughtful. But one in the middle of the pack was capricious and mischievous.

Thus the Angelics were born or made; ten dozen distinct, free-thinking entities all working to create a perfect world using the Song established by their creator. Groups split off and some went to carve out valleys and bury ore in the mountains. Another went to create sea monsters. Still others worked on sunsets and gentle breezes. Over the years, each Angelic determined their specific area of interest and worked to make theirs the best, most perfect for the Radix Cordam and his new people.

By this time, the choir had chosen names for each other. Claudia loved animals, especially those that lived in the ground. She amused herself by creating large burrows for her weasels, groundhogs, and ants. Marius was a grand builder, who enjoyed working with stone. He made cairns of rock that seemed to sway in the wind and yet never tumble to the ground. Juliana loved colors and ensured fields and forests alike teemed with colorful flowers, plants, and bugs. Stahd focused on light, as it was the root of life. He proved himself to be so careful and meticulous that the Radix let him set the heavens and determine the placement of the stars to tell stories and pass the seasons for the people. Rasulo was crafty and brought variety to all projects; although, he rarely focused on one area for long. He established the element of surprise within Telaria, introducing everything from rainbows after storms to volcanos.

During this time, the Radix Cordam relaxed his supervision over the Angelics trusting them to continue to structure and hone the world he began. Instead, he focused his new melodies on sentient life, creating one species to represent each of the main elements of life. Dwarves were born with the durability and steadiness of the earth. Mer had the flexibility of water. Fiery humans were protective and passionate, while the elves were broadminded and focused as a sharp wind. Additionally, he made the faerydae to compliment the light and centaurs to watch the skies. He doted equally on his new creations delighting in creating a variety of forms and faces within each group. He watched them establish family groups and settlements ensuring that Telaria was able to provide for them and only instructing the Angelics when something in the environment needed tweaking to accommodate specific needs. It was a brief period of perfect harmony.

Eventually, Rasulo came to resent the people of Telaria and how they disturbed the Radix Cordam's focus on grand works. Their foibles and petty drama distracted the Creator from directing the Angelic choir to expand his power to new realms. They were an anchor holding the Radix in place. Rasulo felt stymied and restricted. Too many eyes were watching him, keeping him from fully experiencing the range of his talents. No, the Angelics and the Radix needed to move on. He had no interest in making something new, preferring existing works and corrupting them like a cancer.

In the still of the hour before dawn, he crept down to the Pond avoiding scattered sleeping forms and nocturnal animals. At the edge, the Song resonated with such ferocity he could almost touch it and see the vibrations in the air around him. He traced down a specific melody, one that controlled deep ocean currents. Pulling it out gently, he manipulated the tones and set several a half step lower than they had been, as accidentals. Inspected on its own, it would be difficult to determine the root of the problem due to the speed of the melody and how well it was buried. When combined with the other melodies of the sea, it created a subtle dissonance. Hali would not appreciate his modifications, but it was a start.

Over time, he added dissonance to most major systems of the world. The forests were overrun with rodents that ate the undergrowth. Mountains cracked savagely forming the ridges of the Spina Ardus. Each Angelic worked frantically to fix the faults in their areas. The faster they worked the more problems appeared. Rasulo offered to help many with their repairs and introduced compounding problems under the guise of aid, only the heavens remained untouched. Stahd's systems were built precisely and contained multiple redundancies to hold the world on its proper path. Any changes would be located and fixed immediately.

The people complained of the damage to their world. They became unhappy and in turn made the Radix Cordam frustrated. Initially, he worked to meet their expectations, but the demands only grew. Faced with endless whining and no gratitude, he cut off his Song and moved on to start his work again in another place. The echoes remained, but he refused to add more effort to an ungrateful world. Without his support and guidance, the Angelics began to leave. At first only one or two moved to follow the Radix Cordam, slowly the rest followed. Until finally, only Rasulo, Stahd, and Hali were left.

It never sat well with the Lady of the Seas that her waves were the start of the dissonance. She could hear it constantly. It fairly screamed at her across the ocean every time a wave crashed. She painstakingly pulled out each melody and examined them individually for a variance, but so far they all sounded as she made them. She sighed and sat on a rock in the dusk hearing her failure every time a wave met the rocks below. Stahd joined her sitting just off to one side.

"Any luck, my lady?" Stahd asked in his quiet, firm voice. His eyes were troubled and his heart heavy.

"None." She answered in a despairing tone. "Your heavens amble on in their perfection and yet this mean earth slips further toward chaos." She tried to contain her jealousy as she stared alternately at the appearing stars and her ocean. "So many have abandoned us. Most of our brothers and sisters left without a backward glance at the demise of their labors. And what of the people? The Radix created them, but they haven't the understanding to fix this world themselves. Were they created as nothing more than playthings? So easily discarded, as he moves on to the next shiny world."

"I would fix the dissonance if I could, Hali. You know

this," Stahd assured her. "But we are only treating symptoms. Even Rasulo can't seem to find the cause of these changes and he has been involved in more repairs than any other Angelic."

"How ironic that the master of surprise is the one focused on bringing stability to Telaria." Hali moved her gaze back to the distant horizon where the moon was just rising. She tilted her head to one side as she listened to the moon and the waves. "Stahd!" She whispered urgently. "Listen to my waves and your moon. What do you hear?"

"Did we not tune them when I was made lord of the sky?" he inquired after listening for a moment. "Your waves are flat. Not just flat," he said, listening more closely. "Are they in a different key?"

They had set the moon and waves to complement each other in perfect fourths so that one affected the other in a constant push and pull. The additional accidentals had shifted the melody just enough that it no longer harmonized. Hali pulled out the deep root melody of all waves and corrected it. Immediately, her waves fell in perfect time with the pull of the moon again and her ocean slipped back into its rhythm.

"How could it have slipped into a new key? Melodies don't change like that. Shift over time? Possibly. But that was intentional." She mused out loud. "It wasn't a completely new key. It was a few precisely placed flats that shifted its base slightly."

"Who had access?" Stahd hissed through clenched teeth and took a moment to think. A sudden realization slammed into his mind. "No, don't tell me. It was our good brother."

"Indeed. We are betrayed not only by our brother, but by our Radix and the rest of our kind. None cared enough to fight for this world, but I will see it restored. We must be quick." With that Hali took off along the beach toward the Pond knowing Rasulo would be lurking there. Her long legs ate up the miles without tiring. Her black curls streamed out behind her as her ebony eyes flashed with the rage of a thousand stormy seas. Stahd followed without comment willing to let her deal with their wayward brother and support as needed.

Reaching their destination with the moon still low in the sky, they found Rasulo spread out on a rock near the edge sampling different melodies for possibilities and grinning to himself as he changed them subtly and wove them back into the Song. Never one to admit his fault, he boldly met their gaze. Hali rushed at him, eyes wide, nostrils flared in rage. She stopped just short of striking range held back by Stahd. She growled. A snarl warped her beautiful face into a furious mask.

"And here we few are gathered at last," Rasulo sneered, twisting a new melody around his fingers as he taunted them.

"Put it back, brother. We can fix this world and leave it in peace." Stahd tried to defuse the escalating tension in the air.

"Or what, Stahd, most perfect of all creators? You could never delight in the unexpected or appreciate serendipity." Rasulo slowly stood and moved to place the rock between himself and an enraged Hali, while keeping an eye on both of them.

"Hardly serendipity with you forcing the alterations," Hali spat. "Nothing is more changeable than the sea, but rules must exist or the world will tear itself apart." She pulled her arm from Stahd's grasp and shifted to one side to block the miscreant from closer access to the Pond as Stahd countered the other direction.

"But that is the point, is it not? To experiment. To see how far we can push before all is lost. Why are we here if not to see how far is too far?" Rasulo responded by shifting his stance and gaze between his adversaries.

"And sacrifice the people of this world for what? A game of cosmic chance? No. I will not allow that their lives and our work are forfeit to your amusement."

Hali moved to the very edge of the water aiming to use its power to contain her brother. No other Angelic had ever been restrained or punished by the others and she hesitated as the weight of the necessity bore down on her. Hali's eyes closed and her features strained as she focused on her task. The shoreline of the Pond moved up around her feet leaving a peninsula of dry sand around her as it reached out to reclaim Rasulo and his abilities.

The corrupted Angelic was surprised by her resolve at enacting such a permanent solution to his antics. He reacted almost without thought and sprinted toward his sister with arms outstretched. Stahd let out a yell and her eyes opened just in time to see Rasulo bearing down on her. Startled, she lost her melody as he struck her full force. Her body flew several feet landing in the water, immediately dissolving her back into the essence of the Song as the waters closed over her.

"Hali!" Stahd screamed her name from the edge. Its boundaries increased by a miniscule amount and he took a hurried step back as his toes were singed. He could feel his connection to the Song leak away through his wounds. In his anger, he failed to notice that the loss continued after he moved from the water.

"Dark-hearted monster! You murdered our sister!" Stahd turned on his brother consumed by his fury. "You trick or corrupt everything you touch. Redemption is beyond your reach."

Shoulders hunched and staring across the glassy surface, Rasulo seemed stunned by his own actions before he gathered his wits. "Losses were expected," he stated flatly as he turned to his brother unprepared for the backdraft his thoughtless words provoked.

Without a sound, Stahd's rage-fueled focus enabled him to pull the moon into a lunar eclipse overhead. Unnatural shadows ate across the landscape consuming everything in their path. Stahd could not bring himself to end his own brother's life regardless of his actions, so he sought to imprison him. With the shadows rapidly approaching from behind, Stahd reached down and splashed a great handful of water at Rasulo, distracting him from the real threat. Screams mingled from both Angelics. Stahd lost his hand and Rasulo clutched his scorched neck and arms. The cost was enormous, but Rasulo was encased in shadows; his countenance frozen horrifically.

Stahd released his pull on the moon and shifted it back to its correct location in the heavens. The carnivorous shadows dissipated without a trace of their prey. The lone Angelic staggered slightly feeling his connection to the Song weaken with every step. For the first time since gaining sentience, the Lord of the Sky was unsure of how to proceed. How could he, damaged and broken, protect this world? Until this very encounter, they had not even known Angelics were vulnerable. Now in the space of an hour, one was dead, one banished, and one mortally wounded. His mind raced as he stumbled through the trees to the nearest settlement; a plan formed in his mind.

As dawn broke cold and grey across the horizon, Stahd staggered upon a handful of souls setting up for market day. At his appearance, they all stopped and gathered to render assistance. One kind woman wrapped his necrotic stump in a cloth. A young boy fetched a cup of water, as several men carried him inside the closest home. For a short while, it was mass chaos until a commanding figure stepped through the door and told everyone to hush. She was not especially tall or beautiful, but she was regal and her confidence oozed from every pore. Sybilla was the settlement leader and was in charge of directing the town's defense and industry since the Angelics left. Slightly widened eyes were the only sign of her surprise as she took stock of Stahd's condition. With a word, she dismissed everyone except her second, Sigurd. She began her inquiry immediately, barely waiting for the door to close behind the last eager observer.

"How have you come to be here? You were all thought

to be gone." Ever incisive, she cut through all pleasantries and straight to the meat of the issue.

Had he the strength, Stahd would have smiled. This was a person he could use to protect others. "We found him, the cause of the dissonance. My sister, Hali, was lost in the confrontation. Pushed into the Pond by the traitor, Rasulo. I have trapped him for now, at great cost to myself, as you can see. I will not survive for his eventual return." Stahd pushed through each sentence with effort. "You must prepare. I estimate his return within the next one hundred years at the next eclipse of the moon. I have pushed that eventually as far into the future as I could."

Alarmed, Sigurd spoke for the first time. "But you are essentially asking us to fight a god. What would you propose we do? Throw rocks at him or pray he is in a merciful mood and just leaves us alone?"

"Peace, Sigurd," Sybilla stated calmly. "I doubt he suggests any such thing. What do you have in mind, Stahd? From your statements about the moon, I am guessing at your identity."

"And you are correct, madam. This will work. I am losing my connection to the Song at an alarming rate through my wounds. When it is gone, there is no way to recover it, so we must act quickly. I will imbue those we can gather with the ability to hear and manipulate the Song, just as Angelics have done since the awakening. Although, I can only give you a fraction of the abilities I once had, I will drain myself. As you grow in your abilities, you will be able to accomplish great things. I will establish the two of you as a bondpair, able to work in tandem as a single force. Additionally, I will stretch your lives, enabling you to greet Rasulo personally as he emerges from his prison. Do not allow him to gain a foothold. He will likely use his imprisonment as a time to recover his abilities. He has been gravely wounded and will never be as strong as when he was created. Take heart in that. However, he is wiley and will find a way to overcome his deficiencies. You must also." This long speech gave Stahd an intense fit of coughing. Sybilla moved to help him sit, over her shoulder she instructed Sigurd to gather the people in the square immediately and send the first two strong people he encountered in to help her carry Stahd. Unwilling to proceed without doing everything to ensure future success, the Angelic begged for a slight reprieve as his eyes lit upon a large silvery basin in the corner and an idea formed.

Shuffling over to the dish, he tuned the basin to the Song slowly leeching out of his body. The surface of the metal smoothed out and coppery radial bands were exposed and straightened in even sections. As he brushed his fingers along each, he could hear and feel the perfect pitch of the basin. Stahd was pleased with his work and summoned Sigurd to take possession of the relic, briefly explaining that it was an amplification tool and obtaining the man's vow to protect and use it wisely.

Within the hour, Stahd was moved to the auctioneer's platform in the center of the plaza supported on either side by two burly dwarves. The entire town was gathered before him with expectant faces and questioning eyes. Sybilla moved to the podium and squared her shoulders. Stahd noticed that she did that often before addressing anyone. It was her way of gathering her thoughts and projecting confidence. Looking just below the surface, her mind was a whorl of interconnecting thoughts and emotions. Each tumbling around and feeding on the others. When Sybilla squared her shoulders, she forcefully ignored all of the possibilities and focused exclusively on the task before her. It was not that she was comfortable commanding others; it was that she recognized her flaws and moved forward for the betterment of others in spite of them. It was this trait that gave Stahd hope that his gamble would pay off. That he was not just delaying the inevitable by imprisoning Rasulo. That one day someone would do what he could not. He hoped it would be Sybilla and Sigurd.

As she addressed the crowd, keeping her voice sure and her anxieties at bay, Sybilla assured them all that though there was a threat, it was in the future. They had time to devise a plan and develop as a community. Their abilities when working together would be their strength. With that she turned to Stahd and he forced himself to stand and move to lean on the podium. He looked at the crowd of faces before him. Every race was represented in some form or another. Admittedly, there were fewer Mer than the others, as this town was on land, but no race would be left out.

"Listen well, all of you. The Angelics have passed and their time here is at an end. While my sister, Hali, and I would have stayed to protect this land until the Dissonance was removed, we were blinded to the true culprit of our downfall. We trusted Rasulo until the last. Our blindness is now your responsibility. To that end, I will give you what I can. The Song is everywhere. It touches everything and everyone at all times. You are never truly alone, but connected to your world in the most intricate of ways. Open your ears and hear its call. Do not be afraid."

He moved slowly from the platform supported on either side by Sigurd and Sybilla. He began humming in concert with the elements that he felt around him first the earth at his feet. The dwarves all shouted as a new awareness hit them. Next the air melody, several elves stood taller and closed their eyes in response. The humans responded to the fire he pulled from a nearby blacksmith shop. Finally, the mer reacted as he mimicked the water flowing from a small fountain in the square. The centaurs and faerydae at the edge of the plaza seemed to understand what he was doing, but he carefully taught them to hear light and the skies respectively.

Before long groups were forming, each imitating the songs that they heard before running across to hear what another group was doing. A great cacophony grew in the square each sound overlapping with others drawing tighter and tighter until they all understood each element. By the time Stahd and his helpers reached the edge of the town, the sound was almost deafening. The Angelic smiled for a moment and then rushed back to the Pond with urgency.

The entire trip was spent teaching Sybilla and Sigurd what he could about the Song and what he remembered about the different systems placed by the Angelics. He recalled many of the songs that his brothers and sisters used in working with animals, plants, or even his in the heavens. Those in the town would have the ability to hear those melodies, but there was no time to teach them to use what they heard. Sigurd suggested that they pool their knowledge and research different melody forms, which reassured Stahd that his sacrifice would not be in vain.

Upon reaching the Pond, he rested for a moment leaning against a boulder. His long grey hair flowed out behind him, pale as starlight in contrast with his dark skin and eyes. The weight of his decision bore down on him as he realized he would no longer exist after his last act. Just listening to the Song gave him comfort. Listening for pleasure and not to work for the first time in eons, he smiled. He had forgotten how beautiful the world could be. Each rock and flower stood in stark contrast to the ones around it. Colors coalesced and split again. The wind kissed his weary face and caressed his hair lovingly. He took in the work of his brothers and sisters as a whole and felt all of them around him again for a moment, working in concert to aid him again.

Levering to his feet, Stahd moved to the edge of the Pond flanked by Sybilla and Sigurd as support. It would always need to exist in some form or another, but he could not just leave it in the open for any to manipulate. With more Users, the potential for corruption and misuse increased dramatically. Ideally, the Pond could remain and be used to further great works in the world, but Stahd could not run the risk of Rasulo having access again. As a contingency, the Pond would be hidden.

Sigurd and Sybilla remained quiet as he focused his song on the bedrock below the water. Similar to the melody used to move the moon, Stahd syphoned away every drop of Pond water underground and pulled it away. It raced along, called to another location under mountains, grasslands, and rivers until it finally settled locked away from the world as protection from its power. Every drop of moisture wicked away leaving a crackled, baked surface behind.

The Lord of the Sky crumpled to the ground from the strain of his final act. Sybilla caught him and cradled his head in her lap weeping. She could feel his connection to the Song blink out to nothing. He shuddered a breath.

"I would do it again to right the wrongs of my kind against yours, but I have never felt such silence." Stahd blinked and stared at the moon just rising over the horizon. "Even she is silent. My favorite child cannot even speak to me." His eyes slid shut and several tears leaked out spilling over his worn cheeks and splashing warm against Sybilla's hand.

"We will not fail you," Sigurd promised solemnly.

Stahd did not wake or acknowledge the promise; he let go. The remaining pair worked together for the first time to bury the Angelic in the former site of the Pond. Calling to the earth, they split a channel deep enough for a burial and created a cairn of stone as a marker. Silently, they headed back to begin the task entrusted to them.

CHAPTER 5

This was it. It was the day. Safara paced in her chamber and tried to gather her scattered thoughts. She was too nervous to eat and with an hour before sunrise, she saw little point in attempting to go back to sleep. Her acolyte test was scheduled to start in two hours.

"How am I going to do this? I'm not even classified yet. I'm not ready." Safara's thoughts tumbled about her head in an endless loop. She could never hope to pass because no one knew how to train her. Consequently, she was forced to take both Vocalist and Canticle training. The Masters hoped to force her orientation to assert itself through the coming days' ordeal, but Safara doubted the plan would succeed. Her purpose would remain a mystery and she would be one failure from expulsion.

At thirteen, facing the acolyte test was practically unheard of. Most were sixteen by the time they were deemed ready. The Masters only pushed Safara and Ryl because of their parents. Talents, especially bonded pairs, of that caliber rarely produced more than one child. Because both Ryl and Safara were beyond gifted, the entire school was practically salivating to see how far they could go. Safara alone carried a double course load on top of personal weapons training. Ryl was slightly better off, as her Canticle designation was beyond doubt. Her bondpartner was already being sought and she was only ten. Although Ryl seemed to think the school would be unsuccessful. She insisted she already had a bond, but as it was unverified, on went the search. Safara felt a wave of nausea wash over her. She doubled over to put her head between her knees, but it was too late. She retched into a nearby waste bin and stumbled to the wash stand to rinse the acidic taste from her mouth.

"Get it together, Fara! Momma and Papa both passed. You aren't a coward. Do what you must and show everyone what you can do. Designation or not, you have talent. Use it!"

With that mildly rousing pep talk, Safara attacked her snarled hair. She could not find her regular hair ribbons, so she improvised using the leather necklace from her father. Her determination grew as she twisted her hair around it. She hurriedly finished by tying it as a headband at the nape of her neck and braiding the rest of her straight brown hair down her back fastening it with a leather thong. Surveying her work and satisfied that her hair would not get into her face, Safara exited her room and jogged up several flights of stairs to the roof. She planned to greet the day and center her thoughts before presenting herself on the training commons.

The roof was chilly and pre-dawn cast an eerie light across the battements. Safara headed for the opposite wall to her favorite spot. From that vantage, her view over the water was unobstructed and one could almost see Syreni on a clear day. So intent on the view, Safara failed to notice a dark figure detaching from the shadows to sidle up to her.

"I bet Ayo two silver you would be here." An amused voice boomed much too loudly considering the solemnity of the day.

Safara nearly jumped out of her skin in shock. "Dammit, Terris! You have got to stop sneaking up on people. What if I had shrieked and accidentally attacked you?" Her scowl and anger were augmented by her nervousness. "What are you even doing in this building? And at this hour? Even being Parke's son won't keep you from punishment when you are caught."

Terris shrugged and leaned against the half wall of the parapet nonchalantly. His escapades were legion and most chalked it up to his being almost bored with his training. The ease with which he mastered his coursework bordered on unfair. Terris had passed his acolyte test at fourteen and, as the most talented Vocalist of his class, he was allowed some leeway. It had always irked Safara. Mostly because he seemed to view his privileges as rights and he was so self-assured. She envied his sense of place.

She tried to ignore him and focus on the sunrise. The beautiful pinks and oranges contrasted against the fluffy purple clouds. All reflected in the calm, glass-like sea below. She would have a temperate day for her trial in any event. *"Breathe in... breathe out,"* she thought and concentrated only on that for several moments with her eyes closed. Sighing in resignation, Safara squared her shoulders with a determination she did not quite feel and focused her gaze on the horizon.

"You'll be fine, you know," Terris stated reassuringly. "They wouldn't risk a failure on your part. You are so far in your training that there really isn't a choice."

Safara rolled her eyes, not needing to state the obvious.

"No one will know how to proceed with you unless you are classified," he continued. "Everyone knows it. Just do your thing and it will be fine."

"I appreciate the attempt, Terris, but that doesn't help. What if I complete the task and my abilities don't hone? It'll be almost worse than it is now." She spoke without taking her eyes from the water.

Terris nudged her arm with his elbow until she looked at him. He gave a quick half-smile at her annoyed face and quickly stated, "I had a reason other than the bet to come up here. I heard my father and uncle talking. Your trial is going to be different because you are so...different. I thought you might need these." Terris handed her a pair of long leather gloves with a wink. "I like the hair." With a quick tug on her braid, he walked away and left her gaping after him.

Safara quickly shook off her shock at the unexpected help. Determination settled over her like a cloak. "Different, eh? I can do different." With a final look out over the sea, she turned on her heel and headed back down the stairs.

Feeling more confident with each step, she stepped into the common room for some bread and fruit. As she munched, it occurred to her that her test might last all day. She quickly tucked away a flask of water and several handfuls of jerky in the pouch at her waist. With a final check for her knife and new gloves, Safara walked the last hundred yards to the center of the Commons.

Parke, Deckard, and Lucia were waiting along with a smattering of students, who had cut class to watch the start of the test. As most of the teachers were just as interested, their absence would be ignored. A murmur rose from the crowd as she approached, pulling on her gloves as she went. The action was marked by Master Parke, whose eyes flashed around the crowd to find his son. However, for once, Terris was in class. That alone was enough to confirm Parke's suspicions.

Safara stopped before the Masters and bowed at the waist. The wind whipped her emerald green cloak around her thick leather boots and leggings. With a huff and a smile, she tugged it free and awaited her instructions.

Deckard returned her smile and began. "Good morning, my girl! I am pleased to see you in good spirits. Confidence is your ally in this challenge. Keep in mind it is my utmost belief that you will fly through this test." He stopped to give her a quick wink and a shrug.

Lucia nudged him gently with her sleek black flank and took over. Her centaurian height allowed her to easily gesture over the heads of the other masters on the platform outside the Choral Tower. "Safara. You know the difficulties we have faced in your schooling better than anyone. And you are aware that the cycle is advancing at all times toward a peak. We cannot delay the training of any competent User at this juncture. That is why you are being tested today. The Song resonates in you, but it is muted. Through this test, we hope to not only award you Acolyte status, but to also unlock your potential. You are an untapped spring, bursting for freedom. Seek your freedom today and unleash the woman you are meant to be."

With that final word, Lucia handed Safara a map and eased back to join Deckard. Parke moved forward. He motioned briefly to the gloves and stated, "I do not know what rumors you have been told, but keep in mind that each trial is different and tailored to the student. Your strengths will be assessed and your weaknesses exploited. Your objective is simple: retrieve the purple stone from the top of the tallest spire on the High Mesa. You have three days to get to the Mesa and back. Your time starts now and sunset on the third day is the end. You must be through The Band before the last ray of the sun is gone."

Parke gave her shoulder a squeeze and stepped back. Safara immediately ran for the stables and called for Parsifal. While she saddled him, Ayo and Ryl ran up to hand her a packed saddle bag and bedroll.

"How did you know? No one else has ever been sent outside The Band for their test before."

Ryl quietly hugged her sister, burying her face in Safara's chest. Her shoulders trembled as she fought to hold in her tears. Ayo answered in her chirpy Mer voice, "Terris, who else? I didn't believe him, but Ryl insisted we pack for you. I'm glad we did, but now I owe that insufferable canker two silver!" Ayo attempted a chuckle, but failed. She quickly hugged Safara and stepped away to allow Ryl some time.

Safara slowly pried Ryl off her midsection and took her face between her hands. "Oh, Ryl," she soothed, "it isn't so bad. We used to love camping and Parsifal will see I come to no harm." Parsifal flicked his ears forward and nickered in agreement. "You will see me in three days. Keep heart and trust I will never leave you, Bean." Safara gave her baby sister a kiss on the forehead and stepped toward Parsifal.

"I'm sending Nyx with you. I can't go, but the Masters can't hope to control a faerydae."

Safara started to protest, but Ryl cut her off. "I'm serious, Fara. If it makes you feel better, Nyx is put out about it, too. So as I see it, you both deserve each other."

Nyx dive bombed at Ryl with an angry tinkling sound.

She deftly caught him and begged him to do her this favor. Safara laughed as she could actually hear when the resigned note entered his chiming. Usually, she had no clue what he was saying. Nyx ruffled his favorite's short midnight hair affectionately and dutifully took a seat between Parsifal's ears.

"I love you, too, Nyx. At least try to save her from herself." At her elder sister's protest, Ryl laughed. "You know what I mean, Fara. Be safe. Without Iyna, you are my only family."

"I know, Bean. Ayo, see that she tries to sleep. Love you both. Tell the canker we are even now."

With another quick hug, Safara swung up on Parsifal and headed to The Band. She only looked back once to wave. After a quick survey of the map, she stowed it and gave Parsifal their route.

"Head for the Long Road. The spot marked on the map is just west of the Great Marsh. If we are lucky, we can make it to the foot of the Mesa by nightfall. I can start the climb in the morning." Parsifal whinnied in agreement and Nyx let out a brief chirp that could have meant anything. Most likely disapproval.

Four hours later, they reached The Band. It was the first and most imposing line of defense for Sonaris. Safara called for a halt and climbed down from Parsifal to give them both a break.

"Alright, P, let loose for a bit." She said affectionately as she removed his saddle and bridle. Parsifal kicked his hooves and took a quick roll in the grass. Then he set about the business of grazing to his heart's content. Nyx busied himself finding a few berries for his meal before settling on a rock to sun himself.

Safara grabbed a hunk of bread from the supplies packed by Ayo and relaxed in the shadow of the wall at her back. She took in the imposing edifice. It soared just over one hundred feet in the air, its grey stone facade as smooth as a blanket. The parapet at the top was dotted with guard posts every quarter mile with the main guard quarters above the only gate cut into the facade. The gate itself was currently open, as was customary during the daylight hours. While the gate was wide enough to allow two carts to pass without incident, it still seemed dwarfed when compared to the mountainous facade. The top of the gate could not have been more than a third of its height. Safara knew from her entry into Sonaris that the portcullis, when down, was studded on the outside with spikes of varying lengths. The outer gates were iron and covered in bas relief sculptures of the creation story. Stahd and Hali were central figures and Sybilla and Sigurd had their own panel below. With her bread consumed, Safara heaved a sigh and called Parsifal and Nyx.

With a final look around, the three left and continued on toward the gate. The guards in the barbican waved her through and shouted encouragement. The Captain of the Watch, Palmer, saluted and called, "Best of luck, Neophyte! According to the letter from Master Parke, we will look for you in three days. Be safe!" His relaxed, smiling face was a welcome sight and eased her stress. Safara smiled back and called out a cheery thank you. She had occasionally seen the Captain since she and Ryl arrived in Sonaris five years prior and she vividly remembered his kindness and care for two lost girls with no home. Both considered him as close as family.

Parsifal kept up a steady pace for the next several hours. He began to flag as they approached the northern edge of the Mesa. The face of the rise was dotted with trees, but there was no way a horse could make the ascent. The rider-friendly approach was a week or more ride to the south. Climbing was her only option.

Finding an enclosed copse of trees, Safara unloaded the saddle bags and set Parsifal free to eat and get a drink from a nearby stream. After taking an inventory of the gear, she joined Parsifal at the water to soak her feet. Nyx remained at camp as a sentry. After cutting up an apple, Safara shared it with her faithful mount. Parsifal gave her a gentle nudge in thanks and followed her back to Nyx.

As they lay down for the night in the rapidly growing twilight, Safara was lost in thought. The cliffs above her went from green and brown to orange and grey. The climb was at least a thousand feet if it was a foot. How she was to make it up and back in a day was beyond her. Safara curled up with Parsifal and offered Nyx a place under the saddlebag with her handkerchief as a blanket. He chimed at her and settled in.

"What am I supposed to do? Fly?" With a rueful laugh, she turned her cheek to Parsifal's side and gave him a pat. Quietly humming, she wove a large blanket of grass and leaves and suspended it on some saplings. With that final thought, she drifted off to sleep.

At dawn, Nyx woke Safara with a bright tinkling sound and a smile on his dark face. The sunlight caught on his wings and sparkled merrily. It was the first time she could ever remember him seeming pleased with her. Taking it as a good omen, she stretched and accidentally knocked down the makeshift tent startling Parsifal. He surged to his feet and trotted away quickly. He shot her an accusing look and Nyx practically folded himself in half laughing. Safara hastily apologized and smothered her own laugh in her hand.

"Sorry, P." She let out a quick huff. "Well, boys, let's do this. Nyx, you are with me. Par, you stay here and remain out of sight. Guard the gear we can't take and don't let yourself be taken by nomads. I'd rather risk a walk back to The Band and retake the test next year than risk losing you. I'll whistle for you when we get back down."

Parsifal flicked his ears in understanding and simultaneously pawed the ground in protest.

"I know, Parsifal. I want you to come too, but you can't make that climb." Safara threw her arms around her oldest friend in a fierce hug smoothing her hands along his smooth grey neck and mane. She stowed the gear under a bush and shouldered her pack. "If I'm not back in two days, head for The Band and get Palmer. Love you, boy." With a final glance over at Parsifal and the north, she turned her back, squared her shoulders and hiked into the foothills of the High Mesa.

The start of the climb was gentle and the early morning

weather was beyond perfect. If she did not know better, Safara would have been enjoying herself. As it was, she did not have enough time. "Four days would have been barely enough time, but three? Impossible. What is the key? How can I move faster?"

Safara grabbed a fallen walnut branch and used a flora melody to smooth it into a staff. The leaves at the end, she preserved as a reminder of its original state. Nyx tinkled his approval and turned a stone into a faerydae crystal for the top. It sparkled in the early morning light and almost seemed to cast its own glow. "Oh, Nyx! Thank you! It's perfect." Safara continued to hum in happiness, unconsciously imbuing the staff with her tone and tuning it to her. She had little practical experience making artifacts. The first she attempted blew up and left her brows scorched for a week. At least this attempt ended successfully and left her in possession of all her hair. Another good omen.

The sun was just past the tops of the Spina Ardus when they reached the foot of the cliff. "Might as well rest. I can't climb a cliff on my own and your wings can barely carry you." Nyx huffed a chime in protest, but they both knew the real test had just begun. "A straight climb would take hours. I need speed," Safara thought out loud. She closed her eyes in concentration. "We don't even know what I am, so how do I know if I should design or build? That is exactly why I was given this challenge to force me to choose. But I can't! Both feel the same to me. Blast and damn!"

Safara picked up a rock and hurled it at the base of the cliff. It almost crushed a sapling desperately trying to grow in unfriendly territory. She felt like that tree. Focusing on the sapling and its losing battle, Safara let out a frustrated howl of sympathy. The sapling responded, shaking with the force and intent of her call. It sent out roots and shot another foot into the air. She jumped back and Nyx flew to inspect the tree. The root system now covered twice as much ground as before and the entire plant seemed to be waiting for her next move.

"That's it! Holy Stahd! Did you see that? How far up do you

think we can get it to go?" Safara considered her options and the implication of what she was considering. A giant tree was problematic. At some point either her focus would run out or the structure of the tree would become unsound. She could not bring herself to sacrifice the tree, so her best option would be to grow several at intervals along the rock face like a big, branchy ladder. She was nothing if not nimble. Combat training was the one area where her lack of classification did not matter. Master Falstaff had her working with the Acolytes for the past two years. Scaling a tree or even jumping between two was no problem.

Safara gathered a few seeds from the trees nearby and stowed them in her pack. "I'm going to do this, Nyx! This will work," she said more to herself than her companion. She tucked the staff close against her side and focused all her hope and will on her tree. She started her song low and soft. The roots of the tree thickened and embedded themselves deep in the earth. She spent several minutes on the foundation, knowing the stronger it became the further she could go before starting on a new tree. She was not even sure if she could germinate a tree using just her abilities. When she felt the roots hit bedrock, she sent a few down into a couple of cracks as extra anchorage and then changed her attention to the body of the tree.

Her words became more lofty and the pitch and tempo increased. The base-heavy sapling responded with an almost twenty foot jump in height immediately. Not expecting that fast of growth, Safara struggled to contain her shock and keep her focus. She made a split second decision and latched onto a thick and newly grown branch. Pulling herself to straddle the branch, Safara continued her song, but slowed her urgency. She did not want to risk anything in an unnecessary rush.

The tree grew smoothly along the cliff face at a rapid pace. By the time she needed to stop to drink, she was already a quarter of the way up the mesa. As Safara took a long swallow, she asked Nyx to assess the tree's strength. He gave her a happy trill, which she took as confirmation her tree was at least stable.

She felt woozy from the effort, but gamely proceeded with her next phase. She selected another tree on a shelf even with her position. It was scrubby and windswept, but it was closer to the mesa wall. As she rose on her tree, she realized that the taller it got the farther she was from the wall. The mesa stair stepped away toward the west. She needed to change trees fairly often from here on out to keep the gap from becoming unmanageable. The initial rise was around a quarter of the way up the cliff, so starting a new tree was necessary. The branchy dome of the first tree would help her close the distance to the next, but just barely. She was stranded until the new tree was at least on level with her. Jumping on to a growing tree seemed like a terrible idea, but with a tree that scrubby she was not sure it could withstand the shock of growth twice and the tune was getting harder to focus the more tired she became. *"Jump it is,"* she acknowledged internally. She started the same as before, low and slow, focusing on the root system of a small tree struggling for a foothold against the rocky wall. She hit bedrock almost immediately and switched to sending out anchor roots as before. The cliff split in a few places as Nyx flew down to inspect the work. He gave a half-hearted trill and Safara changed the tune to growth topside. This tree was less eager to grow, but soon it was approaching her level. She stood and flexed, bobbing lightly on the balls of her feet to maintain her balance. As the crown of the tree passed, she ran along her branch and leapt through the sunlight to her new perch. For a moment, time stood still and she heard nothing but her song and a supporting chorus of wind. Her hair whipped back and she felt right for the first time since leaving home with Ryl.

All too soon her moment of nirvana was over and she was hurtling face first into a prickly, pokey mess of branches. Her song faltered while she scrabbled for a hand hold. Her relief at not falling was so great that she almost gave a yell. Grinning, she shimmied across the depth of the tree to the cliff side and settled in for a ride. She maintained the tree for almost a hundred feet, until Nyx warned her it was becoming unsound. She repeated the process several more times until it was almost dark and she was feeling faint. Climbing off the top of the tree, just shy of the summit, Safara considered her options. No saplings were available this high on the cliff face, just a few bushes and weeds. She could free climb the remainder, but in the waning light, she would never make that height before she was left in darkness without her next handhold. Another option would be to camp for the night and continue in the morning, but she had to make it back to The Band by nightfall. That seemed unlikely to happen if she did not at least reach the summit by night. Her final option was to plant and germinate a whole tree.

Safara munched on a quick meal and replenished her fluids as she thought. Really her only option was the third. With a determined sigh, she dug an acorn from her pack and carefully planted it several feet from the cliff face. She even watered it for good measure. She stood using her staff for support and asked Nyx to monitor the seed. He nodded and stood on the ground to one side of the displaced earth.

Her song started in a mid-range, singing of nature and the beautiful land stretched out before her. She endeavored to entice the seed to break forth and experience the world about which she sang. Nyx chirped and jumped back. A tiny sprout burst from the ground and began to grow. It was slower than its predecessors, but grew steadily. Safara encouraged it and focused on the roots and upward growth equally. One last time, she hitched a ride on a rising branch and held her song firm until she saw over the edge of the mesa. She leapt and landed with a roll less than five feet from the edge just as the last rays of sunlight faded from view over the far side of the plain upon which she was now standing.

Scrambling to her feet, Safara shook the dust from her clothes, as Nyx flew up excitedly to join her. They set off in a westerly direction hoping to spot the objective: a purple rock on the tallest spire. "Is it cheating if you fly up to grab the stone?" Safara asked facetiously. He tinkled a warning. "I know, I know. Everyone would know and I just bet if I have to retake the test next year, no amount of begging by my sister could get you to help." He gave an emphatic nod and pointed her onward.

In the waning light, she hummed gently at her staff and the faerydae crystal took on a soft glow allowing them better night vision. Two or three miles from the cliff, towering clusters of rock spires rose from the ground. The closer she got, the fiercer the wind pushed at her, as it howled between the structures blocking its path. The noise was intense and little pieces of sand whipped at her face and any exposed skin. The gloves from Terris not only protected her from the rough bark of the tree, but also the harsh weather. Nyx hid himself, under the flap of the pack to ensure he was not blown away and rang out his displeasure. Safara needed no translation to understand. Safara cupped her hand around the opening of the pack to protect Nyx as she spoke. "We will stop at the base of the closest spire for the night. With no trees or bushes for shelter, we have no other option. If you think of any bright ideas on how to get to the top of one of these monsters, let me know. This challenge just gets worse and worse." He agreed and settled in for a bumpy ride.

To approach the spires, Safara aligned herself with the closest and used it as a break to allow her some relief from the constant push of the wind. At its base, she carefully set down the pack and opened the flap, so that Nyx could poke his head out. He flatly refused to leave shelter. Both shared the remaining bread and a few sips of water from the skin before settling for what little sleep could be found with the constant noise around them. Just as she was drifting off, Safara could have sworn she heard the cry of an eagle.

In the predawn hours, the temperatures on the top of the mesa dropped to dangerously low levels. Nyx woke Safara with a quick tug on her matted braid. "Ouch, you little mosquito! Can't you ever be kind to me? I will never understand how you can be so gentle with Ryl and so nasty to the rest of us." She rubbed her scalp. Nyx stuck his tongue out and looked supremely unsympathetic before he dove back into the bag to preserve what warmth he could. He hefted the last apple toward Safara's head for good measure. She took a bite and surveyed the landscape. From this angle, she could not tell which spire was the tallest and the previous evening night had fallen too quickly for more than a brief viewing before the tops were shrouded in darkness. "Upward to go onward, I guess," she muttered. Again a free climb of the spire before her was risky, but possible. Options were as limited as the time left for her task. Taking the entire day was not going to work with her schedule. The wind pulled at her and she saw a few torn leaves and some grass rise high above her, sparking an idea.

Picking two spires that were deep and tall, she called to the earth. Her tone was rich and deep. She concentrated on the solidity of the ground and urged it to form a wall between the rocks on either side and move up behind her. The base of the wall was curved to channel all of the air from its easterly course and push it straight up. As she had hoped the wind was caught and began to swirl upward, but she was still too heavy. Safara turned her back to the raging wind to protect her face and provide her a moment to think. Considering the leaves being blown about, she used several leather thongs to attach her cloak to the bottom of her leggings and along her arms. As she turned and spread her limbs, the pockets of material filled with air and she rocketed up the channel at an alarming rate. Within seconds, she cleared the top of the shunt and was hurtling back to the ground.

Based on nothing more than instinct, she leaned heavily toward the top of the nearest spire. When she got close, she brought her arms and legs together to collapse her makeshift sails and hit the edge hard against her stomach. With a whoosh, all of the air was pulled from her lungs and she was momentarily stunned, half-on and half-off the top of her target. Nyx burst from the satchel chiming angrily at her as loud as he could. "Merciful Stahd! That could have gone better," Safara gasped fearfully as she hauled herself up to lie on a cool stone face. Nyx agreed readily and flicked her ear so she would understand just how little he appreciated being taken along for the ride.

She finally forced herself to sit up with a grimace, knowing she would have a lovely bruise all along her abdomen and sincerely hoped that nothing important had been ruptured. Gingerly, she loosened her cloak from her ankles and arms. The wind, unencumbered by the closely packed spires was calmer at this level, though still very much a constant presence nudging her in an eastern direction.

She glanced over her shoulder to the east and froze at the sight. Even from the top of the Neophyte's Tower, she had never seen such a sunrise. It looked as though the entire world was stretched out before her. The Spina Ardus was painted purple at the base and faded up to a bright yellowy-pink at the tops. Even Sonaris was barely visible in the distance to the northeast. That view more than anything hit her with a wave of homesickness. The eight central towers melded into one large silver point at this distance and twinkled at her with promise. "Tonight, you sleep in your own bed and hug your baby sister. Now get a move on!" Speaking out loud to no one felt odd, but encouraging, and she turned back to the west to find the tallest peak.

Away to the south and a little west of where she stood, a cluster of peaks rose much higher than any of the others she had seen to this point. With a tired huff, Safara shouldered her pack and moved to the edge of the rock to consider how to cross without falling to her death. The next spire to the south was less than ten feet away, so taking a hold of her staff she moved to the northernmost edge and tightened her pack. Without giving Nyx a warning, she took off at a sprint and pole vaulted over the chasm landing with a grunt of pain and earned herself another pull to her braid from her angry stowaway.

"If you don't like how I travel, you can brave this wind yourself, but I think we both know you are stuck with me." Safara refused to apologize to the crotchety faerydae and after a few moments heard his ring of consent. She walked slowly to the other side of the spire. This one was wider than those around it and there was a section off to the east side that was about ten feet higher than the level where she had landed. As she walked past she heard a chuff and a low warning bark. She quickly backed away toward the edge as an enormous, feathered head poked over the side of the cliff and what she now recognized as a nest. A large claw soon followed the head out of the nest and with no other options, Safara took a battle stance with her staff out in front of her.

The griffon looked at her with a question in its eye and squawked when it saw the soft glow of the staff. The griffon's talons uncurled and it hopped down from the nest to investigate. Upon closer inspection, Safara realized that it was an adolescent and extremely curious about her and the staff in particular. She remembered how fascinated the kittens in the stable were whenever they saw a reflection off of the water in the troughs and considered that this griffon might feel the same. She held herself very still and allowed the creature to approach. Its large rear paws and front talons seemed much too big for its body. It was not the most graceful animal she had ever seen. The feathers on its head were also snowy white and they bristled with equal parts fear and fascination as it padded forward. When it got close enough, Safara extended her arm and let the griffon take a sniff. It sneezed and backed up startled. She responded by waving the crystal in a circle. The griffon's head and eyes followed the motion and it had to shake its head to dispel the dizziness that followed. Safara giggled and the griffon looked sharply at her as though waiting for her to make another noise. It cocked its head to one side and sat with a thud on its haunches to wait. Not knowing what else to do, she spoke.

"My name is Safara. I come from Sonaris." She pointed with her finger to the shining city near the horizon. "I am a neophyte at the school there and have come here for my acolyte test." She felt supremely stupid for explaining herself to an animal that obviously did not understand her language. But rather than attack or move away, the more she spoke the more interested the griffon looked. He, as she could now tell, swished his tail in anticipation and scooted toward her. At this point, Nyx shot out of the bag and flew straight at the griffon chittering away and trying to shoo him off. But the griffon yawned and pounced, deftly caging the little faerydae within his talons.

"Nyx! Oh choirs, let him go will you? I think you understand me. He is annoying, yes, but he is also a friend."

With an unimpressed look, the griffon released Nyx and looked at Safara mournfully, as though she had denied him the highlight of his day. "Thank you, you big lug," she said as she edged closer to her new friend. "Are you alright, Nyx? I appreciate the help." Nyx was in no mood for her platitudes as his pride was quite damaged. He scooted back around behind her and sat on top of the pack nursing a sore arm and wiping dirt off of his iridescent wings.

Safara slowly reached out to touch the griffon and he responded by extending his beak under her hand. She held her breath and waited for contact. As they touched, warmth enveloped them both and the griffon gave out a happy cry while dancing around her with joy. Safara did not entirely understand what had happened other than that the griffon had apparently decided they were friends. "What should I call you?" She asked as she gently stroked the feathers above the griffon's beautiful inky, black eyes. He blinked his eyes and waited. "Horus?" That suggestion earned her a thump on the leg with his heavy white tail. "Okay. That one was no good." She looked deeply into his eyes and said, "Daichi? That's your name isn't it?" She knew she was right, but for confirmation he blew softly in her ear and made her giggle. "Glad to meet you, Daichi. I am Safara and I am honored to make your acquaintance." She bowed formally and burst out laughing when Daichi did his best impression of her bow.

"Why thank you, good sir," she stated with affected formality. "My companion, Nyx, and I are on a quest to obtain a purple rock from the highest peak in the spires and return it to The Band by nightfall. Would you care to aid us along our journey?"

Daichi jumped in the air and unfurled his wings in response. He looked happy to be asked and eager to join. He quickly moved alongside Safara and bumped her with his extended wings. She quickly ducked under them as he was pushing her to the edge. As soon as she was behind his wings he stopped, looked at her, then pointedly at his back, and then right back to her, his neck swiveling like an owl.

"Ride you? Are you sure you can handle my weight? I don't want to hurt you." Daichi responded with a sniff and repeated his unspoken instructions to climb aboard. As she complied, Safara could not help but notice how soft his immaculate coat was. The feathers on his head gave way to a pillowy mane that was just starting to grow. She patted him trustingly as she settled behind the wing joints. Nyx let out a trill and she felt him climb back inside the pack as a precaution. "Good idea, Nyx. Alright, Daichi, if you know where the highest peak is lead on!"

With a scream of delight, the griffon launched himself off of the spire and into the gorge below. He caught an updraft and was soon flying south toward the rock formations Safara had noted earlier. He was fast and she loved it. Banking to the right and left just for the sheer fun of flying, Daichi was careful of his rider, but also wanted to show off a bit. Safara laughed at his antics and encouraged him to show her what he could do. As the high spires appeared, he pumped his wings again and again to gain altitude. Safara hung on for dear life, gripping the flanks between her legs and leaning forward into the griffon's neck. Just as she felt that she could no longer hold on, he leveled out and began to circle around the topmost spire. In the very middle of it, she could see a pedestal and upon that rested a spherical, purple rock that caught the morning sun.

Once again, Safara carefully weighed her options. With the addition of Daichi, she no longer wondered how they would make it home in time. However, getting the stone without dropping it was a serious concern. It was nestled in a slight depression at the top of the spire, but it caught the light like a beacon and the facets threw out beams of purple in all directions. The wind from the coast buffeted the spire and she saw the stone sway, but not come out of its seat. Safara was most comfortable working with fire, but she could manipulate earth, flora, fauna, and wind with varying degrees of effort. Wind was her weakest area of study. With a gentle tug on his feathers, she directed Daichi to fly west of the spire in a direct line.

"Turn around now, please! And head straight for the spire. The wind will pick up, but try to maintain speed. Use the rock as a windbreak and stay below the top of the formation. I'm going to knock the rock off with wind and catch it below. Ready?" Safara took a deep breath and searched for the words that would focus her song. With fire, she could focus her intent with the minimum of effort. With wind, she had to be very specific and use lyrics lest her focus falter.

Daichi signaled his understanding by banking to the left and peering over his shoulder to give her a quick look. He took off back toward the stone like a shot and picked an elevation twenty or so feet below the top.

Safara started her song carefully and stared at the stone to help direct the wind she was enhancing. Thankfully, the wind was already strong, as she could never have started a new wind stream on her own.

"Wind strong and wide

Let me guide

Focus small

And the stone fall"

While not the most clever of lyrics, they were the best she could compose on such short notice. Luckily, it seemed they were good enough as the wind picked up and focused on the rock. She saw it wobble and then tip out of the western side of its perch. Daichi and Safara both realized at the same time that it fell too soon and at their current rate they would miss the catch. Daichi took a dive and angled his underside at the rock face. Safara clung to his back using her knees and arms under his wings. After a few moments in freefall, he reached out both claws and snatched at the purple stone. He fumbled a bit, but managed to keep a hold of it. His wings snapped open and the force of their lift almost knocked Safara loose. She desperately grabbed at his feathers and accidentally pulled one out in her panic. Daichi's roar of pain was earsplitting and he shot her an accusing look once he leveled out.

"I am so sorry, Daichi! That was an accident." Safara quickly soothed away the pain and gently rubbed the stinging patch of skin. He chuffed his acceptance of the apology and made a beeline to the edge of the mesa. At the edge, he soared out over the cliff and made a quick descent along its face. He flew just above the stream where Safara had camped two days prior. He let his claws drag in the water and then let the rock drop softly to the sandy bottom with a plop. A short distance away, he landed and Safara clambered down while unhitching her pack. Nyx emerged as she set it on the ground and she shot to the stream for the rock. She had to search for several minutes to find it, as it rolled several feet before stopping.

The rock was the size of a fist and a deep clear amethyst purple. It was surprisingly light and Safara let out a crow of triumph as she held it aloft from the middle of the stream. "We did it, boys! We did it!" Her shout alerted Parsifal, who came thundering up from the direction of their original camp. He whinnied in relief and greeted his young charge enthusiastically. Daichi, however, was not about to let a stranger around his new friend and moved to block Parsifal's approach. Anticipating a problem, Safara moved quickly between them both to facilitate an introduction. "Don't you two start any of that. Parsifal, this is Daichi, our newest friend. He has been a big help in getting this stone. Daichi, this is Parsifal, my oldest friend. He has been my friend and guide since before I could walk." She gave each a quick pat and waited for both to acknowledge the other. Each seemed to assess and accept the new acquaintance.

"Good. With that out of the way, we need to get back to The Band. I will have to ride Daichi in order to make it on time.

Parsifal, please follow at your own pace. I don't want you hurting yourself. Can you take me back to where we stored the rest of the gear, P?" She hoisted her pack and mounted Parsifal bareback. He took off and stopped at a familiar tree no more than a mile to the south. Safara quickly dismounted and saddled Parsifal, stowing the remaining gear in the saddlebags.

"Nyx, I want you to stay with Parsifal, but I won't boss you around. I just don't want him left alone any longer," she explained. Nyx chimed his assent and flew to his normal perch between Parsifal's ears. "Thank you. I could not have gotten half so far without each of you. I will see you both at The Band tomorrow sometime. As it is, we will barely make it in time. Be safe." With a hug to Parsifal and a smile at Nyx, she mounted Daichi and took off to the north. Daichi let out a call as he gained altitude. Safara squealed with happiness and hugged her arms as far around the griffon's neck as they would go. The sun had begun to set behind them, but at this rate they would make it. The wind whipped past and pulled Safara's cheeks tight against her bones, her braid streaming straight out behind them. For the second time in as many days, she felt free and right and connected.

The Band loomed in front of them growing ever closer and ever more imposing. At the same time, it was comforting. It was the start of home and a whole new chapter of her life. The gate was still open for the day and in front she saw a crowd of soldiers and Sonarians awaiting her arrival home. Captain Palmer was watching from the top of the gatehouse wall and sent out a call to open the gates. Daichi let out a screech for good measure and raced toward the goal. He landed just short of the gates with a thud and proudly strutted through with Safara perched laughing on his back.

"Well met, Acolyte!" Deckard's voice boomed across the gatehouse yard, his freckled face stretched with a wide smile. Safara dismounted with an answering grin and greeted her favorite of the Masters. "Greetings, Master Deckard. I think you wanted this?" She held out the purple stone for his inspection.

Almost reverently, the master took the gem from Safara and weighed it in his palm.

"I knew you could do it, my girl! Your mother could scarcely have done better." he enveloped Safara in an unexpected, but welcome, hug. "I am so glad to have this trial past us. Watching your progress has been one of the most aging experiences of my life."

"Watching?" Safara queried. "How could you have been watching? I thought I was alone."

"Never alone, my dear. It would have been too risky to send you out alone at this time in the cycle. You had some unseen minders, who frequently sent back news of your progress. Had I known that you would attempt a mid-air jump at those heights along the mesa face, I would never have agreed to this trial. Much less, befriending a griffon. Griffons are usually a menace, not a blessing." With this pronouncement, Safara realized that Deckard had not taken his eyes off of Daichi and was very wary of his presence.

"Don't worry about Daichi. I'm not sure how, but he and I understand one another. I gather that his pack left him and he decided that I am his family. You always said I could take a familiar."

"Incredible! Well, as long as he is friendly, he is more than welcome to make his home with us at Sonaris. It seems that your affinity to fauna has affected more than just your squirrels and your horse." Deckard made a move to address Daichi. "Welcome, Daichi. As you have designated yourself as Safara's protector, you will have a home and family here. Safara, your quarters will have been moved to the Acolyte's Tower by the time we have reached the city and I believe, we will place you on the top floor, so that your companion can make his aerie on the roof."

Safara's grin could not be contained. Not only was she through her trial, but her new friend was going to be living in close proximity and not relegated to the stables. She slowly moved through the crowd of well-wishers and made her way to

Captain Palmer, who wrapped her in a warm reassuring hug. He felt like home and safety.

"Well met, Captain," she said softly with a grin still plastered on her face. "Parsifal and Nyx are following us from the base of the Mesa. Can you please provide a warm, dry place in the stable for Parsifal? Nyx will usually see to himself, but bread and fruit are his favorite foods. I will stay at The Band until their arrival here, if I may, but I can barely keep my eyes open."

"Yes yes. I well remember all of your preferences. I will see to it. And I will say that I had every confidence in your success! Although, the griffon was definitely unexpected. Come with me and I will see you to a chamber where you can wash and rest without interruption. It seems like everytime you come inside The Band you are in desperate need of a bath." The captain laughed, his straight white teeth contrasting pleasantly against the dark color of his skin and beard. He motioned for her to follow him toward some stairs embedded in the wall structure. "Master Deckard brought a pack of clothes from Jameson and no one is expecting you to do anything other than sleep for the rest of the evening."

"One moment, please, Captain." Safara rushed back to Daichi and gave him a quick hug. "I am going to sleep now in one of those rooms up there. You won't be able to fit, but I'm sure you can either sleep on top of the wall or pretty much anywhere you choose. I'll call if I need you. Thank you, Dai." The griffon chuffed in response and gently swatted her with his tail to assure her he would be fine. As she moved up the stairs, he ambled off to eat the fish provided for his dinner and find a place to bed down for the night where he could see the door through which Safara disappeared.

The stairs opened onto a hall that ran down the middle of the wall with chambers off of it on either side. The room that she was given was warm and a quick peek out the shutters confirmed that she was above the level of the top of the gate. With a groan, she began to untangle her hair with the brush provided by Ryl. Luckily, the leather headband and braid had held most of her hair in place, but she briefly considered shaving her head bald to save the time it would take to untangle it all. After her wash and a new change of clothes, Safara fell into a dreamless sleep once she lay down.

In the morning, she awoke with a start and threw off the bedding in a rush to get to the stables. As she had hoped, Nyx and Parsifal were waiting for her and greeted her with such a cacophony of noises that Daichi poked his head in to investigate. He added a loud screech to the noise, effectively waking up everyone in the gatehouse and scaring all of the other livestock. Safara quickly moved to calm her three companions and moved them out into the stable yard for their reunion. Captain Palmer and Master Deckard headed their way after Daichi's restive paws and tail settled.

"Good morning, Acolyte Safara!" Deckard boomed. "We need to make our way home this morning. Captain Palmer assures me that your mount has had a full night's rest and seems no worse for the wear." Parsifal whinnied his approval and stamped his feet in expectation of leaving.

Safara grinned in relief and assured Captain Palmer and Master Deckard that she would be ready to leave within the hour. She rushed back to her room and gathered her things returning her hair to the style of the previous day. Her travel clothes had been laundered, so she added the cloak, boots, and gloves to the leggings and loose tunic that she was already wearing. Grabbing her staff, she was ready and headed down to the yard to wait for her escorts.

Nyx took up his perch on Parsifal's head and Deckard requested the use of Parsifal for the ride back to the city, as he had made his original trip with a delivery cart. Daichi was anxious to move on and as soon as Safara was settled he bounded into the air careful to keep within range of the ground mounts.

"Might as well use this opportunity to practice flying. Show me what you can do, Dai," Safara laughed into his feathery mane. Daichi let out a scream of delight and they spent the next hours practicing loops, dive bombs, and aerial passes that just about stopped Deckard's heart. But Safara was fearless and as they approached the school, Daichi landed and calmly walked side-by-side with Parsifal.

Safara's ever present grin faltered as she made her next statement to her mentor. "You know, we didn't solve our problem. We still don't know if I am a Canticle or a Vocalist. I may have completed the challenge, but I still don't fit."

Deckard drew Parsifal to a stop and waited for Safara to meet his gaze. "It does not matter. You are as you are and you passed the test. We will have to reassess your current workload, but with becoming an Acolyte you have proven that there is much to who you are and what you will accomplish. Your differences are your strengths and maybe that will be the making of this cycle. To be honest, I thought the whole theory of forcing your nature to pick a side was ludicrous, but I was overruled by the others. Forget the set path and make your own." With those words they both entered the courtyard of the towers to cheers and gasps as Daichi became visible.

"Fara! Nyx!" A cry rang from the steps of the Neophytes' Tower and Ryl charged to her sister in a flurry of flailing arms and flying skirts. Jumping from Daichi, Safara met her halfway but not before a tiny black ball zipped past her and attached itself to Ryl's shoulder with a loud tinkle. "You're back! All of you and in one piece." Ryl hugged both of them and buried her face in her sister's side crying in relief. Safara was hardly in better shape trying to reassure her sister and feeling a bit guilty that she had not made her way home the night before. Daichi silently padded up for an introduction and the crowd dispersed as they realized that the sisters had no desire for outside company.

Deckard summoned several stable hands to take care of Parsifal after Ryl greeted him and he asked that they put a store of hay and blankets on the roof of the tower in anticipation of Daichi's residence. He quietly stated to Safara that they would discuss her course load in the morning and gave her, Ayo, and Ryl the day to do as they pleased. Before he left to meet with the other Masters, he watched the three trot off to check out Safara's new home in the Acolyte's Tower.

CHAPTER 6

"Wait, Stahd's Breath, Fara! Wait up!" Terris followed Safara out of the Sonics Tower as she angled left to the Practice Tower path. "Seriously, wait." He took off at a slow run to catch her up, lightly grabbing her shoulder and stopping her. "Please, Fara. You have got to stop beating yourself up like this. Ayo and Ryl are both so worried they are thinking of taking this to Jameson. Why are you pushing like this? We all want to help you, but you have to let us. In the three years since your acolyte test, you have barely slowed down at all. What are you rushing toward?" He ducked his head and crouched a bit to make eye contact, as Safara seemed unwilling to look up.

She relented and looked him in the eye shrugging. "I'm stuck. I can't move forward. I can't be anything. You know your job, so you can't possibly understand. Same with Ryl and Ayo. How am I to learn to focus like I need to, if I have no target? I feel fractured." She took a deep breath and gathered her thoughts for a moment, unconsciously tapping out the rhythm of the stone beneath her feet to calm herself. "Hold on. Why ARE you here? Your schooling is done. You should be assigned somewhere."

"I'm assigned to Captain Palmer at The Band. I came back last night with the latest reports for the General Council. My dad requested I play messenger boy occasionally, so that I can visit. I saw your sister this morning and she looked more pensive than usual. Ayo was the one who admitted why they were so concerned." He paused and motioned her forward again. He fell into step beside her watching her out of the corner of his eye. "Do you want me to talk to my father?" He asked almost reluctantly.

"No," she sighed, releasing the tension in her shoulders. "I talk to Deckard almost weekly and he is well aware of my stress. He, too, has told me to settle down and find a rhythm. He said a forced breakthrough isn't worth the rush."

"Maybe you could take a break from vocal training for a bit," he offered gently. "I mean when is the last time you took some time to just have fun without having some doomsday clock ticking off the beat in the background? Take your sister and Ayo. Go camping. Go to the market. Hell, sing a song for fun and not to manipulate the elements." He grinned at her. "Some people do, you know. Sing for fun, not to build or attack. Just to make a lovely noise with feeling."

"I honestly couldn't say. I have tried to remain on goal. Ryl is so convinced that Iyna is out there and I have to find her. My parents would expect it."

Terris could see her pulling back mentally and doubled down on his suggestion before she could think about it. "Even your parents wouldn't expect you to never have fun. Didn't you say they were always joking with each other and seemed happy? I doubt they would want you existing like this without any time to relax." He brightened and snapped his fingers at an idea. "Meet me at the top of the Acolyte's Tower in fifteen minutes."

"What? No, I have weapons training this afternoon. I can't miss that." Safara protested, but was cut off when Terris ran past her yelling he would take care of it.

"Fifteen minutes!" He shouted over his shoulder.

"But...and he's gone. Dammit." She headed back to her Tower and went to her room to drop off her books and grab her bag. Knowing Terris whatever plans he had would be well-intentioned, but not thought out. She stuffed a canister of water and some fruit into the satchel with a book just in case he got them stranded somewhere. After a moment's thought, she added a hooded cloak. She was already dressed for the cool spring day in grey leather leggings and an embroidered blue tunic that hit just above her knees. It was slit up both sides to her hips to allow for free movement. Her boots were thick and came up just below the knee secured with laces along the back of her calves. After fitting on her bracers, she barely made it to the roof before Terris.

"Are you ready?" he asked with a grin flinging his navy cloak around his shoulders.

She tried not to smile in response and failed abysmally. "Suppose so," she said and looped the strap diagonally across her chest as she walked across the stone pavers to him. At her voice, Daichi screeched in excitement from his aerie and came bounding out to greet his person. She laughed and offered him a mouse from a bin by the enclosure door. "Hi, Dai. How are you this lovely spring day? Have you been out hunting yet?" She kept up some chatter as she rubbed his beak and wiped some dirt from his otherwise pristine white coat. Daichi was a fastidious griffon both in his person and his enclosure. He chuffed at her happily until Terris approached. Immediately, Dai pushed forward between Safara and Terris, pushing her back and covering her with his wing. "Stop it, Dai. You know him," she admonished, as she tried to push his wing out of her face.

"Can you ask him to take us somewhere?" Terris asked nervously with his eyes downcast to avoid presenting a challenge.

"Yes, just a moment." Safara ducked under the wing, sputtering and spitting feathers. "Dai. Daichi!" She called his name several times to get his attention. Finally she reached up with both hands and pulled his beak down to her level. "He's a friend, remember? Can you fly us both on a trip? Not far. Just for the afternoon." Daichi grumbled his consent and turned around offering his back to them both.

"Don't we need to saddle him or something?" Terris

asked as Safara swung her leg over the snowy, white back having used a nearby stool to mount.

"Would you care to ask Dai how *he* feels about a saddle?" Safara shot back with a small laugh at his incredulous face. "Didn't think so. Climb up here and grip with your knees. It's easier to stay on than you think. Just don't let go." She really did laugh then at his unsure face. "This was your idea after all," she reminded him.

"When I said have fun, I didn't mean laugh at me," he muttered petulantly, but quickly cheered up, as he saw the afternoon off was working.

"Where are we going anyway? You should tell Daichi. Oh and don't pull his fur, he hates that. You will have to hang on to me. I can hold on to his wing joints if needed." She leaned forward and scratched the griffon where his fluffy mane faded into the soft fur of his body. His whole torso vibrated with his purr and he gave a stretch shoving his front paws out and bowing down with his tail up. Terris muffled a yelp and tried to lean back enough to keep from crushing Safara.

"Tell him to head for the trader's market near Knolhaven. I have a friend there I think you should meet."

Diachi was listening and immediately took off for the edge of the tower. He dove off the side with a screech of happiness. The wind rushed up toward them until the large wings snapped open and caught. The griffon quickly established a strong beat and soon carried them up above the top of Sonaris. Their departure was noted and Safara saw several of the students, including confused looking Ayo, wave at them from below. They circled higher and finally set out southwest.

Knolhaven was a small town within The Band populated mostly with Hearers and their families. Many engaged in trade and training in the market. The population fluctuated seasonally, as many parents chose to remain close during school sessions. Only some children stayed year round at the school; many were only present for half the year and then rotated home before returning the following year. These families tended to live in areas with Sonaran enclaves and defenses. Knolhaven was less than a half day's carriage ride from the school and a steady stream of ravens and messengers traveled between the two on any given day. The town itself was unremarkable. The buildings tended to be low, one or two stories with thatch roofs and timber beam construction. Several were made of local stone. Knolhaven was located on a cliff overlooking the Endless Ocean and boasted a thin rocky beach between the sheer rock face and the water. A narrow switch back path provided the only access to the oceanfront north of The Band. The rest of the coast around the Sonaran peninsula was honed to a vertical drop into the water. True locals could often be found resting on the beach in the afternoon or during the evening watching the sunset out over the water.

The griffon attracted some attention as he landed to one side of the town plaza. Several children scampered in close as their concerned minders tried to keep them back. Daichi was amused with the tiny things and did not mind their petting and crawling around his feet. He chuffed happily at them and flicked at them with his tail. His riders carefully dismounted and Safara told her familiar she would whistle for him when they were ready to leave. Daichi's response turned into a squawk, as a small elven girl pulled on a tuft of hair on his hock. He gently shook off the children and made a break for the edge of town to find some lunch and a nap.

"This way," Terris nodded to a small street that emptied into the town plaza. It was narrow and gated. The two story buildings on either side were of a smooth grey stone carved with knots and swirls. As they entered, Terris rang a bell off to the side three times in quick succession. The sound bounced off the walls and reverberated as they turned a corner and opened into a small, circular courtyard with a fountain spraying merrily in the center. A barn door off to the side slid open and a elderly mer approached them.

"Mister Terris! So good to see you again, lad. I heard your ring and bless if I didn't say to myself, 'Roggle, my ears must be false. Indeed they must. Our lad isn't due back for another month!' and yet here you are!" The black eyes of the mer twinkled happily and he moved to embrace Terris in a mighty hug. Roggle was medium height and pole thin, as most mer were, with short cropped purple hair and pointed, fin-like ears covered in earrings of gold inlaid with shells. "But who is this you have brought to my corner? A seeker, perhaps? I always say to myself none can find you if they don't look. So here you must be, my dear."

Safara had no ready response to such a declaration and just nodded as the old gentlemer graciously grasped her hand and bowed over it. She mumbled something to the effect that she was thankful for his kind attentions and silently pleaded with Terris to make some sort of explanation. The wretch had the nerve to wink at her and compliment Roggle on the fine welcome they received. For well on ten minutes, she had to listen as they volleyed effusive compliments and thanks back and forth, each more ridiculous than the last. Finally, she could take it no more and burst out in laughter. She leaned against the fountain for support and wiped tears from her eyes. Her companions eventually did the same. Terris shrugged sheepishly and introduced her.

"Roggle, my good sir, this is Safara. She is an Acolyte up at the school and was in need of a break from her regular training. I spirited her away for the afternoon and brought her here to learn about your particular skills. Would you be amenable to showing her around and imparting some of your great wisdom?" Terris pulled Safara forward to stand in between them.

"Without a doubt, you need only ask! My great honor, of course." Roggle offered a shallow bow and swept his arm toward the door he had exited. "Follow me to the shop and we shall see what we can learn, my dears." He stepped forward with an agility that belied his age. "This way, this way!" He called as he ushered them through the door and closed it behind them. The interior room was narrow and led directly to another set of doors. Once the exterior door was secured, Roggle moved around his visitors and opened the second, careful to shut it again as soon as they were within.

This room was far larger and had a two story ceiling height. It was an octagon and made of stone with the thatch roof supported by thick timber beams which met at a point in the center of the roof. Halfway up each wall was a balcony about five feet wide that ran around the entire perimeter and was accessed by a spiral staircase near the door. Most of the balconies were covered with bookshelves stuffed with all manner of books, scrolls, curios, and memorabilia. A thin metal track encircled the top of each bookcase and spanned the niches between. A narrow ladder on wheels was positioned so it could be moved around the track to reach any of the items needed. Transom windows of stained glass topped the shelving and allowed light to spill down into the work area on the floor without the worry of nosey neighbors. Each depicted a different cycle story and how Rasulo was defeated. The 7th and 8th windows represented Stahd and the founding of Sonaris. Safara's jaw went slack as she moved toward the middle of the room, turning slowly to take it all in. Small motes of dust floated down in the soft colorful light and she relaxed for the first time in ages.

"What is this place? It is wonderful!" She turned slowly in a circle trying to memorize each transom scene in order. Her voice came out in barely a whisper as she felt rather than heard the Song in the room. It was almost tangible and it was clearer than ever before.

"This is a Songforge, Safara," was the simple reply. The funny man cocked his head to one side and waited several minutes until he was sure she was listening to the symphony channeled into the room. "You can feel it, yes?" He asked knowing the answer, as she was lightly swaying to the sound.

"It is so clear here. How is this possible? Why haven't I been here before?" She would have been upset at having been excluded from this experience, but was so content that she could not muster even mild annoyance.

"Not many come to the Songforge, few at all. It is a great secret even among the Hearers in Sonaris. You heard the bell Terris rang at your entrance? That is a signal. Any that approach the forge without a proper check tempt their death. These treasures are well guarded, I assure you. I have spent my life gathering this trove and I do not share well, do I, my boy?" At this Roggle elbowed Terris in the side and moved to pull Safara further into the very center of the room. "The sound is best here. Please sit. Sit, sit, I insist. I can't have you falling over when the full force of the cacophony hits you, no no indeed!"

Safara gratefully sank into the floor and closed her eyes at the aged mer's insistence. Within moments, she was swept away by the most beautiful blend of sounds: earth, fire, water, wind, light, shadow, flora, and fauna elements all called out simultaneously in one voice, but she could hear each distinctly. Mingled within were a few elements she did not recognize. They were softer, but definite. The rhythms were practically visible as the vibrations focused toward the center of the room. Under several of the balconies were workstations. One appeared to be a desk covered in papers, scrolls, inkpots, quills, and other writing paraphernalia. The second was a smaller version of a blacksmith's forge, but the hearth contained a fire of rainbow colors and the bellows were made of pipes. This work area seemed to have all manner of metallurgical tools spread across a bench near the forge. The pipes were connected to a keyboard in yet another area. The last area was filled with test tubes, phials, and preserved specimens.

Quietly, the songsmith motioned Terris over to the keyboard and the bellows. The mer studied the girl taking in all aspects of her dress, bearing, and personality. After a few minutes, he roused her from the trance she was in and began asking questions.

"Now to start the work, this will be a great work. I always say you feel when genius will strike and how can we slip and fail to impress our new miss?" He pottered over to the hearth and took a look at his materials. "What do you want more than anything, Miss Safara? Your drive is not purposeless. I would wager my ears on that!"

"I want my sisters back together. I want to find Iyna." She answered honestly. The Song in the room shifted slightly in response.

"What motivates you in this mission?" came the unexpected follow up.

Safara started to answer and then stopped herself. She thought the answer was obvious, but she sensed Roggle would not ask if it were a matter of course. "Love, I would hope. I love my sisters. I loved my parents even though we don't know what happened to them. I have to assume they are gone or my mama would have found us at the school by now. Papa never would have left us either. Knowing what I know now, he would have eventually found us at the school, as well. It has been eight years. I know they are gone. But Iyna is out there. Ryl has felt her and we need her back." Again the Song changed.

"How would you accomplish this goal?" her host asked the question with finality.

"I will fight and do whatever is required to get her back. Rasulo can burn this cycle for all I care. I would give anything but Ryl to get her back." Tears shimmered in the corners of her eyes as she boldly met the narrowed gaze of the mer. The Song picked up tempo and he nodded.

"Very very well, young acolyte. Your determination has picked for you. It knows what you need and we will make it, yes, no question. Terris, my boy, start the bellows. If you will move this way, we can talk about my craft. This is the Songforge, you see. The fire is made of pure Song channeled and refined into colors representing different elements based on what is being made. For now, just know that your answers sorted the colors. While I make all sorts of baubles, I specialize in weaponry. You strike me as a close combat fighter, yes?" At her nod, he smiled mischievously and winked. "Always can tell, you know. Now back to business, knife fighting is an art, more dance than a quick stabbing, at least it should be. You should use two slender stilettos in a reverse grip. I like that idea, unexpected. But we hide them in your bracers. Remove them and let me see what we have."

Safara did as she was told and watched with interest, as her leather bracers were examined. After several minutes, he placed the bracers and two lumps of silvery metal into the forge. The colored fire in the forge reacted to both, but did not burn the leather. Roggle moved to Terris and whispered something in his ear. Terris, in turn, began to play a tuneless melody on the keyboard. Greens and blues exploded through the forge and the metal began to soften into the molds that Safara only then noticed. Roggle now approached Safara and pulled her forward.

"This is your part. To make these blades truly yours, completely yours, you must insert part of yourself into them. You must use your voice to forge them. It will be uncomfortable, but the earning is worth it. They will respond to you, specifically to your voice. Now tell them what to do, child." Roggle backed away and busied himself at another work bench. Terris kept plugging away at the pipe-bellows. Teal and lime green fire sprang out toward her face.

Safara focused on the blades on what they represented.

She let out a clear, high note, pure and without vibrato. The effort was like trying to sing with a mouth full of syrup, but as she focused, the tone honed and pierced through. That note rippled across the liquid metal and slowly sank into each surface evenly. The note represented her care for her sisters and her desire to have them together again; it asked for nothing for herself. Each blade took on a slightly green hue and the color became more vibrant as she approached it. She smiled and looked to Roggle for approval. He gave a slight nod and removed the molds from the fire to cool. Now he focused on the bracers. The leather seemed to stretch under his expert fingers. He occasionally called on water to soften the leather further and sculpt it as needed. When he was finished, each bracer spanned her forearms from elbow to wrist. The tops were covered with intricate knot work as was found on the buildings around the forge. Some of the knots were silver and others a faint green. The underside contained the most useful changes to the armor. The mer inserted a small, flat spring loaded tube to the bracer, just wide enough to receive the corresponding stiletto. With a small practiced movement, Safara could press a release on the heel of her hand to eject the blade, point first. With a small burst of song, she could slow the blade enough to grab the hilt either just as it emerged or shortly after to reverse her grip. The crossguard was narrow and round to reduce friction.

The mer elder explained that while each blade was tuned to Safara; they could be used by other people just like any other weapon. However, Safara would have better control using them and she was unlikely to lose them for long. Songforged items have a way of turning up. Safara nodded appropriately as she received instructions for how to care for her new blades. There was the usual information about keeping them clean and dry, but also how to keep them tuned. Occasionally, she would need to renew the song she laid into the blades by singing to them the same melody (or in her case, single tone) that she impressed upon them originally. From what she understood, the blades were not sentient, but neither were they inanimate. When the new blades were loaded into the bracers and tested for the first time, Terris finally left the pipe-bellows and joined the other two toward the center of the room. Safara hit the button and the right hand blade shot across the room with some force pinging harmlessly into the stone wall.

"Use the tone. The tone you picked for this one. Start as you push the button." Roggle reminded.

This time the blade emerged sluggishly and stopped before the hilt was out. Safara tipped her arm down and caught the handle as it fell.

"Too much, too much. Dial down. You are talking to the knife, you know."

Safara reloaded that blade while Terris went to fetch the other. Within the hour, she could slow one blade enough to grab it, but could not seem to master catching both at once.

"Ah well. Too much to hope for that success today, dearie. But you did well. No cuts yet!" Roggle smiled as though he had expected something different. "You will train with these constantly until they both obey you intuitively. Learn different techniques from the trainers at school. Be different. Don't just depend on your song. Depend on all of you." Again he cocked his head off to one side as he said this. "You will come back and visit me, yes?"

"Of course, Roggle! I would be honored." Safara bubbled over with enthusiasm and impulsively hugged the mer. He returned the hug with genuine fondness and patted her back.

"Your bell will be four dings, I think. Short, short, long, short. That will do nicely. Don't forget!" He said this absently and moved to make a note of the change to his security system.

Terris moved quietly to Safara's side and said they should leave soon if they wanted to make it back to Sonaris before lights out.

"Of course, you are right." Safara was disappointed to leave and gave the transoms one last review in the setting sun light. "Roggle, I will be back to visit on my next free day. Thank you for your gift and guidance." The old mer just kissed his fingers and waved them at her before returning to his notes.

Safara and Terris moved through the double doors, careful to open and shut them in the reverse sequence of their entrance. Once back in the plaza, Safara let out a shrill whistle, which was answered momentarily by the happy cry of Daichi. He had been cruising about nabbing bats in the twilight and was quite pleased with himself. They mounted and took off for the school again. Safara was content and relaxed for the ride. When she was not admiring her new bracers, she spoke to Terris about possible uses for them. In general, she was so altered from that morning that Terris could not help hugging her as they dismounted on top of the Acolytes' Tower. After checking Daichi had enough water and food for the night, they left the aerie and leaned out over the parapet wall to watch the stars emerge.

"I really do need to thank you, Terris." Safara changed the tack of their conversation suddenly. She looked down and picked some imaginary dirt from under her fingernails to cover her embarrassment. "You saw I was drowning and did something about it. And not just anything…something meaningful." She brandished her right bracer under his face; the silver knotwork catching in the soft moonlight. "You are a great friend and I am painfully aware that I haven't been completely fair to you over the years. Pax?"

Terris gave a small smile and shook her hand. "Pax," he said solemnly. "You always were my friend, at least in my head anyway. I was an ass when you first got here. I wasn't used to sharing my dad or uncle's attention outside of classes. I have been trying to make up for that; at least now we truly are even. In fact, you may even owe me because of the gloves." He laughed and she joined in knowing he did not mean it.

The air suddenly felt charged and Safara felt like her world tilted. Not knowing how to respond to the change in atmosphere, Safara saluted and yelled her goodbye over her shoulder as she darted for the stairs to her room. Not waiting for a reply she rushed through her door a floor below and slammed it behind her. She wondered sourly what in Stahd's perfect heavens possessed her to salute. Shrugging she headed to wash up and climb in bed, unsure of why she was castigating herself.

CHAPTER 7

The rush of metal swords and the creak of leather filled the thick afternoon air. There was a light mist present, which oddly made the heat more oppressive. Ryl was off to the side of the practice yard working on her mounted archery with Parsifal. He rushed past targets at different speeds and she did her best to hit them. Nyx sunned himself lazily on a large boulder off to one side of the field. He ignored most of Ryl's combat training except when an arrow rushed his direction pinging off the rock below him. He picked up his head and jangled a nasty retort for the fright before lying back down.

"Arrrrgh!" Ryl let out a frustrated yell. "I am no good at this!" She nocked another arrow and let it fly toward a brightly painted hay bale hanging from a tree branch. The arrow whisked to the side and hit the tree instead. Having hit only three of ten targets on the course and none of them inside the outer ring, she wheeled back around to the start where Master Lucia waited occasionally digging her hooves deep in the sod.

"Honestly, this is the most frustrating exercise, Master! Why can't I train in another combat proficiency? Safara got to choose hers." Ryl started to whine, but Lucia cut her off fast, responding in her patient, unhurried way. Even Parsifal seemed unimpressed with her pity party.

"You, small one, need to learn to get out of your comfort zone and stretch yourself. Your sister's path is her own and quite frankly none of your concern at the moment." Lucia stopped to observe her pupil absently swatting a fly from her flank with her tail. "Your training has progressed at a remarkable pace for your age because you are so adept at the skills needed to be a good Canticle. Combat training presented a unique opportunity to provide you with controlled frustration. To force you to make a choice and quickly. You are perfectly capable of using your instincts, but you choose not to. That will get you and your bondpartner hurt. Working as a bonded pair is complicated, but most of it is instinct. Knowing yourself and your partner so well that you can anticipate what should be done. This isn't an exercise in torture. It's an exercise in adapting. Failure is a powerful teacher that the naturally gifted often miss. Roll your eyes again and I'll add an hour of martial training to this afternoon." Parsifal nickered in approval, stamping his foot to underline his agreement.

At that pronouncement, Ryl quickly schooled her features and apologized. "I am sorry, Master Lucia. I'm just not good at this."

"Understood, but regardless, try again."

She moved to a table and handed Ryl another bundle of arrows to complete the course. "Another two times at least, I think. Then retrieve all of the spent arrows. A hint, if I may?" Ryl nodded sullenly. "Although you have to shoot arrows, our rules say nothing about using your abilities to help them along. In fact, as a Canticle, using your wind to aid a machine or existing function is exactly what you have trained to do." Lucia laughed as the idea took root in the girl's mind.

For the next hour, Ryl ran the course of her own free will several times. By the last run, she hit seven out of the ten bales and one of them was in the middle ring. She grinned from ear to ear. While not the best showing on the course, it was a vast improvement on any previous attempts. Generally, combat training was not her forte and she avoided it at all costs. With a happy heart, she jumped down from Parsifal and began to walk the course to retrieve all of the arrows. Her mount trailed contentedly behind. At the first target, she tugged the arrows free and packed them into the quiver on her back. When she turned to hook the bow to the saddle, she removed the bridle and scratched Parsifal's chin affectionately.

"You might as well get a snack. I'm going to be a bit finding the ones I missed," she said as he snuffled at her hair. She giggled and trotted off to finish her work before the sun faded. Ultimately, she managed to recover twenty-eight of the thirty arrows she shot. *A new personal record!* She thought as she stowed all of her equipment and took Parsifal back to the stables for his dinner with Nyx languidly trailing behind.

* * *

Zing! Zing! Thud! Thunk! The blades sang across the room. Safara stared intently at the target on the opposite wall dissatisfied with her showing.

"The left one is pulling a bit to the side," Ayo called from her place in the viewing gallery above. She had just finished her training and was waiting on Safara to go to dinner. "Did you tune it before you started, Fara?"

"Yes, of course I did," came the terse reply. Safara hated off days. She had been flat and she knew it. Being perfectly healthy, she had no excuse like a cold or even a headache to blame it on. She just felt…off like there was an invisible ceiling blocking her progress. "They are being weird today. I think I'm done. Are you ready for dinner?"

Ayo flipped herself over the polished balcony rail and slid down the side of a buttress by the door landing just behind Safara. "Dumb question. I love food. Get going." She pushed the door open and held it as Safara retrieved and loaded her daggers. "You know you were the tiniest bit flat, right? That's not you." Ayo's blue-green ponytail bounced around her shoulders as they jogged down the stairs of the tower. She looked concerned and watched carefully as Safara unstrapped the bracers.

"I know. I know. It was weird. My practice sessions have been going so well lately that I think I was being lazy. But mostly I feel restless, I guess. Like I should be doing something not here. Come on…if we miss the blessing and have to eat separately, Ryl will murder me."

Safara's training was complicated and specialized, as she preferred close combat before Roggle made her daggers. However, they had a ranged option that was foreign to her instincts. Usually, sparring was easiest when the other combatant was near your level of competency, but no one else in the school used the same technique as the one suggested by the Songsmith. Many times, Safara ended up practicing alone. Another complication was dexterity. The spring release was tricky and releasing it unintentionally could result in a punctured foot, lost eye, or other maiming. Safara had to release the blade and precisely close her hand over the hilt of the blade as it came out. Most of the other students were unwilling to risk injury just to round out her training. Ayo helped occasionally, but only if Safara used wooden dowel rods instead of the stilettos. The substitutes would not respond to Song, so it rather defeated the purpose. As it was, Ayo regularly had a few small round bruises on her arms and legs from being shot with the padded tips.

Additionally, Safara made a few modifications with the help of Master Deckard over the last weeks to enhance her capabilities, which made her unwilling to subject anyone to sparring. She could now load the daggers with the point going either direction. They added a slit to the outer edge of each tube for the edge of the blade to swing out as she grasped the hilt. Slowly, she was becoming comfortable with having a forward grip in her right hand and a reverse grip in her left. Pairing her song with the daggers allowed her to manipulate their trajectory or stop it all together. Using the blades became as natural as breathing. After allowing Ayo to try them out earlier in the day, the girls discovered that she needed to tune them after. The songforged blades were now legendary in the student body, as no other student was allowed their own weapons in their room or outside of the armory. Safara was allowed to keep hers, but not wear them outside of the practice yard or combat tower.

The sun sank slowly below the horizon as twilight spread across campus washing the area in dusky light and a warm, salty breeze from the east. Ayo asked Safara's opinion on their latest homework in Sonics and how she discovered that for her a high pitched tone with a slow vibrato could turn water into ice. The possibilities were completely distracting to both of them. Safara's interest was theoretical, as she had never managed to create so much as a ripple. After comparing techniques and their schedules, Ayo suggested that they take a short trip. Both had a rest day coming in two days and they planned to take Daichi to Knolhaven to visit the beach, if Ryl wanted to go. After changing, they just barely made it in time for the blessing and Ryl shot them both a relieved smile. Nyx sat contentedly by her plate ignoring the rest of the group, as usual.

"I was sure you would both be late and then I'd have to eat with Marcus and Jillian alone again. Ever since Marcus showed up as a Canticle last semester, she has been in hot pursuit. It's no wonder he hangs out with me. He knows we can't bond and I think the pressure is a bit intense for him. I told him to tell Master Lucia, but he doesn't want to complain. He's like, what? Fourteen." Ryl stopped and grabbed a roll from a passing platter. "Jillian is seventeen, almost graduated; it's beyond ridiculous. Here they come. Fara scoot over a bit, so he can squeeze in." Ryl muttered most of this under her breath, but turned and greeted Marcus in a loud voice. "Marc! Over here! Saved you a seat. I know you wanted to ask Fara about Daichi." She casually patted the empty space her sister made as Marcus gratefully smiled in their direction. He quickly slid into the space between the sisters. Jillian let out a huff and rounded the far side of the table to sit by Ayo, who was amused and ready to watch her older classmate make cake of herself over a pubescent boy. Canticle or no, at sixteen Ayo preferred her partners (vocally or otherwise) to be a bit more mature.

Safara smiled reassuringly at Marcus and asked after his studies. She saw him occasionally in the Focus Tower when she had Canticle Training with Master Lucia. After thwarting several attempts by Jillian to elicit a promise from the young dwarf to join her for training in the next week, Safara gained herself a devoted friend. Ryl was too disgusted by Jillian's blatant attempts to find any humor in the situation, but Ayo called it the most entertaining dinner of her life. Marcus on the other hand took Ryl up on the promise to show him around the Neophyte's Tower and give him some pointers on how to fend off some of the more persistent vocalists. The Masters had been trying to pair her for years and she still managed to hold her own.

Marcus was a late admission to the school from the Dwarven capital of Tark-Delve, which was located on the western side of the Spina Ardus south of the Great Marsh. Outside of Sonaris, it was considered the safest stronghold for Users and Hearers in Telaria. Marcus' parents decided to tutor him at home when he was identified as a Canticle. His father was the head of the Smithing Guild and his mother was a ranking member of the Tark family, one of the two founding families of the Dwarven Alliance. She served on the Ruling Council and had opted to keep her son close until his grandfather finally insisted he be sent for formal training and pairing. Marcus liked Sonaris well enough, but he found the lack of subterranean buildings and general openness of the campus to be unsettling. He was tall for a dwarf around five and a half feet with strikingly black hair and just the hint of a beard starting. His eyes were small and narrow, set deep into his face. When he smiled, they practically disappeared because of how they crinkled up at the corners. His skin was a deep brown and he had dozens of small, intricate tattoos on his hands that indicated his House and rank in the Dwarven Alliance. He was generally considered friendly at home, but Sonaris had taught him caution in trust. The Masters all wanted what was best for him, but under it all, he knew that they would put the survival of the cycle over his wishes for a bondpartner. Thus it was up to him to defend himself and his own pairing. Ryl treated him as an equal and a friend. She wanted nothing from him and in return he gave her his friendship, trust, and loyalty. She reciprocated with the same gifts, but added on her own bonus of foiling pairing attempts whenever she could.

With Marcus in mind, Safara and Ayo changed their plans from Knolhaven to a picnic along the cliffs several miles from the school on the east coast facing Syreni. It was Ayo's favorite place, a small hill covered in boulders with a few trees for shade. From that position on a clear day, she could see all the way to where the Spina Ardus met the shore, which marked the location of her underwater home. Parsifal was recruited to carry Ryl and Marcus with Diachi soaring above with Safara and Ayo. Nyx flitted around for a while, but eventually settled between Parsifal's grey ears for the trip. He had no interest in being flown by another and was almost fond of the large horse. Occasionally, he flicked his wing against the horse's ear just to see it twitch and tinkle out a laugh at himself.

"Honestly, Nyx! It's a reflex. He will do it every time. Leave Par alone for a bit." Ryl chided from the saddle. Nyx chattered back in his defense. "I know you are just messing with him, but fight fair." She reached forward and patted the Parsifal's neck before offering her hand to the faerydae. He climbed on begrudgingly. She put him up to her face and ghosted a kiss over his cheek. "You know I love you, even if you are a weasel sometimes." He tweaked her braid and flew off ahead silver sparkles spreading out behind him.

"Do you really understand him?" asked Marcus. "It just sounds like bells or whistles to me."

"I know what his intentions are, if that's what you mean. But no, I don't understand actual words. It's all feelings and impressions. I think he makes me understand because I never learned his language that's for sure," Ryl answered thoughtfully. "I think he would make Iyna understand, too."

"Who is Iyna?" Marcus asked innocently just as they arrived at the top of the hill. Safara and Ayo were already waiting and had a blanket spread out and were unpacking lunch. Both of them heard the question and swung around to face the new arrivals.

"Iyna is our sister." Safara answered slowly gauging Ryl's willingness to discuss their sister in public. Ayo was aware of almost everything, but she had never discussed the third sister with Ryl.

Ryl took a deep breath. "She is my twin specifically and..."she paused for a moment. "You absolutely have to promise not to tell anyone, but Iyna is my bondpartner, as well. That is how we know she is still alive and well. I can feel her on the other end of the tether."

"Is that how you have managed to avoid being paired for so long? I thought they tested you against almost every available Vocalist at school." Marcus seemed to be processing the information quickly. He seemed concerned, but not disbelieving, which made the others more inclined to share.

"For the most part. The Masters don't know of the pairing. I didn't realize what she was until we came here and I had been in training for a few years. I think Master Lucia may suspect because I report to her whenever I can feel Iyna more clearly, but they still try." Ryl sat on the blanket and started making herself a sandwich from the contents of the basket. The others joined her as Diachi and Parsifal wandered off to nap and graze respectively. "Iyna is my opposite. She is sunny and quick. The impulsive twin with practically white hair and light blue eyes. She always made me laugh and want to be free. She was the one who suggested we should try to make a berry bush grow together out of season. It worked, we bonded, and she got trapped. But when we went back she was gone and then Mama was gone. Papa never came back or came here to find us. That's why we think our parents are dead. They would have found us here. But Iyna...she never knew this place existed. So how could she know to come here?"

"Are you going to find her?" asked Marcus after swallowing the last of his first sandwich.

"We will," said Safara with Ryl and Ayo both nodding.

"When?" came the innocent reply. The question hung in the air, begging to be answered. Safara tried to answer several times, but did not want to lie.

Ryl shook off her malaise and answered with certainty. "The next time I feel her pull, we go. We know too much and have been training too hard to just stay here and get assigned around Telaria after graduation. Fara, you and Ayo only have another year left before your assignments. I think we have to go now. Before *we* are split up."

The rest of the group agreed and lapsed into silence as they considered their options. Marcus was the first to speak. "I know I haven't been here long and you have no reason to let me, but I want to come. I think I can help." When the others began to protest, he pushed on. "Hear me out. I am a Canticle, so I can help even if I'm not bonded to anyone. Plus you three are some of my only true friends in the school, if you leave I have no interest in staying. Add to that, I'm the only one of us to have spent significant time outside The Band and on the continent in the last several years. Ayo goes home, but that's a swim across the bay, not inland travel. I can help."

"That's kind of you, Marcus. But you need to train here. What will your parents say?" Ryl asked gently.

"My mother would expect me to help. My father, too. No

worries there," he replied with a slow grin. "So seriously, when do *we* go?"

"We will need a diversion to get away from the school with supplies. A picnic basket won't get us far and we can't go doubling up on Parsifal all the way to Iyna." Ayo pointed out initial problems with her usually efficiency.

"It will have to be a big diversion, but not something that can get us expelled. We will need to be welcomed back once we have our sister, who knows what condition she will be in." Safara thought out loud for a moment. "I bet we can get Terris to help us get outside The Band, but we will have to coordinate carefully. It's no good to get away from here and be stuck inside. It takes half a day to ride from Sonaris to The Band and we can't let them send any ravens to warn Palmer. He wouldn't let us out even if he agreed with our mission. Jameson might help, but that is risky, too. She mothers Ryl to death and still makes me report to her weekly on my progress."

Ayo stared out across the bay toward Syreni twirling a lock of blue hair around her finger thoughtfully. "What about an out of season blizzard?" At their shocked faces she laughed a bit and explained. "Think about it. Ryl is awesome with wind and I just learned to make water into ice. We just have to pick a rainy or misty day and BOOM! Instant snow storm. Everyone would be so interested in the weird weather that they wouldn't even notice us leave the stables."

"And by the time everyone stopped wondering what was going on, we would be out of sight. All the Masters will assume we are messing around with the rest of the students hopefully. Regardless, they will assume we are still on campus somewhere." Safara picked up the thread of the idea and ran with it. "You and Ryl can work from the top of the Acolyte's Tower away from everyone else and Daichi can fly you down to us. Marcus and I can head to the Stable Tower and saddle Parsifal and another mount to bring with. Dai won't mind carrying two. I can let Terris know that on the next rainy day after you sense Iyna, we will head for The Band and he will have to get us through. Maybe Nyx can fly ahead and let him know we are coming?"

A slight tinkling sound was heard from the rock where Nyx had been sunning himself.

"He'll do it," Ryl confirmed. "I think he wants Iyna back just as much as I do."

"I can work on stockpiling some food and gear. The Masters don't know me well enough to have an idea of what is odd behavior from me," Marcus offered. "We will need water skins, a tarp, and several blankets. Not to mention food that will keep like jerky or dried fruit. I have a few packs from when I moved. What about weapons?"

Safara thought for a moment. "I have my bracers, but I think we should leave weapons to Terris. He has his own now that he is graduated and stealing from the armory here just seems like a bad move. Food they would forgive, weapons maybe not. We will also need cloaks, boots, and leather gloves. Dress in layers. During my acolyte test, the weather at night was the worst."

Soon everyone had their assignments for the trip. No one wanted to discuss the problem of finding Iyna once they were outside of The Band, but that it hung over them all. Ryl and Ayo moved off to one side to practice making a blizzard. Nyx shook a partially plugged water skin over their heads and they practiced in the sprinkles that came down. Marcus and Safara moved to the top of the hill and discussed the logistics of getting the gear to the Stables Tower without being noticed. In the end, they decided to store everything in their lockers at the Choral Tower and run it over during the storm. Marcus said he had a mount in the stables as his familiar, so they did not need to worry about stealing a horse. Satisfied that they had as much planning done as possible, the four moved back together and all solemnly swore to keep their plans a secret. If anyone asked about the extra food or gear, they were going to plan a diversion camping trip as a cover. The return to the school was filled with more discussions and plans and they all parted to their rooms with a new purpose.

❋ ❋ ❋

Several days later, Safara heard a familiar rippling sound overhead and looked up just in time to see a stream of water settle over her position. She took in a breath to push it away with wind, but ended up choking on a mouthful of the stuff. Coughing, she sputtered for her next breath and whirled around looking for the culprit.

"Terris, you ass! Why? I like this tunic and now I'm a sopping mess." She flipped her hair out of her face and hoped he would see just how infuriated she truly was.

"Oh come on, Fara! I called your name twice and no answer. You were really out there. I had to do something. You look just as pissed as you did when we were little." Terris jogged up to her and tried to wipe her face a bit with his sleeve. She slapped his arm away.

"Seriously, now you want to be helpful? Get your snotty sleeve away from my face. Who knows what nastiness you have on there?" She pushed his hand out of her face and then laughed a bit, but continued petulantly, "You are so odd. Next time use a gentle breeze or something. Seriously, even my socks are wet!"

"Fine, no more water snakes hanging over your head. And my sleeves haven't been snotty in months, so you know." Terris crossed a hand over his heart. "What were you so focused on?"

"Not here. I'll tell you later. Can you meet me and Daichi after classes?"

"Sure. I'll go meet with my dad and see you later," he agreed easily and jogged off toward his father's office, as Safara trudged on to class despite her soggy attire.

When they met on the roof again, Safara was teasing Daichi with the faery crystal from her staff. He pounced on the light no matter where she moved it and always seemed confused when it refused to stay under his paw. He squawked at it and swiped at the stone floor of the aerie.

"Go easy, fella. She is messing with you." Terris stated as he moved around the griffon to Safara. "So what is so secret that we have to meet up here? You have something going on. I've known you since I was ten. Spill." He plopped down on the storage bin next to the one Safara was perched on.

"I hope I'm not that obvious to everyone or Ryl will kill me. We are going after Iyna." She clapped a hand over Terris' mouth to hold in his protest. "You need to listen; once I'm done you can comment." When he nodded, she removed her hand and started back up. "Ryl bonded with Iyna when we were kids. Literally on the day we fled our house. She can feel Iyna out there sometimes and knows she is alive and needing us. Ayo and Marcus have agreed to come with us and search for her since we can't risk waiting until Ayo and I graduate and are assigned. We have to go now…before they split us up. Ayo and Ryl have been working on a diversion. It's good, but probably better if you don't know what they are doing in case it doesn't work. Marcus and I are gathering travel supplies and will be in charge of the mounts. We do need your help." Safara paused and looked Terris directly in the eye. "To be honest, I wouldn't feel right about going without you knowing. We need you to get us out of The Band. We will head your way on the first rainy day after Ryl next feels a pull to Iyna. Nyx will fly straight to you and let you know we are on our way. Once you see him, we will only be a few hours behind, so whatever you can do to ensure we can get away, do it without getting caught or in trouble. Will you?" Safara was close to tears at this point and Terris could not say no.

"I'll do it." He assured her and took her hand. "But I am

coming with you. I cannot in good conscience let four students out into the world without protection. Let alone a Canticle like Ryl."

"Two Canticles." Safara amended.

"Stahd! You never make things easy. My father will murder us both when we make it back. And I mean possible, real murder." Terris dropped her hand and ran his through his hair. He stood and paced for a few minutes. "Fine. Never mind, doesn't matter. I will still do it, but you keep all of this secret. Don't worry about the camping gear. I can stow some outside of the gates with a few bows and arrows. You bring your daggers and staff, but the others will be stuck with whatever else I can scavenge."

"I'll let them know. Marcus and I were worried about weapons. Stealing from the armory is a bad plan if we want to be readmitted."

"Who is this Marcus and why is he coming?"

"He is a fairly new arrival, a Canticle. Trained at home in Tark-Delve. Now half the school is chasing after him and he has attached himself to Ryl since she has no interest in him nor can she pair with him regardless. Ayo thinks he is harmless. But he pointed out that he is the only one of us that has lived outside The Band in years, much less traveled it."

"Interesting. Introduce me at dinner. He sounds decent anyway. I'll get a map from my dad's office so we have an idea of the best routes around Telaria. He won't even notice I have it and if he does, I can say I'm thinking of asking for an assignment in Arcem and wanted to see how to get there fastest."

"That might work, if Arcem weren't straight down the Long Road from here at the west crossroad. Make it Galston instead. That would work." Safara slightly amended the plan. "He would never approve that though. Try and sell it anyway; that's a long enough trip to make a map necessary."

"Agreed. So we have a plan?" Terris looked at her for signs of sincerity and was satisfied.

"I've never been more sure about anything."

* * *

The opportunity to act almost came too soon; barely a week after Terris returned to his duty station, a light sprinkle started. Ryl felt Iyna calling the night before and was ecstatic. It was the 7th day of Growth and the weather had been favorable. Just after breakfast Safara and Marcus rushed back and forth between their dorms and the Practice Tower frantically packing away food and supplies like rope, a lantern, and a medical kit. By mid morning, the mist turned into a decent rain. Large fat drops pelted down over every surface in a steady tattoo. All of the doors and windows were shut and most of the residents of the school were attempting to wait out the shower wherever they ended up. The Choral Tower and Stables were practically empty, as lessons were scheduled for the morning with physical training after lunch. Transferring the packs was simple with no onlookers.

Safara glanced over her shoulder at the stall holding Marcus' mount.

"What in Stahd's Name is that?" She asked with a laugh.

"Who? Mynock?" Marcus did not pause his work saddling his massive ram. Its large shaggy head peered over the stall door with his tongue lolling out of his head. Mynock appeared just as interested in Safara as she was in him. He brayed softly and she moved to briefly scratch his nose, careful to avoid the long curling horns that jutted out just above his mouth. "He is my best friend and is ready to be back out in the world."

"He is so sweet. Is he fast?" Safara resumed saddling Parsifal, who seemed affronted at her defection until she gave him

144

a carrot and kissed his nose. As they packed the saddle bags full and checked that they left no debris, Marcus filled her in about rams and their desirability as mounts in the Spina Ardus. They possessed speed and amazing agility over rough terrain. Mynock was a birthday gift for his tenth birthday and Marcus was allowed to keep him at Sonaris as his familiar. Both riders moved carefully to the stable door on the southwest side of the building and waited for the snow to start before trotting across the fields to the road. They attempted to look casual for the first mile before breaking into a canter once they reached the bend in the road.

❊ ❊ ❊

Ryl and Ayo headed to the roof of the Acolytes' Tower when it started to sprinkle. They found Diachi ready to carry them away and started to create their unseasonal weather.

"Nyx," Ryl called to the ever present faerydae. "Go find Terris and let him know we will be there soon. Fly safe and don't get caught up in this." The younger girl nuzzled his nose and watched until he was clear of the Focus Tower before telling Ayo to start.

The pair had not been able to practice as much as they would have liked. To be honest, neither felt particularly safe about how the storm would act. At first the rain refused to change, but once Ayo was fully focused on the task, flakes began to form around her. First a handful, then a small flurry just around them quickly melted away by the surrounding rain drops. Ryl called up the wind around them to push away the interfering rain and to push Ayo's ever growing bubble of snow out over the center of campus. Once it was large enough, both amped up their volume so that they were practically scream-ing into the storm. The sphere broke free of the wind caging it and dumped snow all over campus. Every tree, bush, and path was covered. No surface was left clear. Yet they kept growing the storm. Ryl seemed to notice the loss of control first. She tried to pull back out of the wind, but it kept cycling and swirling around them. She managed to slow the storm. Ayo was still changing the rain to snow as it came down; she caught every drop. However, she focused so hard on freezing that the drops began to turn into hail. They ranged from pea size to that of a large grape and dropped hard over every surface bouncing off the stones below or shattering and shooting shrapnel in all directions.

With difficulty, Ryl managed to pull completely out of it and the wind ebbed. She grabbed Ayo's arm shaking it. The mer's eyes had been closed and the strain of maintaining the melody showed in every line on her young face, which flushed to a pale yellow with the strain. At Ryl's insistent jostling, she slowly opened her eyes and let go of her melody. The storm swirled away to the south and began to break up without their guidance.

"Come on, Ayo. We have to go now. It won't take anyone long to figure out that was fake." Ryl winked and climbed up on to the confused griffon. Ayo sluggishly clambered on behind and held on.

"I don't feel well. Be kind, Dai," begged the mer.

The griffon responded with a chirp and leapt off the west side of the tower. The bright white wings snapped open and pumped powerfully. He gained altitude above the storm as quickly as possible to hide in the clouds, soaking both his passengers despite their cloaks and traveling gear. The griffon corrected course due south and soon they saw the welcome sight of Parsifal and Mynock galloping the same direction just below them. He screeched at the sight of Safara and she gave him a wave before bending back over Parsifal's head. As they reached the halfway point between Sonaris and The Band, the storm finally passed to the south and all traces of the faux snow were gone. The warmth returned. Although the sun shine was welcome, it also meant that their wet clothes were sticking uncomfortably and everyone felt sweaty despite the mild day.

When they broke for lunch, gloves, cloaks, and any other non-essential clothing was removed and stowed. The saddle blankets were checked and had remained dry under the saddles thankfully. After a brief rest, Safara and Ryl took off on Daichi leaving Marcus and Ayo to exit through the gate. Palmer was not nearly as familiar with them and was less likely to demand an explanation. As it was, Ryl had a hard time leaving Jameson that morning and insisted on leaving a note for her. Nyx had delivered it to her room as Ayo and Ryl were climbing up the Acolytes' Tower. Fortunately, the guardswoman had an assignment for the entire day and was not expected to return from Knolhaven until early evening. Daichi walked happily along with the other mounts until Nyx approached about a mile from the gate. He let Ryl know that Terris was waiting with a distraction whenever they were ready. Ryl greeted him as though he had been gone for days, not hours. He also seemed relieved to see his pet before flying back off to signal Terris. Daichi took off straight in the air and Ayo encouraged Parsifal to trot with Mynock easily keeping pace. Both were nervously excited. Ayo loved a challenge and Marcus was just grateful to be away from the school and its machinations. She grinned at him and winked.

"Ready for this?" she called just over her shoulder.

"No, but I will be," he called back with a grin.

"Good. Terris has some gear stowed outside the wall, but I don't think approaching at a gallop will work. I think we should go through at a trot, what about you?"

"Agreed. I haven't known Terris long, so what do you think he will do?"

"Likely something wildly unexpected and unnecessary,

but it will get the job done. He's been pranking most of the Sonaran population since he could walk."

They were within sight of the gatehouse towers and tried to keep calm and act natural, which meant both looked nervous and unsettled. Luckily, their appearance did not matter as the entire gate house area was empty. Not a soul was around to stop their progress and they rode through unimpeded. Off to the east, they could hear raised voices and some creative swearing, but neither bothered to investigate. Terris met them on the southern side just through the gate and smiled proudly. Nyx hovered nearby with his smokey wings flapping occasionally to keep him aloft, until he could settle between Parsifal's ears.

"I assume the girls took the aerial route?" At Ayo's confirmation, Terris wheeled around and motioned them to follow. Once they all passed the first stand of trees and were hidden from observation, he stopped, dismounted, and threw an additional saddlebag across his roan mare's back and handed a couple of bows and two quivers to the other riders. The mare seemed calm and unperturbed by any commotion her rider may have caused earlier. Both groups met up at the stream where Safara camped during her acolyte's test and Terris filled them all in as they set up camp and redistributed the gear into even pack sizes.

"You didn't give me much time to figure out a decent distraction. I have to start by saying this is not my best work." He paused to drive a stake into the ground for the tarp, which they were using as a tent for the night. Safara made a firepit and started their fire with a tiny peep of Song. "So Nyx showed up this morning clanging away at me like a tower bell, I almost forgot why he was coming and was momentarily worried that Ryl was nearby and injured. Then I remembered this harebrained idea and realized I had two hours or less to clear the gatehouse for you all. It wasn't easy, first of all. And second, I broke so many rules I'm fairly certain I will be reassigned to the Great Marsh for the next several years."

"Will you just get on with this?" Ayo almost snapped at his showboating.

"Yes, yes," he responded. "You may not know my full complement of affinities, but I inherited the ability to form and manipulate mass for brief periods of time. My grandmother used the same ability to create the frescos in Sonaris, but she was much stronger than I am. I digress." By this time, Ayo looked ready to drown him and he hurried up. "I built small golems out of earth and set them loose in the kitchen gardens. I don't know if you have ever seen or used a golem, but they are extremely stupid and crash through everything in their path. I probably made a hundred of the tiny things and set them loose all over the place. You should also know that the garrison cook is an extremely crotchety old crone, who hates anything being out of place. She raised such a ruckus over her newly growing garden that Palmer thought she was actually under attack. He summoned most of the garrison to dispatch the golems and I got rid of the rest of the guards by riding through and reporting a fire at the stables." He paused and laughed at their shocked faces. "Don't look at me like that. I didn't set a fire. I dropped a fire ball into a vat of water and pulled the steam into the air with song. It was only steam." He held his open hands palms up in front of his chest to underline his innocence. "Fara wouldn't tell me, but what did you all do?"

Ryl bounced up and down with excitement. "We made a snowstorm using the rain! Ayo was amazing. I just aided her with wind to really get it going and give her the room to work, but it was fantastic. We probably dumped a good inch all over campus."

"Really?" Terris looked suitably impressed. "You will have to teach me that one."

"I am willing to try, but it was rough going for a bit." Ayo replied good naturedly and with a faint purple blush at Ryl's praise.

They all settled around the campfire to eat and discuss their next moves. Ryl said it felt like Iyna was in danger. Her call had never been so strong, but it was cut off abruptly. She felt the pull coming from the south and slightly east, even at that moment she felt as if she could point the exact direction and pointed off through the trees. She even spun herself around to make herself dizzy and with her eyes closed she still picked the same direction several times.

"Where is the map?" Safara asked Terris. He pulled it out of his backpack. It was made of leather and was about the side of a dinner plate when unrolled. Safara oriented the map north to south and asked Ryl to point her finger directly at Iyna's location. When she lined the map up with that direction, a straight line bisected the Great Marsh, Tark-Delve, and the Spina Ardus. It ended directly on Mount Profana.

They all sucked in a deep breath and stared at the location in disbelief. Safara shook off the surprise first.

"Stahd's Breath. She can't be there. How are we supposed to get her out of there? It's *his* place." She bit back the start of a sob at the thought of her baby sister being trapped and raised by a monster for the past eight years. At worst, she had thought Iyna had been caught by traders and slaved. It never occurred to her that a worse option existed than that. Safara looked at Ryl, who seemed to be the calmest of the group.

"We will get her out. I'm just relieved to know we have a location." Ryl traced her finger over the map and gently tapped the place where she knew her twin was. "We have to try."

"You are right. *We do.*" Safara turned to the others. "We understand if you want out. This went from a bad idea to insane. That has to be the worst possible location for her to be and there are only five of us." Nyx let out a jangle of protest at the number of able bodies. Safara corrected herself. "There are only six Users here. Please do not feel obligated to come."

The others all immediately assured the sisters that they were still invested in recovering Iyna.

"Whatever happens, I could never leave you two." Ayo pulled both into a tight hug. "You both have been my family for years and although I haven't ever met her, I consider Iyna family, too. You don't leave your family with a monster."

"Agreed," said Marcus softly. Everyone was holding back tears at this point. "Maybe we should all get some rest. My father always says that problems seem less impossible in the morning."

With that, they all grabbed their blankets and spread out under the tarp and around the fire. Safara cuddled up next to Daichi and Ryl lay right next to her. The griffon covered both of them with his wing and purred softly at them.

CHAPTER 8

He moved determinedly down the stairs, robes occasionally catching on the rough stones protruding from the walls. He ignored the inconvenience and padded silently through the halls. At the false wall he stopped and checked his surroundings carefully. None of his lieutenants knew of this particular project. Mason and Greyfinger were away on assignment which left only Faustus scuttling around the keep. Assured of his privacy, he slid behind the panel leading to the winding tunnel and closed it behind him. As it closed he flicked out a mote of fire and aimed it at a narrow groove in the wall. Light filled the passage as the fire licked its way down the tar lined channel chasing away the shadows until it reached the boulder blocking the vault.

Rasulo heaved the boulder out of the way slightly and ducked inside just as it rolled back into place. The binding was doubled on the enormous stone and moving it was a challenge for his recovering abilities. He lit the tar groove as he moved to the pedestal in the middle of the room building his song slowly to gently acclimate the form to his process.

She was tall and slender with a vaguely humanoid form. No specific facial or body features to identify her race or general looks, but she was definitively female with two arms and legs. Her hands were molded to her sides. He worked slowly to separate each finger and her palm from where it was adhered to her outer thigh. The surface of her body was fragile and the slightest wrong move or breath removed the top layer of what would be her skin. It was delicate work, but this Angelic was known for his attention to detail and appreciation of the finer things. So he concentrated and was able to separate out each of the fingers on her left hand and even create fingernails. As the night wore on, his voice grew tired and he eventually tamped out the flame in the vault and up the curling tunnel as he returned to the castle above leaving her, alone and unmoved.

* * *

"Samal!" Iyna whispered, as she shook the mer's arm. "Wake up! The guards will be here soon to take me and leave your breakfast." Samal woke slowly and pulled herself up into a sitting position.

Darek was already up and puttering about the room in his usual routine. He had brushed out his beard and braided it again for the day. He took advantage of some extra water in the trench to wash his work clothes. Samal dragged herself out of bed and ran a brush through her lime colored hair. Time out by the mills was turning it more yellow this season and she was still losing her voice.

Iyna stopped both of their preparations for the day and pulled them to the table.

"I can't take much more of this. Both of you are sick and getting worn down. We need to make plans to get out of here and soon. Faustus is running out of lessons for me and once he is done I will have to train directly with Rasulo." She took a deep breath and pushed the hair from her face to make eye contact. "He scares me." She admitted in a small voice.

"Of course he does, girl," came Darek's terse reply. She could tell he was angry with the situation, not her. "We need a distraction. A big one. As long as that cursed Angelic is in the castle, no one is going anywhere. The sycops are used to letting you out into the woods, but they know if you don't return, they shouldn't neither."

"The only thing that could draw him away is power or the potential for more power." Samal was thinking out loud.

"But his power is growing. The farther into the cycle we get, the more he improves and gains back his abilities." Iyna stopped to think. "The last time I was summoned the slightest noise called up the Song. What could he possibly need other than time?"

The guards banged on the door and thrust their daily ration through the grate at the bottom. The ugly gimlet eye of the sycop guard peered in to take a head count. None of them had names that Iyna knew of. They were all covered with different scars and markings allowing her to differentiate. This guard was new and seemed more focused than their last, which was disappointing considering their escape plans. All three set to eating quickly without resolving their dilemma.

When she was done, Iyna rapped on the door and was released for training with Faustus, which was frustrating as usual. He made no allowances for typical teenage attitudes or issues. As it was, Iyna was in no mood to listen to his harangues and kept intentionally going flat to annoy him.

"None of that!" He yelled, his voice ricocheting across the training room, spittle flying with it. "I have told you thousands of times that focus is the only skill that matters across affinities. If you cannot do that, you cannot work with the Song. Don't think I have failed to understand that this is all on purpose." He paused to take a deep breath. "You, Miss Iyna, are stuck with me as a tutor until you have mastered your affinities. Do you understand that? Stuck. With. Me. Once I have nothing left to teach, we can both abandon this farce. Now, again. Try the melody again. I, for one, cannot wait to see what you suffer with him. Training is dangerous when your partner is significantly stronger and He will not make allowances for weakness."

"Yes, Master Faustus." As much as Iyna disliked Faustus, she preferred his rage to the calm cruelty of the Angelic. She had no intention of spending any more time with Rasulo than necessary. Not a month past, he sent a gang of mine workers out into the forest and forbade them to return. A week later she found some of them on her way to the tulip grove, dead and looking as though the life had been sucked out of them. It was the binding. Darek had discovered if a worker was denied a source, their life would slowly eek away and leave a dry desiccated husk behind. The interim was unbearable for the addict. They could feel their connection to the Song leeching from them and were powerless to stop it. Some took their own lives when the pain was too much. Others attempted to make it back to the stronghold, but were kept out by the patrols.

Sometimes the call of the Song was intoxicating and she could not help but perform to her best ability. In those moments, as with the tulip trees, Iyna betrayed her progress and moved one step closer to being Rasulo's personal slave and constant attendant. She shuddered at the thought. He may not look like it, but he was a monster: proud, exacting, and brutal. He had admitted that he was taking special pains to make this the last cycle, slowly and carefully rebuilding his strength and hiding his plans from all.

Iyna started her call to the earth again. Her tone was rich and full with little vibrato, as she slowly raised the pitch. Small stalagmites appeared all over the floor in front of her. Each stalagmite was thin and tapered to the top. The entire group covered an area of several square meters, all of the available space between Iyna and Faustus. He hit back with his own earth song designed to disrupt hers. He changed the composition of the material from rock to sand and many of them crumbled, unable to hold their shape. In response, Iyna caught the ones that fell and pushed them out again; this time growing them at an angle directly toward Faustus. He had not counted on her swift reaction and was caught off guard for a moment.

He quickly recovered and changed his tone to create a small earthquake which shattered all of the formations scattered across the floor. As some of the points fell, Iyna caught them up with her hands and threw them across the room at him.

"None of that!" he screamed. "Song only!"

"That is ridiculous." Iyna spat back. "There is no good reason to not use other resources. You said to always take stock of my situation. I am perfectly capable of maintaining my melody and throwing some dirt."

"I make the rules of these duels. You are to follow them and see if you can defeat your opponent fairly. Cheating only sets you back." Faustus was practically apoplectic and spit again flew from his mouth with every hard consonant, his wiry body vibrating with anger and frustration. "Just go. I don't care what you do for the day, just leave and go away."

Iyna was more than willing to comply. She fled the room in a flurry of white hair and black robes with such haste that she almost fell down the first set of stairs. She caught herself and pulled back just in time. Her instinct was to head back to her cell, but no one was there. Years of incarceration left her feeling adrift and unable to decide for herself. Eventually she redirected toward the library. She had never been allowed inside without an escort before. Faustus' fit of pique played into her hand, as the guard did not stop her or return her to her cell. She took cautious advantage of her freedom and eased into the library with her guard remaining outside. Sycops were forbidden from entering and as there was only one exit, she could not get away from him.

The room was more of a cavern set deep into the heart of the castle. All of Rasulo's writings and knowledge of the Song and Telaria were contained within. He was as fastidious with recording his history as he was with his clothing. The room was silent, cool, and slightly humid to keep the tomes from drying out. The room had no windows and fire was absolutely prohibited. Instead, glowing crystals were used all over the room and maintained to provide enough light to read, but not enough to fade any of the books or scrolls on the shelves. The rare books were kept in glass front cabinets to keep them from getting dusty.

Shelves covered every available wall and niche, each was custom built to fit around the curves and angles of the natural cave walls. Unlike other caverns in the compound, this one was dry and free of mold and other fungi. Iyna loved this room. It was the only place on the grounds that felt calm and restful. She hurried across the empty floor, her shoes clacking on the stone and reverberating around her. Tucked at the back of the room was a shelf that contained Rasulo's personal notes and journals. He recorded his thoughts in the Angelic language, not Common. Iyna had a rudimentary grasp of the language, as most of the music in the castle was written with notations in Angelic, so some exposure was necessary as part of her training.

She flipped the cabinet door up and grabbed one of the journals at random to search for anything that might help. Copying the text would take too long and she could not risk stealing any of them. She knew she would eventually be found in the library and would never be able to pass off her presence as leisure time if she stole a book. The journal she picked was from the 5th Cycle. Rasulo was faced with a bondpair named T'Chort and Kyayote at the end of the 4th, dwarven females with a strong fauna affinity. According to this record, they summoned every wolf in Telaria into a pack and overran Profana, tearing Rasulo to shreds. His body was eviscerated and scattered, but his spirit took refuge in the mountain and he spent the next years reassembling his body and regaining his strength. Iyna had wondered about the small white scars that covered Rasulo's face and hands. This account explained them in detail.

She closed the cabinet and moved around the corner to hide behind some shelving. The next several pages were not as interesting as her understanding of Angelic was not equal to the contents. The word "Pond" was repeated over and over along with the name "Stahd". There was a rudimentary map on the next page that contained many crosses and blots. Iyna decided to take the map and carefully removed that page from the diary. The back side was covered with a list and some notes in the margins. She carefully folded the page and decided not to tempt fate further. After reshelving the book and securing the glass door, she moved back to the entrance and walked out with a confidence she did not feel. The guard did not stop or search for her. Although they ran into Greyfinger, it was close enough to the end of Iyna's normal training day that no one questioned her late trek across the courtyard back to her cell.

She paced nervously as she waited for Darek and Samal to return for the day. Their dinner arrived at the same time, which meant they would be left alone until morning. After the meal was finished and the guards were gone for the foreseeable future, Iyna pulled the map from her sleeve and set it on the table for her companions to see.

"I managed to get into the library unsupervised today," Iyna said to start. "I found Rasulo's journals and this was inside the one I skimmed. My Angelic isn't very good, but the map seemed important as he drew it himself. I couldn't decide if he was looking for something or if this were attack points. What do you think? There is a list on the back."

"I can't read Angelic at all, but that looks like a search. See how all of the scribbles are in different inks and widths? Like the person had a different pen and ink each time. The underlying map was drawn all at the same time, but the other marks were added later, as though checking each spot." Samal held the map up to the light for several moments and then passed it off to Darek for his assessment.

"I haven't read Angelic in years, not since my capture any-way. Give me a few moments." Darek bent over the paper, his lips moving slowly as he sounded out each word in his head. His eyes became round and he flipped the paper over several times to consult the list on the back. When he got to the bottom of the back page his eyes narrowed and then his head snapped up to meet their confused faces. "He is looking for the Pond! The Pond! Stahd's Breath! It must be a real place if he is looking for it." At this point, the wrinkled hands of the dwarf were shaking as he held the map. "Praise and blessings that he has not found it." Darek took a moment and calmed himself. "The Pond is the origin of the Song in Telaria. The original Angelic chorus used it as a sounding board to amplify their songs during creation. I thought Stahd had destroyed it when he finally had to leave. But it must still exist for the Song to function, so either he hid it or moved it. This map shows all of the places Rasulo has searched for it. The note at the bottom of the list is more recent it is dated eight or so years ago, stating that Loch Fel does not contain the Pond. Iyna, that is where you are from, is it not? He was looking for the Pond and found you instead." Darek's eyes were filled with compassion as they all realized Iyna's imprisonment was a fluke. Rasulo was not out to collect more workers. He was merely checking a location off his list.

Iyna blinked back a few tears and kept a hold of Samal's hand. "It doesn't matter how I got here. I am here. We are all here and shouldn't be. What matters is how we get out. Do you think we can use this?"

"Practically, no. It gives us an idea of Rasulo's endgame, but it does not help us get away. He would leave if he knew where to find the Pond, but I don't think our lives are worth that trade." Darek fingered the page for a moment. "We should burn this, commit what we can to memory, but we cannot be caught with this kind of information."

"No, we can't. We may need to know where he looked in the future." Samal protested quickly; she started pacing as she considered their next move. "Iyna can take it out of the compound on her next excursion and give it to Celeste to hide."

"That is risky. When is your next trip to the grove?" asked Darek.

"It should be this week. I can preserve the page in a leather scroll and Celeste can take it into the woods and hide it. I don't know that it will last out in the elements, but you are right, we cannot keep it here. Rasulo would kill us all just for peeking at it. Speaking of, how do you know how to read Angelic, Darek?" Iyna asked, genuinely astonished.

"It was part of my training in Tark-Delve. My family name is Delve. I was trained at home by some of the best trainers outside of Sonaris. My father died when I was young and I became head of our family and unable to attend the school. I was taken during a scouting trip near Profana a few years after the start of this cycle. My responsibilities would have fallen to my brother and cousins after I was lost." He shrugged and looked as though he did not care to say more.

"I'm sorry for the years you have lost, Darek," Samal tried to comfort him, unsure how to react to his vulnerability.

"Don't you girls start to worry over me. I would have picked capture to know what we have just discovered and to keep you both safe if I had been blessed with foresight." He gave a tight smile and became thoughtful again. "If that lynx of yours is willing to take the map and guard it, do you think she could take it to someone?"

"Who could we send it to?" Iyna sat up and considered the possibility.

"We send it to Lyssanna Tark. She is the cousin of the Tark chieftain and a ranking council member. Other than me, she is the best at reading Angelic outside of Sonaris." He pulled his beard forcefully as he thought, nodding at each new thought that occurred to him. "Lyssanna will come up with a plan. Her sister, Scoria, was part of the last bondpair to face Rasulo. Between the two of them, they can figure out what is going on and possibly get us out. They will know someone is here. We dare not put our names on anything, as if it is found, we are dead. Celeste should take just this page. Do you think she will understand?"

"Maybe. I don't know. It's not like she can talk."

"No, but she is your familiar. She should be able to understand what you want. Familiars feel compelled to help their people. It will be harder to convince her to leave you than it will be to get her to know what you want."

"What is a familiar? And how do you know she is one?"

"Faustus probably doesn't have one and that is why he never told you. Many Users have a familiar, usually an animal that is highly attracted to your song. In your case, Celeste was attracted by your trees. If she could stand the binding, I guarantee she would be in this room now and following you around. Instead, she hangs around the one spot she knows you will come back to. All you have to do is find a moment with her during your next training session. We will make a collar and attach the page for you to give her. I will teach you Lyssanna's base melody and the cat can use that to find her inside Tark-Delve. Lynx are notoriously hard to spot, so sneaking in the city will not be a problem."

"I like this plan. It keeps the page from being found and we don't have to destroy it." Samal was hopeful for the first time in years. Darek grunted and said it was their best option.

"I'll arrange to go to the grove tomorrow. Faustus was angry with me today and won't want to see me."

"Then I suggest we all get some rest. It has been an unexpectedly eventful day," the dwarf elder said as he leaned across the table to pat both of them on the arm, which was the most demonstrative he had ever been with either of them.

The next day was foggy and cool. As predicted, Faustus had no desire to see Iyna for training and she was sent off to the woods. Her standard complement of sycops accompanied her. They were to keep her in sight, but she was otherwise allowed to practice as she wanted. Iyna wandered toward the trees trying to make it seem as though she had no plan or purpose in mind. Celeste was around watching, she could feel it. The lynx picked up on her agitation and twitched her tail in response, otherwise holding perfectly still.

Iyna climbed up into the tree and settled a crook within the canopy. Celeste climbed up beside her and purred gently as the girl scratched her ears and played with the silver tufts of fur on the ends. Then she determinedly made eye contact and began to speak quietly.

"Celeste, I need you to do something for me. I need you to leave this place." At that pronouncement, the lynx pulled her head back and grumbled slightly. "Just listen. I need you to go to the big dwarven city in the mountains, Tark-Delve. There is a lady named, Lyssanna Tark, who can help me. I need you to get a message to her. It is on this collar." Iyna pulled the collar out of her pocket; a small tube was affixed to it with the map sealed inside. Celeste sniffed at the collar and batted the tube gently. "Yes, that is what she will need." Iyna scratched the lynx's chin as a reward. "I am going to hum you a melody that Lyssanna uses. Can you remember it and use that to find her?" The lynx meowed softly in response. For the next few minutes, Iyna hummed the melody over and over until Celeste pawed at her arm to signal she knew it. Iyna fastened the collar around Celeste's neck and hugged her tight taking comfort in the purr emanating deep inside her chest. With a soft lick to Iyna's forehead, Celeste slithered down the tree and blended into the long grass at its base. The only sign of her passing was the bend of the grass. Iyna lost track of her as she jumped across the river and disappeared north into the mountains. Feeling suddenly lonely, Iyna climbed down from the tree and walked slowly back to the compound surrounded by her guards.

Days later, Iyna was summoned to a late night training session. She dressed quickly and tried to put on a brave face for Samal and Darek, who were both concerned with the unexpected change of schedule. When she arrived at the training room, Faustus was standing at the far end of the rectangular room. Rasulo was seated in the center along the long wall. Something felt off about the room. In her nervousness, Iyna chalked it up to Rasulo's presence.

"Enter, child," said the Angelic in a cold, calm voice; the now familiar buzzing sensation crept around the edge of her awareness. "This is your training assessment. Do not think to present anything less than your best work or I will know. Faustus thinks you are sabotaging yourself, but I *know* you would never do anything so foolish." His tone implied he knew what she had been doing and expected it to stop immediately. Whatever time Iyna had bought herself was now at an end. "Move to the end of the room opposite Faustus. You will duel him and we will see where you are. No rules apply. You will compete until one of you passes out or loses their voice."

Iyna walked slowly to her end of the training room and took several deep breaths to consider her options. She knew Faustus could use wind, earth, and water, the last only if there was a source. She spotted a small carafe on a table beside Rasulo's chair. It would have to be emptied to limit his attack options, but lashing out near the Angelic was also something to avoid. She reached the end of the room and turned to face her opponent. She touched a finger to her forehead to signal that she was ready and Faustus did the same. A high, steady tone rang across the room as it faded a low buzz was left exposed. It did not fade.

Faustus lashed out with wind hoping to drown out Iyna's Song before she could start, but she opted to defend with an earthen bulwark behind which she hunkered down and considered her options. She felt Faustus tearing at the wall from the other side with his own earth melody. She shifted her song slightly and pushed a section of flooring up under the back legs of the table beside Rasulo. The carafe of water toppled to the stone floor and shattered. The liquid inside was quickly absorbed between the stones. Faustus let out a frustrated yell when he saw the water source was gone. He bent the yell into another wind attack and Iyna's wall blew back toward her and pelted her with fist sized stones. She brought her arms up to block her face and felt several cuts open from wrist to elbow. She cried out and lost her focus as she twisted and curled up to protect herself. Rolling to her back, she levered herself up and dodged a push of wind narrowed to a point and shot at her like an arrow. She grabbed a few of the rocks behind her and feigned a throw, as she hoped Faustus flinched and moved to roll away giving her an opening. Frustrated with herself and wanting to be done, she poured all of her loathing for the other occupants of the room into her Song. She called on fire and sent it out from her position in a swirling cone aimed directly for her opponent. At the middle of the room it split and flanked Faustus on either side, containing him within a ring of fire. He attempted wind and earth to tamp out the flame, but volume won the day. She pulled the noose tighter and tighter around him until it licked at his robes; then she extended the walls of the cylinder to the ceiling and he passed out as all of the air in his cocoon was consumed.

As he fell, she released her melody and he fell to the floor with his robes smoldering and choked out a breath. Iyna's face was grey and raw as she released all of the anger she had been holding in for years. She shook with the depth of her revulsion and sat hard on the stone floor, shaking and upset. Faustus was her main torturer in this hellhole, but he was not the cause of her enslavement. He was the symptom, not the root of her problems. Until that moment, she did not realize just how much she hated those around her and she was frightened. A light clapping noise permeated her senses.

"Excellent." Rasulo looked mildly pleased and stepped over Faustus without a glance. He held out a hand to help her rise, which Iyna reluctantly took with a shiver dropping the connection as soon as she could. "We start tomorrow afternoon. You will be an asset."

With that pronouncement, another Mason pulled the unconscious Faustus out of the room by his arms and off to his chambers. Iyna was immediately escorted back to her cell and locked in.

CHAPTER 9

Morning light crept over the camp, after the excitement of the previous day all five of the fugitives were exhausted, but equally sure that they could not linger. The denizens of Sonaris would have missed their presence by now and Terris' absence would be noticed when he failed to report for duty that morning. The Masters were not dumb. They would know all five of them were together and gone. Hopefully, the note left with Jameson would offer some reassurance, but Master Parke would be especially furious. Terris did not like to think about the consequences of their current adventure.

Marcus woke first just as the grey light of pre-dawn was easing away to a full burst of color over the mountains to the east. He sluggishly moved to gather their things and disguise their campsite. The others soon awoke and joined his endeavors. It would be impossible to completely mask their presence, but foolish to give away their location unnecessarily. As they packed, they decided to cut east and skirt the northern side of the Great Marsh. While it would be easier to follow the Long Road south and turn east after they passed the marsh, which was the most direct and easiest route, but a band of guards from Sonaris would be sure to follow that route and stop them before they could reach Tark-Delve.

Marcus insisted that they stop at the city to resupply and because he thought his aunt, Scoria, could be of some help. She was an understanding woman and knew the land on the east side of the Spina Ardus better than any other dwarf. He was unsure of a route through the mountains and traveling around the southern end of the Spina would take them through the Paphiae Myrti and on into the Low Plains. The plains were usually crawling with sycops and the open area would not provide much cover for their approach. Regardless, they all agreed that the eastern trek was the best way to avoid detection for the current leg of the journey.

They mounted and sped off before the sun was fully up. Once they crossed the Long Road, the Marsh appeared on their right. The ground was an odd mix of sand and turf. The hoofs of the mounts made little noise and the company was silent. Ryl and Safara had mixed reactions as they made their way along the northern side of the Great Marsh. It reminded them both of their arrival at Sonaris. Ryl was calm and interested in the ever changing landscape of the marsh. Safara remembered their difficult trip and sincerely hoped that this journey would be easier. The others were all distracted by the interesting array of noxious smells that frequently wafted their direction.

They kept a decent pace and stopped to walk occasionally to keep their mounts from tiring. Daichi scouted ahead with Safara and Ayo on his back. They swung around to the west and checked for any followers after the midday meal. Keeping up in the clouds ensured they would not be observed while allowing them to get a good view of the Long Road. No search party followed their route, but several riders were moving quickly to the south. Neither girl could tell if they were Sonaran guards, but the chances were good based on how fast they were moving. They circled back around and met back up with Terris, Marcus, and Ryl at sunset. There was no choice but to camp in the open near the stink of bog water.

The night was temperate, but the smell made it almost impossible to sleep. They stayed awake long into the night discussing the implications of the search party headed south.

"My parents will be upset, but understanding when they hear why we left the school. They may try to send us back, especially Ryl and me." Marcus was seated by the fire poking at it thoughtfully with a stick.

"I'm not going back without Iyna. Your parents can't make me," Ryl stated defensively. "Will they try to hold us?"

"Maybe," Marcus admitted.

"Regardless of a search party, I can guarantee a raven has already been sent to Tark-Delve and Syreni. No one at the school would allow our disappearance to be kept from your parents." Terris moved closer to the fire to add another log and was thinking out loud. "Sorry. I don't want to discourage you all, but it is true. Word would be sent as soon as they knew we were all gone. Especially as Marcus' family is so prominent and he *is* a Canticle. You two," he pointed at Ryl and Marcus, "are what will get us in trouble. Not only did we all run away, but we took two, young Neophyte Canticles with us. You better come back paired or we won't be forgiven." He let out a short laugh.

"Be serious for once, Terris." Ayo shot him a dirty look as he started laughing again.

Safara piped up for the first since they set camp. "He is being serious. If they come back paired, I bet that they consider it your acolyte test and decide it was a fair trade for field experience. The rules are incredibly flexible when a pair bond is the result."

"Avoiding a bond is part of the reason I came on this thing!" Marcus started to complain, but then thought better of it. "At least I like all of you, so I guess, if it does happen...it won't be so bad."

"Why do you mind so much? Bonds don't happen without a connection between both." Ayo was curious, as Marcus' reaction was strong every time a pairing was mentioned. "Most Users would kill to be paired. At least for a Canticle, it is practically guaranteed."

"My cousin was paired and his bondmate died during training. It was a freak accident." Marcus stared into the fire speaking in a flat, detached voice. "He blamed himself for her death. While their connection was strong, his abilities far outstripped hers and his melody overwhelmed her harmony. His secondary was water and she had no affinity. His melody did not account for her lack of ability. They were holding back a subterranean lake, so that a dam could be worked on. The water broke free and she was swept away along with several other workers."

"I am sorry for your cousin, but that doesn't mean it will happen to you," Ayo said gently. She bumped his hand with a water skin to get him to take a sip.

"I know that," he said. "But it doesn't feel like it. Being a Canticle is odd. You are at the mercy of the framework you are given. I can add in my harmony to strengthen a work, but if the base is faulty I can't fix that." He took a long drink and Ryl took over.

"He is right. We Canticles can work on our own and establish our own structures, but our best contribution is amplifying what is given to us. Sure I could build a song, but if I enhance an established melody, then we can create truly great works. Being a Canticle isn't about brute force, it's about understanding possibilities."

"Subverting your ideas in favor of someone else's?" asked Terris.

"Yes and no," said Safara. "As I understand it, you aren't sacrificing or destroying your melody. Instead, you are working your thread of harmony into the melody already present. Kind of like turning your melody into a harmony." She shrugged. "It's hard to explain. But I know that within a pair bond, it is much easier to accomplish. The connection between both is so strong that the Vocalist can sense where the Canticle already wants to go and attempts to provide a way for both of them to work. My mama always said she had to make allowances for my papa. She was significantly stronger than him and I think that was part of what worried her so much about their bond. She couldn't be sure he wouldn't be hurt."

"You never told me that." Ryl seemed almost upset that she had not considered the possibility before.

"It never seemed like a good time to talk about them, Bean. I didn't mean to keep a secret. Sometimes I don't remember that you can't recall everything that I do." She moved over to hold her sister's hand.

"I understand, I guess, but I still wish I would have known." Ryl shook herself out of her thoughts. "I think we should go to bed." With that she moved away and cuddled up under her blanket next to Parsifal. Nyx rode along on her shoulder and quietly trilled at her.

Everyone else settled around the fire while Safara moved to check on the other mounts one more time. Daichi was off catching his dinner, but Mynock and Cerridwen, Terris' horse, were resting comfortably and seemed to have finished grazing for the evening. Safara moved over to Cerridwen and introduced herself to the lovely roan.

"Hello, girl. How are you doing after our exercise today?" Safara offered a carrot to the horse and scratched around her ears and neck as the mare munched happily. "I thought we should meet since we are going to be together for a bit." She hummed a bit and the horse's ears twitched forward in response to her fauna melody.

"Don't you go bewitching my horse," Terris' voice came from behind her. "Don't think I don't know who is responsible for all those acorn deposits over the years. There aren't enough fauna Users with a vendetta against me to make it a mystery."

"Maybe the campus squirrels just didn't like you much," she returned without shifting her attention away from her new friend.

"Ha! Unlikely. I have never so much as thrown a piece of bark or yelled at a squirrel. They have no quarrel with me. Now their friend, Fara...she is the vengeful type. Always plotting and scheming." He moved around to the other side of Cerridwen's head and stroked her neck. The mare whinnied a greeting and lipped the front of his shirt searching for a pocket hiding a snack. "Oh no, miss. You had a treat. I saw you take it myself," he said affectionately.

"How long have you had her?"

"Ever since I got assigned to The Band. I perform regular patrols on the south side and having a horse was necessary. She isn't a familiar, but we get along well enough." He glanced over at Fara and smiled at the look of contentment on her face as she cared for the animal. "Are you okay? You seemed upset earlier."

"Honestly? I don't know what I was thinking agreeing to this." She bit her lip and looked up at the stars that were peeking out between the wispy grey clouds. "We could all get killed, stolen, or captured. We can't face Rasulo. I only survived my acolyte test because I met a griffon. We can't count on that kind of luck happening twice."

"Woah...slow down a moment. You are jumping about twenty steps ahead of where we are. First of all, no one is suggesting we take on an Angelic. Second, we are nowhere close to our destination. Take this all one step at a time. We will get there and who knows what help we will encounter along the way." He moved slowly around to her side and covered the hand that was idly petting the horse. Her wide hazel eyes snapped up to meet his reassuring blue ones. He gave her hand a single gentle squeeze and then dropped contact. "We will be just fine and so will Iyna. You have to believe that. Now come on, the others will be looking for us if we don't return soon." He turned and started back toward the fire. She followed and rolled up in her blanket near Ayo.

The next several days repeated that pattern. The group

rose early with the sun and set out around the marsh. After the first day the smell was less noticeable and the foothills were lightly forested. Just enough cover to provide fuel for their evening fire and protection from the sun during mid-day. They encountered a few farmers, but no other travelers that concerned them.

On the evening of the fourth day out from Sonaris, they stopped for the night where the Great Marsh meets the Spina Ardus. Gargantuan pine trees towered over them and sheltered the notch between the mountains that contained Tark-Delve. The gap was formed long ago by a massive waterfall that was diverted underground during the fourth cycle by a mer pairing, Pirloo and Ellay. They used the water to create a large subterranean sea and trapped Rasulo for several decades below the mountains before he found a way out.

With the water diverted below ground, the dwarves quickly moved to fill the void. They established a great city built directly into the rock face. Large elevators similar in function to the tram along the top of The Band linked one terrace of the city to the next. Many of the streets delved deep into the mountain, but most of the dwarves preferred to live with at least part of their home on the exposed rock face. Staircases and ladders whipped back and forth between buildings connecting at odd angles as though the city grew rather than was carved into the rock. Bas relief frescos littered the outsides of the buildings, depicting nature and showcasing the dwarven affinity for earth. At the pinnacle of the city sat Council Hall; its domed roof rising above the highest peak of the mountain creating the only truly free standing building in the city. It caught the last glimmer of the sunset and threw them back against the mountains on either side of the approach to the city. The entire area bathed in a soft orange light.

Marcus moved to the front of the group on Mynock and sighed. "Home," he stated simply with a smile.

"Pray to Stahd that your parents are as happy to see us as you are to see this place. Though I must admit, it is a wonder," Ayo muttered as she dismounted and began unpacking for the night.

Just as the others began to do the same, two figures moved into the clearing near them.

"Marcus Tark!" a small dwarven female scurried to his side and pulled him off his ram. "What in Stahd's Name are you doing here? You are meant to be in Sonaris, mister," the female kept up a steady stream of questions punctuated by pokes about Marcus' person as though checking him for injuries, as the second taller figure approached.

"Choirs above! Scoria, let him answer, will you?" asked Fairn in a tolerant, yet exasperated voice.

"I will in a moment. You had better be hurt, young sir, or your mother will have your head!" She finished looking him over and gave him a quick, relieved hug when he appeared to be whole from her cursory examination. "Ravens and riders from Sonaris arrived and said you left school on some kind of trip, but they failed to mention you were coming here!"

"Hi, Aunt Scoria and Uncle Fairn," Marcus began sheepishly, slightly embarrassed that his new friends witnessed this rather embarrassing greeting. "Umm…I left Sonaris temporarily." He held up a hand to stave off his aunt's tirade. "Please let me explain or maybe Safara and Ryl can help when my story gets muddled." He indicated his friends with a wave of his hand. "Apologies. These are my friends: Safara, Ryl, Ayo, and Terris. All current or recent students of Sonaris. We are on a quest to find Safara and Ryl's missing sister, Iyna."

At their names, the tall elf's navy brows pulled together. "Jael and Aries' children? I thought there were only two at the school."

Ryl bravely put herself forward to explain before the

others could move. "I have a twin, Iyna; she is my bondpartner. I can feel her on the other side of the mountains. She has been reaching out to me from there for years, but recently her call has become louder and more insistent. I don't know if it is because we are both older and stronger or if it is because she is in need. Either way, we decided to go and get her from Profana." Ryl pushed aside her natural fear of getting in trouble and boldly met Fairn's silvery eyes as she spoke, only looking away when she finished. Nyx moved out of the shadows to comfort her and the elf's eyes widened at the sight of a faerydae.

It was Scoria who answered. "I would do anything for my Lyssanna, but you are days out from Sonaris, even mounted. The school must be informed of your whereabouts and we can send some fully trained pairs after your sister. Profana is no place for the untrained."

"It needs to be us. I can feel it." Safara insisted, finding her voice. "We left Iyna on accident once; she needs to know we came for her ourselves."

Terris and Ayo had been silent to this point until the stately, blue elf asked them why they were there. Ayo simply answered that Iyna was also her family. Terris shifted his weight from foot to foot before admitting that he would never let Safara attempt anything like that without him. The young vocalist avoided Safara's questioning expression. "We have been friends for too long for me to let her leave me behind."

"Well, I can tell you that your mother and father will have a few words to say about this, Marcus, but I won't presume to stop any of you as you aren't my offspring. I'm just glad that we were assigned patrol duty tonight else you would have already been hauled into the city." Scoria turned to her bond-mate and shrugged. "Maybe we can help them. Lyssanna was all excited about some new intelligence they had from Profana before we left on patrol."

Fairn looked thoughtful and gazed to the southeast in the

direction of the mountain. "No matter what the intelligence, I'm not sure how it will help an adolescent group infiltrate Profana."

"We will discuss this further with Lyssanna, but I feel there is a way forward here." She moved to Mynock and gave his nose a rub. "Don't unpack for the night; you all are headed straight into that city. You can stay with us for the night, but we will all be headed to the Council Hall at first light. Marcus, dear boy, you had better figure out what you are going to say to your parents. Mount up and let's get moving. We are at least an hour out."

Daichi moved forward and squawked at Safara, his gleaming white feathers taking on the orange glow of the sunset as he moved out of the shadows where she had asked him to stay. "You stick close, Dai. No one here knows you are a friend."

"You have a faerydae and a griffon?" he asked incredulously. "I am reassessing everything. You are uncommonly blessed by Stahd. But you are right, Safara, the griffon should stay close until we are past the guard towers, or they might shoot him. We occasionally get wild griffons after our herds."

"Stay away from the sheep and goats, Daichi. Stick to rabbits or deer out in the woods. Do you hear me?" Safara made intent eye contact with her familiar until he chittered an agreement.

They all moved toward the city using Safara's staff for light as the sun set. Ryl hummed at it and increased its luminosity so that everyone could see, earning her surprised looks from both escorts. Dai followed it happily and chuffed every time it bobbed around unexpectedly. After an hour or so they were greeted by the interior sentries and continued on to the gate house. The mounts were all introduced to the stablemaster. Mynock seemed pleased to be back home and greeted his friends with several loud brays. The horses and griffon seemed at ease and the stablemaster offered Daichi a spot in the hay loft, which he could access directly from the outside. The stable boys were running all over the place to accommodate the new guests. Most were wary of the new mounts, but relaxed as they realized that the horses would eat the same food as the rams and the griffon could fend for his own meals.

"We will be back down to see you all tomorrow," Ryl said as she patted Parsifal on the neck. "Be a good boy and make sure Cerridwen has a friend." He answered by snuffling her hair and nickering at Safara, who blew him a kiss from the hayloft.

Marcus led the way to the nearest available lift and they all took off upward to Fairn and Scoria's home near the top of the city. The lifts were nestled against a stone platform suspended over the deep chasm left at the base of the former waterfall. The terraces for the city started about thirty feet above the ground level platform. The few times the city had been attacked, the lifts were pulled up and the population moved inside the mountain for protection against any projectiles.

The lift moved at a decent pace, but it still took fifteen minutes before their host slowed and stopped it. The gates clanged back as they all tumbled out into a plaza. The lift carriage soon moved back down the rails as it was summoned to another terrace. Scoria led the group across the open space, up one flight of stairs, around another corner, and up two more staircases before opening a door to a comfortable home that overlooked the plaza below and out across the tops of the massive forest at the base of the notch.

In front of the house was a small private courtyard. No other staircases branched off, as this was the end of the passage. The north and east sides of the house were made of solid mountain stone which arched out over the courtyard like a porch roof. The courtyard floor was tiled in an intricate mosaic depicting Scoria and Fairn's battle against Rasulo and showed the Angelic encased in the heart of the mountain. The outside of the house was markedly plain compared to the other buildings in the area. The outer windows had decorative trim and the doors had lintels with vine imagery on them which matched the columns along the front of the house. Otherwise, the stone was remarkably smooth. It looked like one solid piece of granite rather than blocks that were built against the opening in the mountain face as were some of the other homes. This home had been formed out of the mountain, not built into it.

Scoria moved all of them inside and, with the help of a maid, got them all water to wash and a late dinner. Over dinner, Terris boldly asked the bonded couple about their own struggle against Rasulo. Scoria willingly told them all about the battle and setting; everything she remembered about the mountain. After she left to show the girls to their room, Fairn approached Terris and Marcus to relay his memories from after the confrontation, which Scoria could not remember and did not like to discuss.

"I think it is vital that you understand the repercussions of the cycles." Fairn made careful eye contact with both of the teens. "You can tell Ayo, Ryl, and Safara, but not in front of Scoria. Do I have your word?"

"Yes." Both mumbled solemnly.

"Thank you. We both carry physical and mental scars from the encounter. Although she looks strong and whole, Scoria occasionally still has nightmares about the days after the fight. She was badly wounded and barely pulled through. My voice was shot and I could barely speak for the first year after. Even now, I have to carefully conserve my attempts to use the Song. It is maddening...to hear the call of the wind and not be able to join a gale as it rushes passed like I used to. I haven't the control to hover, let alone fly a significant distance anymore."

"Wait! Flying is a thing?" Marcus interrupted.

"To an extent, yes. At my peak and with the help of your aunt, I could glide both of us down the face of Tark-Delve and hit the platform using little more than a breeze. It was amazing. Very few bondpairs have the requisite strength in wind and earth to manage that and it isn't really a useful skill for many applications. But I digress." He moved out onto the courtyard and both Terris and Marcus followed. With a wave of his hand, Fairn directed their attention to the mosaic. "Watch," he said simply and bent to press his hand on one side of the tiles on the floor as he started to hum, the tiles moved slowly depicting the scene as Fairn remembered it with a faint wash of audio.

* * *

Heaving to his side, Fairn forced his reluctant body into a sitting position. His silver eyes frantically scanning the scorched landscape for Scoria. She was right beside him as they faced their foe. She was always right beside him, he thought desperately. His bondmate and steadfast supporter.

"Scoria! Answer me, woman. Where are you?" he shouted, voice cracking. His elven eyes pierced through the haze. His deep blue skin camouflaged the bruises already forming on his torso and limbs. A disgruntled moan was his only answer. He dragged his battered body down the mountainside at least twenty feet to where she landed. Her legs twisted at an odd outward angle. Thankfully, both of them had landed on a rocky protrusion and not in a lava flow. Her small stature allowed him to quickly check her for any other wounds or breaks. It appeared that her stocky dwarven frame had protected her from worse injuries. Her legs would heal with time and care if he could keep her in one place for long enough, he thought ruefully.

When finished with his assessment, Fairn surveyed their surroundings. Large swaths of Mount Profana were covered in free flowing lava and fire. The air and sky so choked with smoke that he could not tell if it was day or night. Coughing hard enough to tell that several of his ribs were broken, he tenderly lifted her head so that she could see the prominence far above them, giving him a jolt as he realized how far they had been flung. The side of the mountain looked like a massive Angelic had chopped into it like firewood. At the edge of the crater a polished, black stone stood smoldering in the smoky light, slowly sinking under its own weight into the magma below. The area all around it was coated in thick, slow-moving lava seeping out from the cracks in the mountain side. It appeared as though the beating heart of the mountain had burst forth and swallowed Rasulo.

"Scor? We did it! I don't know how, but we did it. Rasulo is encased up there in the rock. You did that; we did," he soothingly crooned at her.

Fairn carefully reached for Scoria's hand and squeezed it. She acknowledged his news by returning the gesture exhaustedly. A smile cracked her chapped lips, as she pushed her hair back from her dusty forehead revealing a gash and the source of the blood steadily dripping down the side of her face. Her mate quickly used what was left of his cloak to staunch the blood. The cut was deep, but not fatal.

"I hope the bastard rots in that tomb. Song-crafted with our compliments," spat Fairn. A snort of near-laughter greeted his ears. He eased them both into a more comfortable position.

"For a mismatched bondpair, we did good," Scoria rasped smugly.

Her comment was a welcome indication of her recovering spirits to Fairn. He agreed with his own short burst of laughter and then groaned, as he confirmed his ribs were broken. A brief moment of lucidity was all he could hope for in her weakened state and Scoria soon passed out. Taking advantage of her oblivion, Fairn eased himself around her body where he set and splinted both legs. She groaned in protest, but did not wake. Relieved and exhausted, he garbbled out a cry for help to the closest bird he could sense. The large, bloody carrion bird obligingly took off from the sycop carcass it was picking clean and headed north to summon help. With that assurance, the lanky elf allowed himself to slip into unconsciousness.

* * *

Fairn opened his eyes and let his hum fade away. Both members of his audience sat stunned by what they saw as the mosaic shifted back to its resting facade. When he found his voice, Fairn explained, "Everything has a cost in this life. Even doing good can cost you what is precious. Be sure you weigh the possible costs before you charge ahead with this plan. I do not show you this to discourage you, but to create a more balanced pool of information. Rasulo is strong, but he is fallible. He is not all-knowing or the cycles never would have been set. Just...be sure you are willing to pay."

Terris met Fairn's eyes and nodded. "Thank you. For showing us."

"Yes, thank you, Uncle." Marcus choked out.

"You both better head to bed. If Scoria comes looking for us, we will all be in for a scolding," returned the elf, as he moved to hug his nephew and shoo them inside.

CHAPTER 10

With Celeste's departure, Iyna's days seemed dim and grey. She felt the lynx's absence as though a hole were cut into her senses, preventing her from fully experiencing life around her. The loss was especially keen when she trained in the grove. Faustus had introduced a new round of what he called 'distraction training' at Rasulo's behest. It consisted mostly of Iyna avoiding a beating while attempting some intricate elemental work. Sound work was now her focus most days. The Angelic seemed fascinated by the possibilities and wanted to see how far she could expand its application.

"Up, up, you pale bone pile!" Faustus yelled across the training area. Iyna levered to her feet, but immediately dove to avoid a brutal kick to her side. She rolled behind her currently flowerless tree and tried to get her bearings. Twenty or thirty sycops were desecrating her most sacred space with a bloody skirmish. There was not a single being without a wound of some sort. All of them were limping, bloodied, and bruised. Yet they fought on for the love of it. Every pale face would sport a new scar in the coming days. The small vocalist herself sported a black eye and was almost positive that she had a broken rib. Samal would patch her up that evening, but her song would not be the same for days.

Deep breaths were not an option with the condition of her ribs, so Iyna took a split second to consider her options. She ducked behind her other tree and sheltered behind a bush that grew near its base. The leafy branches offered some scant cover. She listened for the sound of the wind and the earth around her.

Neither offered any viable options to end her current predicament. She was desperate. It almost felt like Faustus was looking to get her killed. He was still furious over his defeat in their duel and had been angling for her in the past weeks. Even now she could feel him searching for her, looking for a weakness to expose and exploit. She closed her eyes to shut out sensation.

And then she heard it. She held her breath and concentrated. It took a few moments to identify what she was hearing in the chaos of the skirmish around her. Metal on metal clashing. Grunts, screaming, and howls of defeat and victory. There it was again the beating of twenty or thirty hearts; all thrumming at different rhythms and rates, but with the same sound. *Thump-thump. Thump-thump.*

She was distracted by the cacophony and worked to sort out which beat was coming from what sycop. She picked one and followed the thin thread of sound back to a figure off to one side of the crowd. He was lying wounded and his heartbeat with a gurgling sound. It was this effect that allowed her to differentiate his heartbeat from the others. She reached out with a steady hum of sound and matched his beat gently encouraging his heart to find an easier rhythm and allowing him to calm and remain conscious. She crawled slowly through the brush, careful of her own injuries. From her hiding spot a few feet away, she gave a deeper pulse of Sound in the direction of the sycop. His eyes slowly moved her direction and widened when he saw her. She gave a faint smile and concentrated on the sounds from his heart beat. It had returned to normal and the popping sound faded.

The warrior moved quickly to his feet. He staggered toward her spot and she bit back a scream at his approach, eyes wide in fear. He spun abruptly, turned back to the fight and roared his way back in the midst of the heaviest sparring. He shrugged off several blows before disappearing into the crowd.

"None of that!" came a harsh whisper from Faustus beside

her. "Just what are you doing? You are supposed to be figuring out a way to combat these assailants, not help them." He pushed her out from the plant cover and on to her side. She let out a scream of pain as she landed against her ribs. Her desire to be done with this particular test and her pain focused her scream. She created a high-pitched, straight tone with no vibrato that reverberated across the field. Every single person within a hundred feet covered their ears and toppled over writhing in pain. All of them passed out where they lay.

Iyna slowly stood up and looked around her. Her throat felt raw and shredded, as though she swallowed a handful of nails. All battle noises ceased and she was the only person on her feet save Rasulo, who was watching from the side of the mountain far away. He clapped slowly at her and nodded before turning and going back into the compound. She hobbled off through the carnage praying she made it back to her room before the group woke up, especially Faustus. She was conflicted. The goal of the test was to see if she could defend herself and she accomplished that. Simultaneously, she attacked and wounded thirty people all at the same time.

"What kind of monster am I?" she muttered as she staggered into her cell and collapsed on her bunk. She passed into unconsciousness without discovering the answer.

Morning came too soon in Iyna's opinion. Whatever works she managed with Sound the day before, it was draining and her voice was unusable at the moment. She moved slowly to the water bucket on the stand across the room slowly brushing her hair and re-braiding it down her back. Darek and Samal both checked on her the night before, but let her sleep after ensuring she would heal and had something to eat. She was too conflicted about the results of the test to admit more than that she passed. Neither encouraged her to tell more than she was willing. The young girl felt grateful for their support and understanding, but she knew she would have to tell them at some point. She stared at her reflection in the small burnished mirror on the wall. She did not look like a monster, but she could almost feel one crawling around under her skin. Every day she felt like she was changing at an alarming rate. Soon every part of that sunny little girl from Fel Loch would be tainted, stolen, or twisted beyond recognition.

Iyna knew she needed to get away from him and fast. He was too powerful and persuasive for her to retain any moral compass under his influence. Shamefully, she recognized she would become the weapon he wanted ever since he kidnapped her eight years before. The girl shuddered and lay down again wishing for her sisters and her parents. It was almost enough to make her wish she were never born. Better to have never existed than to bring about the destruction she knew was inevitable if she remained.

Surprisingly, she was undisturbed for the morning. No guards bothered her and the cell was unlocked. She wandered around the compound avoiding the sentries for a while and made her way to the library again. Several of the other trainees were present. None of them questioned her arrival, but neither did they allow her access to any of the tomes lining the walls. Instead she studied a large map hung on the wall and compared it to the memories of the sketch Celeste had taken to Tark-Delve. She cocked her head to the side in thought as she walked closer to take in more detail.

Rasulo had canvassed almost all of Telaria west of the Long Road and everything around Loch Fel. She concentrated her memory on the area around the Low Plaines and Paphiae Myrti. While those areas were relatively close to Profana, the Angelic had never searched for them. There was not much around, mostly farms in the plains and trappers in the woods. Important industries for daily life, but not glamorous. She came to realize that most of the locations he had checked were prominent, well-known landmarks such as the spire forest on the

High Mesa or the Mer Delta . Vallis Lake had also been thoroughly covered. She began to understand that he had weighed his search based on where he would have hidden The Pond, not where Stahd would have hidden it.

Her knowledge of the benevolent Angelic was limited given her residence and trainers, but Darek and Samal had done their best to fill in the gaps. Stahd was said to have been kind and intelligent. After the formation of Telaria, most of the Angelic choir moved on to other challenges or worlds. Over several millennia the population of the choir dwindled to a handful and eventually down to only Rasulo, Hali, and Stahd remaining. Stahd worked tirelessly during his time in Telaria to maintain the Song the Radix Cordam had established. Rasulo on the other hand worked to undo the underpinnings of the Song and hid his dissonance subtly. He was patient and able to wait out his counterparts for it is easier to destroy than to create. As ever, all he needed was time.

Stahd and Hali worked tirelessly to undo the dissonance created by their brother. But the malicious tones spread like a cancer, tainting the once perfect land with disease and death. In the end, Stahd used the last of his strength to move The Pond to an unknown location. Unfortunately, he was not able to cleanse the land and so the deceptive changes festered in pockets and the Hearers were created to combat the remaining Dissonance and deal with Rasulo's reappearance. It was that act of imbuing the indigenous peoples that caused Stahd's death. He gave up his access and ability with the Song, so that it could be carried into the future and used to protect all of Telaria just as he had done.

Over time, abilities were diluted and affinities developed. The first bondpair, Sybilla and Sigurd, could work within all elements and affinities. Manipulating the Song was like breathing for them and the others blessed within their generation. Sonaris was built during the first cycle, before Rasulo reappeared from his banishment. The Sonaran Chorale was over one hundred strong and massive works were accomplished in its time. As the lines of each member of the Chorale thinned and died out, the school became ever more important both as a haven for the uniquely gifted and as pseudo-matchmaking service to ensure future generations had the best chance of retaining their forbearer's gifts.

Iyna blinked and shifted her focus around the room. All noise, except a quiet, persistent buzz, ceased and it took her a moment to realize why before she looked over her shoulder. Rasulo stood, not three paces behind her and smirked at her startled face and accompanying gasp. She nearly fell over in her haste to turn around and back away.

"You will come with me, child." He turned and swept out of the room, his pristine robes moving silently around the door before her mind registered the command. Her feet followed of their own volition and she suppressed a shudder, silently praying to Stahd for strength and mercy. Small beads of sweat broke out across her forehead and her neck felt damp under her braid followed by flashes of cold and then heat again. By the time Rasulo led the way into a new, larger training room, Iyna was thoroughly disoriented and stumbled through the door. There was a deep, almost imperceptible hum permeating the room.

"Sit. Before you fall down. You will listen only during this lesson." He pointed to a chair along the wall. "Your voice is likely useless after yesterday."

Iyna moved to the chair but remained unsure as to how she got there or why the temperature seemed to fluctuate radically. The buzz increased intensity, but Rasulo seemed unfazed.

"Today is about attacks and how to defend yourself against a powerful partner. You will work with me and I *will* always be stronger. Thus knowing how to defend yourself from any residual splashback is prudent, so that I don't kill you accidentally in our first week of training. Understood?"

At her weak nod, he continued speaking and pacing along the smooth stone floor as he went the iridescent sheen of his robes catching in the light of the torches lining the walls. Back and forth, back and forth as the temperature changes continued. Rainbow light shifted around the room. Eventually, her dizziness gave way to nausea, which led to its ultimate conclusion all over the floor beside her chair as she toppled out of it barely conscious. The hum and temperature changes stopped immediately.

"And here is your lesson. Learn it well. I was barely using my melody to manipulate your perceptions and look how it turned out. Imagine if you were next to me during an all out attack. This week you will learn to weave protection into your melodies. You are not a Canticle, so you will closely follow my melodies and repeat them as support and volume. However, you will not be able to weave a harmony into them. Thus, we will be stymied and restricted by your few affinities, which is the weakness of this arrangement. Now leave." He spoke in a calm, detached tone and left with no further comments. Iyna staggered to her feet and back to her cell. On the way, she forced out a pulse to Ryl, repeating it over and over until she stumbled through her cell door. For the second time in as many days, she fell immediately to sleep as soon as she reached her bunk. The faintest residual hum echoed in her ears.

❋ ❋ ❋

It was a familiar path by now. Dodge the guard and slip down the hidden stairs to the vault. As always, Rasulo moved gracefully and without a trail. Even the rats scuttling along the edge of the light barely noticed his passing. With the boulder settled back in place, he moved to her lying on the table. His painstaking work was just beginning to show results. She now had all of her fingers and toes, but her feet were fused at the ankles. After several hours' work, she finally had two distinct feet and he smiled.

"You have competition, my dear." He stopped himself from running a hand along her arm, remembering just in time not to disturb the flaky top layer of her skin. "Ah, no worries. I will keep you both."

With a careless shrug, he left her locked away and silent, pleased with his plan and contingencies.

CHAPTER 11

Morning came early, as it usually does. Scoria was up and around first. She sent a message to her sister requesting a meeting before the midday meal in her office. The raven returned almost immediately with just a time written on the bottom of Scoria's note.

"Ever efficient Lyssanna," thought Scoria. *"I hope she goes easy on these kids, but Marcus will be lucky if he isn't kept home permanently for this escapade."* Scoria shared a special connection with her nephew. She was the reason he was allowed to stay at home for so long. Between the protection of his clan and easy access to a formidable Canticle for training, arguing for homeschooling was easier. However, their family circle could not provide the connections needed for him to bond, nor replicate the opportunities of the school. She sighed and moved inside to wake the others.

Over breakfast, they discussed how to best handle the meeting. Scoria insisted on taking the brunt of her sister's displeasure, both in supporting their mission and for keeping her uninformed of Marcus' arrival overnight. The councilwoman was a person of little expressed, but deep emotions. She made decisions based on risk analysis, but when it came to her son, Lyssanna was known to be uncharacteristically emotional in her evaluations. He was born shortly before Scoria's fight with Rasulo and the damage her sister suffered as a result of that encounter changed how Lyssanna approached all of the decisions regarding the clan. She learned to be protective. Her sister's Canticle designation put her on the short list for the confrontation and after Jael's defection, Scoria was pushed to bond. Fairn and Scoria never regretted their forced connection, but Lyssanna found it hard to forgive the school for removing her sister's options. In all honesty, Scoria was most worried about Lyssanna's reaction to Jael's children causing upheaval for their family again.

They left the house less than an hour before the meeting and opted to walk to Council Hall without using a lift. Every section of the city was accessible without the lifts and living on the top level meant it was faster to use the stairs than wait for an empty lift compartment. Fairn and Scoria discussed warning the sisters about Lyssanna's potential reaction to their presence in particular and decided to hope the councilwoman would temper her response to the children. Marcus hung back when they reached the double doors of Council Hall. His mother's office door was visible on the second floor off on the right hand side of the balcony that opened on the entrance hall. A double staircase wound up twisting in opposite directions. The cupola of the building soared above them ringed with eight small windows that Terris and Safara noticed mimicked the stained glass from Roggle's workshop. Their eyes met and both felt reassured.

"Marcus?!" A voice, equal parts confused and upset, called out from above. "Scoria, what is all this? Get up here, all of you!" It was an imperative command that left no room for disagreement or dawdling. The group hustled up the stairs with no comment other than Nyx chiming gently in Ryl's ear. He seemed to have his own thoughts on Lyssanna, but Ryl did not bother to pass them on. They filed into the room and clumped up near the door while Marcus and his aunt moved to Lyssanna, who was waiting.

"Hullo, mother." Marcus seemed to sense it would be best for him to allow his mother to direct the conversation. She pulled him into a hug and reached up to check his face for signs of distress or maltreatment. Finding none, she turned to her sister displeasure causing her golden skin to darken several shades. She ran a hand through her short, red hair loosening several curls to fall in her face.

"You failed to mention my son's presence in your note this morning, Scor. I deserved to know. When did he get here?" Lyssanna kept a hold of her son as she directed her ire at her sister.

"Last night, Lyssa. Fairn and I found them on patrol. They were going to camp in the forest for the night. We insisted that they travel into the city and stay with us." Scoria was careful in her next statements. "They have come here at Marcus' insistence, as they are searching for a missing child, who belongs at the school. In fact, she is the twin of the younger human girl."

"That doesn't excuse the lack of communication. We had a message from the school that Marcus left with Mynock in the company of a few students. But it sounded like they went on a camping trip, not some rescue mission." She held her son's face in her hands and asked him directly. "What is going on? The full truth, sir."

"It may be best if we all fill you in as a group, I don't want to hide anything or leave out details, mother. We did leave without permission and fully expect to be punished for it when we return. But we do plan on returning to the school." He hastily added the last as his mother's temper seemed to be darkening.

Lyssanna signaled for everyone to take seats at a table near the double doors leading to a small balcony on the front of the building. The sun was up and moving over the mountain causing the light in the room to grow every moment. The inner recesses of the room would not be soaked in light until mid-afternoon, so there were still a few candles lit.

Scoria took the lead and introduced everyone around the table using first names and she included Nyx. If the council-woman was surprised to see the faerydae, she hid it well. Lyssanna seemed calmer, taking her cue from her sister's mate, who was relaxed. She trusted her brother's-in-law assessments and was willing to reserve judgment for the moment. Safara took over after the introductions and gave a brief, but thorough, run down of who they were and how Iyna was lost. Lyssanna's level of concern seemed to increase, but it was something felt, not seen. Marcus took over when Safara started to discuss their escape through The Band.

"I insisted that we come here first, especially once Ryl determined that Iyna is at Profana. No one understands these mountains better than the dwarves and you have the best knowledge of the lay of the country outside of The Band." Marcus quit while he was ahead, as his mother's shoulders began to shake.

Unexpectedly, she broke out into laughter. "Golems! How clever. I wish I could see Palmer's face when he saw them." Wiping away a few tears of amusement, Lyssanna continued after she took a deep, calming breath. "In all seriousness, I don't know how you expect me to allow this charade to continue. I agree that the girl must be rescued, but I have yet to hear a decent argument as to why it must be a contingent of children that go." She raised her hand to stop their protests. "As it happens, we have had the first bit of fresh information on Profana just this last week. It arrived, if you can believe, tied to the neck of a shadow lynx. With such a reticent creature, she must have been directed to me specifically. No one else in the city has seen her. I have told the Council of this development and only allowed the Delve chieftain to actually see the document."

Ryl looked hopeful. "Iyna! Iyna must be involved."

"Perhaps, child, that we cannot know for certain. That is a huge assumption. She would not know me. If your sister is a part of this, then she has been most helpful and we can reasonably assume that she is not alone, as you may have feared." Lyssanna smiled as both Safara and Ryl looked comforted by the idea.

"Now tell me. Why you? Especially, as this proposal includes my son."

It was Terris who answered. "Why, my lady? Because Iyna belongs with us. She is Ryl's bondpartner. If anyone can find her, it is Ryl. Where Ryl goes, Safara goes. Where Safara and Ryl go, Ayo goes. Where Safara, Ryl, and Ayo go, I go. And Marcus has only recently joined us, but he, too, feels that pull. No one will fight harder than us to ensure we ALL come back safe and whole."

"And there is your father talking," Lyssanna thought as she spoke. "He was annoying, but usually right. The question is…are you, as well?" She arched an eyebrow to underline her question as she drummed her fingers against the table.

"He is." Ayo and Safara offered at once. Terris managed to look flattered and offended simultaneously.

Marcus reached over and squeezed his mother's hand. "We aren't just a bunch of kids who ran away from school on a lark." He met her eyes and held contact underlining his sincerity. "This is something that we need to do, not only because Iyna is family, but because anyone would deserve better. Given the same opportunity but a different victim, I know we would all feel the same. That is why it needs to be us, Mother. Please…trust me."

No other argument could have worked better. Lyssanna was proud of her son and the person he had become. From the moment his designation was discovered, she knew that he was not hers to keep. Both parents had done their best to instill their values into Marcus and she found it gratifying and alarming to see that he had listened so well. The councilwoman nodded slightly and squeezed her son's hand back.

"Scoria and I had a few thoughts on strategy, but I am interested in this new information." Fairn spoke for the first time since entering the building. His quiet statement was framed as an inquiry, but felt like an order.

"It is a map. The notes in the margin are written in Angelic and it is rather crude. Nanus Delve agrees that it was likely drawn by Rasulo himself." She let that information sink in and continued. "He has been looking for the Pond." Fairn's impassive face registered surprise as his eyes widened. "Unsuccessfully for now, but the map is centuries old, who knows when it was last updated or if he has noticed its absence. Whoever took it was smart enough to send it here without adding anything that could identify them. The fact that the lynx is still around tells me that she is waiting for something. Additionally, the fact that she only appears to me tells me that she was carefully instructed. There is only one person I can think of who would send that kind of information, but he has been gone for over a decade."

"Darek?" Scoria knew the answer without confirmation. Lyssanna nodded anyway.

"He knows I am the only person in this city who can read Angelic and he likely told the cat how to find me. The fact that she hangs around tells me she was told to do so by a familiar. Darek's familiar is a hawk and he has been here in the Delve compound for the last several years waiting. You cannot have two familiars, so it can't be his." Lyssanna stopped, her eyes widening, as Celeste crept out from behind a sofa near her desk.

The lynx revealed herself completely in all of her silvery gold glory and made a beeline for Ryl and Safara. She rubbed her head against one girl and then the other over and over. If she seemed to favor Ryl, no one remarked on it. Nyx tried to push her off his pet and received a hiss in response. The two sized each other up for a moment before deciding the other was acceptable. Nyx jangled in Ryl's face. He was loud, but clearly happy.

"He said she purrs like Iyna used to sing. He can hear Iyna's echo on her!" Ryl hugged the big cat around the neck and buried her face in its neck. Celeste, who would not allow Lyssanna to touch more than her collar the first day and never again came close enough to pet, seemed peaceful in the girl's embrace. Terris squeezed Safara's arm as she leaned away from him to join her sister's hug. Ayo hugged Marcus and bounced in her seat.

Fairn cleared his throat having spent the last minutes studying the map. "I think we have a way forward. If he is looking for The Pond, maybe we can lure him away with it." At his wife and sister's-in-law horrified faces, he clarified. "Not the actual Pond, but perhaps we could simulate something with the Waveless Sea under the mountains." His listeners relaxed. "No group, regardless of talent or strength will have any luck getting into that mountain with him around. Scoria and I were almost killed the last time we got close. She landed two broken legs and, frankly, my voice has never fully recovered."

"I propose that we split. Scoria and I will head through the Spina Ardus and pick a location near the subterranean lake to send out the call. This group cannot travel the mountains as their mounts, with the exception of Mynock and Daichi, cannot handle the terrain. Your horses would break a leg within your first hour. You all will head around the long way through the Paphiae Myrti and to the south of the mountain range. By the time you round the southern point, we will have reached the Waveless to summon Rasulo. You will sneak in while he is gone and rescue your sister and Darek."

"What about the patrols in the Low Plains?" asked Marcus.

"Don't get caught," replied his aunt shortly.

"Funny, but not helpful," retorted Lyssanna. "You will travel at night and hunker down during the day. The Plains are too open to sneak through in full light even though the sycops are likely to be out patrolling at night, as well. I would send extra guards with you, but the larger the group, the harder it will be to hide. The cat will know the way. She got here after all. Nyx should be able to talk to her." She acknowledged the faerydae with a nod in his direction; he seemed to approve and tinkled out a response. "I am sorely tempted to accompany you, but if the school or the Council finds out that you two are trying to engage Rasulo again, there will be no end to the fall out. No one outside this room can know where you are going and why you are leaving. If I were to leave as well, more questions would be asked."

She took a deep breath and continued making stern eye contact with Safara. "My family has sacrificed much for the sake of yours." As the color drained from the girl's face, she offered some reassurance. "Frankly, it is not your fault and I will not hold the sins of your parents against any of you, but if my sister or son is harmed in this expedition, I will find it *very* hard to forgive. Be sure you know what you are about. Now, let's get you all packed and ready to leave in the morning. It is tempting to keep you here for a while, but the fewer that see you the better."

The group soon left to gather supplies, check on the mounts, and pack. Marcus remained with his mother, who insisted that he stay at home that night and spend time with his father.

Terris was the first to break the silence as they all trouped down the stairs. He ended up beside Fairn at the back of the group.

"Stahd's Breath! She doesn't let her size get in the way of being the most intimidating person ever, does she?" Terris whispered half to himself and half to Fairn. The elf smiled his eyes crinkling in his deep blue skin.

"Indeed not. My sister is...determination personified," he stated. "Either you live up to her or you wish you did. And she was tempering her threat concerning Marcus and Scoria." The last he said only in Terris' hearing.

"But you were not included in that condition." Terris

knew he was prying, but asked the implied question regardless.

"No, and I would not expect to be. Lyssanna has survived and even thrived in her position because she has very few people that she holds in that kind of affection. That sounds like she is cold and harsh, but she is not. In her position, those she loves could be used against her. Keeping that group small is as practical as it is necessary. As my Scoria is offered that protection, I am content."

By this time, they were all boarding a lift to head down to the market which was located on the ground near the stables. Tark-Delve was the largest city in Telaria and many non-dwarves called the city home; three humans and a mer would not stand out in the crowd as they shopped for supplies. In fact, it was the older bondpair that garnered the most attention, which they used to distract from the others. Nyx and Celeste had remained above level at the house to keep from drawing unnecessary attention. Although to be fair, none of them were quite certain that Celeste had remained where she was told. The market was pleasantly busy and the open stalls housed all the wares needed to prepare for a trek around the mountains.

After an early supper, the group dispersed around the house. Ayo insisted on taking a long bath complaining that she was parched after so much time away from a body of water. Ryl went off to play with Celeste in the courtyard and the faint sound of Nyx accompanied them.

Fairn offered to show Terris and Safara their library, which overlooked the entire valley and was filled with mementos from their travels and time at Sonaris. Eventually, the conversation circled around to their cycle fight against Rasulo. Safara stood at the window gazing out absently twirling a globe that stood beside her.

"They ran didn't they?" she asked in a quiet voice. "My parents, I mean. They were the chosen pair and they ran to hide." She sniffed and rubbed her fingers under her eyes to dispel her tears.

Fairn nodded slowly, weighing his response. "They were the most promising pair since Talai and Ceracha, but no, they were never officially chosen." Terris' attention was briefly distracted from Safara at the mention of his grandparents. Fairn began again carefully. "My take on the situation is colored by my role. If Jael and Aries hadn't left, Scoria and I would never have bonded. That outcome alone makes me inclined to view the whole chain of events as fortuitous. Lyssanna, as you may have guessed, resented the need for the drastic measures we took. But we made the choice freely." He smiled across the room as the small, stocky form of his wife entered the room. She seemed to sense the serious nature of their conversation and remained quiet.

"But how did you force a bond?" Terris asked.

"Force is a violent term," said Scoria. "I prefer to say that we created favorable conditions where none previously existed."

"What is it like?" came the shy question from Safara.

"A bond?" Fairn waited for a small nod from Safara before answering softly. "It is everything. It is life. It is purpose. I thought myself whole before, but I never truly knew acceptance or peace until she came and filled in all the cracks I didn't know existed."

Scoria let out a laugh and leaned up on her tiptoes to kiss his cheek. "He is absolutely right. You big romantic!" With another shake of her head and a laugh, she called Ryl indoors, convinced Ayo to leave the water, and bustled them all off to bed.

CHAPTER 12

"I will never understand how you do that." Iyna shook her head in wonder as Samal manipulated the water in the trench to assist with washing their hair. The mer's light hum was enough to separate the water into several sections all contained within the same vessel. Samal winked an acknowledgement never releasing her control of the water. She ran the water over both their heads catching every extra drop and guiding back to its place while keeping their tunics remarkably dry. As they lathered, she called the second portion of water up and rinsed when it was time. She dismissed the soapy water out the drain ensuring it carried away all of the grime and suds with it.

"A pretty, but unnecessary, trick in my home. Underwater no one needs to wash like this. Scrape off barnacles and salt scale, yes, but not this." Samal let out a typically mer laugh, reminiscent of watery bells. It warmed Ryl's heart to hear it. Truthfully, she should not have let Samal use her voice for such a mundane task. Her voice was growing steadily weaker. One day the previous week, she was sent back to the cell to rest when her melody stopped affecting the current. They were all relieved in the morning when her voice was back. But most evenings they made her rest her vocal cords and tried every remedy in their power to keep her strong.

Darek was similarly weak, but he refused to be coddled. Even now he was curtained off in his bunk sleeping and had been since he stumbled into the room an hour before. Likely he would sleep until the guards woke them all in the morning. He was growing pale and his hands seemed to shake if he did not focus on keeping them still. The binding was working its way deeper into his physiology. Even if they could get him out, Iyna now doubted he would make it past the grove before trying to turn back. She tried to blink back her tears and missed one. Samal let out a hum and wiped it away with the song. She gave Iyna a knowing look filled with compassion.

"He does not want our pity. Bear that in mind, little fish," Samal put a gentle arm around her shoulder and pulled the teenager close. "Life is complicated enough at your age without considering the mortality of your family. He loves us. Loves you. Never underestimate what that love will allow him to do."

"I love you both, too," said Iyna. "You are all I have known of family. My parents and sisters are fading memories. Darek has taught me more about how I should be than my own father. How can we even think of leaving if he would be left? I cannot lose my father twice." Her voice sounded young and small even to her ears.

The smooth liquid voice filled her ears reassuringly, as smooth arms pulled her close.. "You can never lose him. He has given too much of himself to you for that to happen. Loved ones are never truly lost. Their echo lives on in you. Every choice you make, word you speak, and desire you have is a direct reflection of the ones who made you for good or bad. So no, my fish, he will always be there."

"Why do you call me 'fish' sometimes?" she asked, needing to change the subject, gently nestling her head under Samal's pointed chin.

"My mother called me that and it seemed appropriate. When you first came to us, it was obvious you had no affinity for water and yet you were never afraid of it. I could tell you knew how to swim and had done so before. The first day I was allowed to bring you to the mill pond, you gave a shriek of laughter and headed for the water to jump in. It was the first time you had laughed or smiled since arriving. You swam and played on the bank all afternoon happy as a fish. So you are my fish." Samal ended the story with a long hug and whispered they should go to bed.

Morning started with a bang, as the cell door was shoved open suddenly and Iyna was hauled from her bed by two color-less, irritated sycops. One grunted and pointed at her shoes the other shoved a hunk of bread and a canteen into her trembling hands. Samal and Darek both woke up, but were kept in their bunks when the guards brandished their weapons. Iyna could feel Darek building a melody and stopped him.

"No! I'll be alright. I'll be back as soon as I'm allowed," she said with more courage than she felt. She moved to grasp their hands, but was dragged out the door by the back of her shirt and the door clanged shut behind them. In the hall, she let her tears fall freely. If the sycops possessed the ability to cry, she had never seen it. Neither guard seemed to notice, but they kept her moving at a steady pace toward the training area.

Rasulo stood within, patiently waiting looking out the window at the far end of the narrow room. That put her on edge; Rasulo was never patient with her. The constant hum droned on blossoming into a full-fledged migraine. Iyna winced and shook her head to clear her hearing. During past training sessions, any failure or delay on her part met with swift and painful punish-ment. Just last week she sustained burns to her left leg below the knee because he wanted to test her reflexes against his abil-ity to control fire. It was a series of precisely timed movements, as long as she could move fast enough and follow his rhythm, she would have finished untouched. But after a half hour, her focus began to drift and she hesitated resulting in her burn. He almost refused her treatment, finally agreeing once he realized a permanent maiming would not help his cause.

Iyna despised his indifferent pragmatism above all things. Cold calculation where a life was worth less than a delay of minutes confounded and enraged her. Had she been any other trainee, her life would have been over. Not that she cared for any of the trainees at Profana, but they were still people regardless of their choice to commit atrocities for a monster. A successful trainee was made into a lieutenant and given sycops to command. As long as they returned from their excursions with resources, slaves, or artifacts, they were rewarded by Rasulo and sent on better missions farther afield or kept back to help organize and run Profana. All these followers were Zealots of Rasulo and forsook their families, loyalties, and consciences to promote his cause: to make Telaria his version of paradise, perfect chaos.

"Ah. And so you finally join me, Iyna. Today, we will work on Sound. I have rarely had a student with this ability and I am interested to see what you can do with it. Please keep in mind that you are not to attack me." He gave her a pointed stare to underline his command. "Move to this end of the room and face the entrance. You will focus on objects on the table at that end of the room."

She skirted around the table and moved to her position as quickly and quietly as possible praying to Stahd that the ordeal would end soon. A servant entered silently and removed the covers from the objects on the table revealing a lighted candle, a leafy plant, and a canary in a cage. Iyna's stomach turned as her eyes swept down the line.

"Now, we can begin." Rasulo's voice sounded much to close behind her and she repressed a shudder. "Start with the candle. Listen for its presence in the Song. The fire will guide you to it. I want you to use your Sound to crush it. Do you hear it? Mid-range. That pizzicato popping noise. So fast it almost seems like a hum, but it isn't." She felt a whisper of silk on her face and moved to wipe it away. "The blindfold will help you focus. Drop your hands and stop fighting me." She relented and went back to the sound of the fire on top of the candle. Inanimate objects had almost no place in the Song, unless they were crafted as artifacts. The wax of the candle had no residual melody, but using the fire, she managed to find the silence where it was. She pulsed out with a low tone matching the rhythm of the fire by rolling her tongue. Once the sounds matched, she pulled back and created a matching rhythm on the offbeat of the fire and canceled it out. She felt it snuff out immediately. She pushed down on the void in the Song and the candle compressed into a useless blob.

"Good. Good." Rasulo praised her for the first time ever. He actually sounded pleased, which was unnerving. "Now find the plant. It is growing. Do you hear the leaves stretching and expanding? Stop it from growing. Tell the plant to just stop growing."

It sounded too easy and Iyna scarcely believed that was all he wanted her to do, but she reached out anyway. Her affinity for flora made the plant shine like the sun in her senses. The vibration of its growth was measured and stable. It was not in a hurry. She allowed her hum to meet the edges of the plant and then using Sound she lightly pushed back, creating an invisible barrier around all edges of the plant and not allowing it to move forward by creating a counterpoint to its rhythm. For a few moments, the plant pushed back and intense pressure built up around the barrier she made. Pushing and pushing and pushing. Then it just stopped.

Iyna ripped the blindfold off her face taking in the destruction she caused. The plant was the same size and shape as before, but instead of being a lush green, it was brown and shriveled. Without the ability to grow, the plant had suffocated and died. She began to cry. This was how he was going to turn her into a monster. Her own affinities warped and honed into the perfect killing machine.

He moved around to her side with a broad smile on his face. "Excellent. Much better than I'd hoped. Now onto the bird."

"No," she stated quietly and with conviction. She shook her head. "No. I'm done. I will not be turned into your doom-herald of a pet." She refused to meet his eyes and stared off at the bird vowing to keep it safe from her.

"We shall see." He summoned a focused blast of wind that snapped the bird's neck with a short note. "You cannot save them. But that is a lesson you needed to learn." He called a guard and told him to take her to a different cell one floor up from Samal and Darek. "There are repercussions for failure. Dwell on that in your new home." He swept out of the room with his robe leaving motes of color behind. Iyna had never felt so alone.

Shut away in her new cell, Iyna allowed herself the luxury of a good long cry. She sat huddled into the corner of the bunk with her back to the wall and her knees pulled up to cover her face. She was glad that it was a new cell and that she would not have to tell Samal or Darek what she had done. Honestly, she was as upset with herself as she was with Rasulo. She had known better than to do as he asked; he had been far too calm through-out the test for it not to be a trick. She expected no better of him, so the failing was hers alone.

"I won't be his puppet again. Next testing session, I won't participate," she whispered into the empty room. She shuddered at his reaction knowing that he may very well end her sorry existence. "What is this all even for, if I die here? Eight years of surviving for nothing."

She started humming a lullaby that Samal used to calm her the first few years in Profana. It was a lullaby that the mer used on their children. It was soft and legato like the tide on a sandy beach during a calm day. She sang it several times allow-ing herself to enjoy the music without using the Song. Each ren-dition increasing in volume and feeling until she was singing at full voice allowing it to echo through her cell and out the door. After the last, she heard dozens of voices calling back along her corridor and down the stairs. Each individual voice telling her she was not so alone and feeding her hope.

❋ ❋ ❋

She was exactly as he left her, not that he expected her to move. The dusty layer of her skin slowly began to harden into a thick outer shell. It was coal black with lighter streaks of grey brushed across it. He imbued his song with strength and durability. As he worked he could feel the melody rushing along her body, filling in the gaps and cracks made by careless handling during her initial transport. The cracks smoothed out creating a polished surface.

When the session ended, she looked like an onyx statue. Her limbs still needed developing and her feet were still imperfect, but she had never looked more imposing. He brushed a hand along her shoulder probing the resilience of her new skin. It was elastic, but impenetrable.

"*Perfect,*" he thought as he rolled the boulder back over the vault door.

CHAPTER 13

Lyssanna was efficient. She and her husband, Pern, had two rams mounted and waiting just outside Council Hall at sunrise. Scoria and Fairn loaded their animals quietly discussing their best route and options before bidding the rest of the group farewell. They planned to head down through the interior of the mountain. That lower gate emptied into the heart of the Spina Ardus. Craggy snow capped peaks rose in the distance and shadowed the deep green valleys. Sheer cliffs emptied into bottomless crevasses where only eagles dared to nest. There were no trails in that area and only the rams were able to pass. Their agility and balance kept their riders alive jumping gaps and leaping over boulders when necessary. It would take months to climb the interior ledges of the mountains and make a way out. However, during summer and mounted on a ram, a competent rider could make it out of the range within fourteen days.

Barring any difficulties, the pair would reach the caves above the lake within a week and a half. They would then have to hike through the caves to the Waveless Sea and prepare to summon the Angelic. Once he was en route, the danger would start for them, as the entrance would be their only exit. If caught on site, their options would be limited: retreat back into the caves or fight. A fight would likely be lost, as Fairn's voice remained weak from their last encounter.

"We will be quick, Lyssa. I promise." Scoria shortened the stirrup on her saddle and made eye contact with her sister across the ram's back. "Do you have it?"

"There would be no point in you leaving without it," she responded practically. Lyssanna held out a large leather pack and helped her sister lift it to rest on the rump of the mount. Inside was a large, silver bowl inlaid with copper radial bands, eight in total, all set equidistant around the rim. "I risk everything by sending this with you. If necessary, you will destroy this before engaging Rasulo, if it comes to that. Do you understand me?"

"Absolutely." There was no hesitation in Scoria's reply. "Fairn and I will both vow to destroy the Basin should anything happen, even if the other is at risk."

Fairn briefly pulled the cover back on the artifact to check its condition and assure himself of what they carried. Every eye widened as the silver caught the eastern sunlight throwing sparkling light in all directions, even Nyx seemed entranced. Fairn blinked and pulled his attention away from it. The Basin Octet was more of a legend than a reality for most Hearers in Telaria. It was created by Stahd himself for Sigurd and Sybilla just before he imbued them with the ability to hear. The bowl was an amplification tool rarely used in modern times. It made its way to Tark-Delve when the current, tiered city was carved and was technically on loan from Sonaris. However, it had been in the city for so long that there was currently some debate on where it actually belonged.

Once Fairn and Scoria reached the lake, the bowl would be filled with water and used to amplify their abilities. A note of pure unison sung by a bonded pair in complete concert with one another could trigger an act of creation. While they would be unable to create much, even forming a speck of dust near the bowl would be enough for Rasulo to feel. Their proximity to a large body of water would further aid their deception. Amplifying the act would also let Lyssanna know they reached their destination in safety. She would send a raven to the other party to ensure they knew, but likely they would feel it, too. The additional risk was that Hearers farther afield at Sonaris, Dryadalis, or Aqua Vadum would hear the summons and set out to investigate.

After a final round of hugs and well wishes, they took off down a path behind Council Hall and disappeared into a cave beyond. Ryl let out a deep sigh and looked at the others. It was clear she was upset, but determined to move forward.

"It will be alright," Marcus' voice was quiet and assured beside her. "My aunt knows what she is about and Fairn has never failed no matter the odds against. Do not start feeling guilty, no matter what happens. Iyna deserves to be free."

"I know, but I hope we aren't trading one prisoner for another," Ryl admitted.

"There is no way to know that, child. And plans are already in motion. You have no choice but to proceed." Lyssanna moved to her side and gave her arm a motherly squeeze. "Now you all need to get a move on before everyone in the city is awake." With that warning, they were down the mountain, mounted, and headed to the far end of the valley within the hour.

The group spent the next day finding a deer track that headed in a generally southern direction. Eventually, they settled on an order. Mynock and Marcus went first, as the ram could easily deal with any tricky footing on the path and warn the others of trouble. Next came Ryl and Ayo on Parsifal with Terris behind. Safara acted as their rear guard because of Daichi's maneuverability.

While they traveled through the Paphiae Myrti, they woke with the sun and went to bed at dark. The days began to run into one another. The landscape was a never ending deep, verdant forest to the west and the rising foothills of the Spina to the east. Initially, they tried to play word games and tell stories to pass the time, but communicating was difficult as they became spread out. Shouting along the line seemed a ridiculous risk for the sake of an amusing tale. Gradually, they sank into silence as they traveled.

The Paphiae Myrti was the oldest forest in Telaria. Soaring toward the sky, the majestic trees spread upwards for hundreds of feet; their canopies merging and twining together. The deep emerald of the foliage blended into black, navy, and violet bark with exotic patterns seen only on the myrti trees. Sunrise brought a murky light to the forest floor. By noon, the occasional sunbeam could penetrate the canopy, but that glow quickly faded, as the sun set. It was never truly light while they traveled, which only added to the befuddling sense of time. Further west, there were places where the sun never broke through. Dark, strange creatures sulked in the shadows. Watching, yet apparently willing to allow passage to those who left them alone. Truthfully, only a handful of people in Telaria ever went more than a mile past the boundary of the trees. Many believed an unknown Angelic set a specific border, as the Myrti had never grown, shrank, or changed in any dimension in recorded memory. Strange purple and blue toadstools grew out of some of the trees. Nyx seemed interested whenever he passed one, but would not reveal why. Occasionally, he would bark out a clang of bells, but Ryl said it was not directed at any of them.

Celeste would frequently hiss and partially disappear or dash away into the brush to the east leading up the side of the mountains. Unlike the forest, the dwarves felt more at home in the Spina Ardus and were frequent visitors. But even they were quick to state that it was not a place to linger or go untrained. The lynx always returned to Safara and Ryl, but she was agitated and on edge. The foothills were also covered in short, sparse pine trees. Regrettably, the ground cover was thick and thorny, so it was preferable to travel under the eaves of the Myrti despite the lack of light, as the undergrowth was mostly ferns and moss.

After a week of travel, the trees thinned and abruptly ended dumping them out on the southern end of the Spina Ardus in the Low Plains. There were occasional clumps of bushes and trees, but the area was remarkably open. Turning east, they crossed the occasional stream running down out of the mountains and across the plains to the River Vimor.

Twelve days out from Tark-Delve, they stopped in the early afternoon to rest and hide. Most of the food crops for the southern region of Telaria were grown in the area and farms dotted all over the visible area. None were close to the mountain range, which provided their only hope of managing the crossing undetected. In a small gully containing a waterfall and pool, they all unsaddled the mounts and unpacked for a rest, as they would continue on under cover of darkness.

Ryl and Nyx went to sleep almost immediately. Ayo offered to take the first watch and Marcus followed her asking about her acolyte's test. She was tasked with keeping Knolhaven safe during a lightning storm. The test had only lasted a few hours, but she managed to direct all of the lightning strikes in the town toward Roggle's workshop and his lightning rod. It was a grueling task as the rod had been moved to the roof of the house and not the workshop, which stood as the tallest building in the town. It took all of her strength and focus to continually push the disinclined forces of nature around to the one spot that would not be harmed.

Terris wordlessly handed Safara a cup of water as he bent to fill his waterskin. She drank without comment before joining him and filling the others.

"Does this seem too easy to you?" she asked quietly after she sent Daichi off to catch his meal.

"In what way? Nothing about the Paphiae Myrti has been simple. My eyes played tricks on me constantly. Even with the mountains on our left to guide us, we lost the path on almost a daily basis," he replied as he stowed the filled skins with the other supplies. "Our rations will be getting slim here soon."

"At least we know we can eat the animals out on the Plains. I wouldn't dare in the Myrti." She shook her head to clear it and bent to wash her face.

Terris sat beside her on the rock and took off his boots to dangle his feet in the water. Cerridwen and Parsifal finished drinking and moved off to the shade to rest. Safara untied the leather strap holding her braid in place and plunged her head under the water suddenly. Terris grabbed her shoulder and pulled her back.

"Choirs above! What are you doing, Fara?"

"Calm down. Just rinsing the dust out of my hair. I have never been so dirty in all my life."

"I don't know. You were a mess on the way back from your acolyte test from what I heard."

"Shut it. You wouldn't know. You weren't there."

"No, but Captain Palmer was and he was very forthcoming when I told him we were friends."

Safara's eyes narrowed, as she pushed the wet hair back off her face and squeezed out the excess water. "I just bet he was. Palmer is protective of Ryl and me; there is no way."

"Fine, he didn't, but I still bet you were."

She laughed at that and admitted that she was filthy, but with no mirror at the guardhouse or in the wilderness, she could not compare the two.

"Fair enough," smirked Terris. "And you look nice regardless."

"That has to be the sweetest thing you have ever said to me."

"What?" he exclaimed. "I say plenty of nice things to you."

"Maybe about me, but not to me. It matters." She went quiet and seemed embarrassed. "But you have always respected my abilities and had confidence in them even when I didn't. I think I would forgive you anything just for that."

He smiled and suggested that they both get some sleep. "I'll take the next watch. You and Ryl need sleep more than me."

At sunset, Safara and Ryl were awoken by a loud call from Terris followed by a watery scream from Ayo and the sound of several bodies crashing through the undergrowth near the waterfall. A handful of sycops spilled into the narrow clearing around the pool and made a beeline for the girls sleeping under the trees. Safara was on her feet first and moved to protect her sister.

"Nyx! Get her away from here." The Faerydae responded by pulling the waking girl to Parsifal and heaving her on with an adrenalin fueled boost. "Par. Take her." Safara did not even spare the horse a glance as she smacked his rump. She heard him take off in the direction of the gully opening just as Ayo, Marcus, and Terris arrived. Ryl was calling for her sister, but the mount would not stop. Safara gasped for air and tried to calm herself. "Ayo, you and Marcus see what you can do with the two that split to follow Ryl. Drown them, burn them. I don't care. Ryl stays safe."

As the two moved to intercept, Terris let out a melody to summon the water from the pool. It barely slowed the four approaching sycops. Safara lashed out with fire, but all four dodged under it and made sure to thoroughly soak themselves.

"We have to work together or we are dead, Fara." Terris stated calmly.

"Fine. Lay out a melody, but keep me in mind," she agreed reluctantly. Terris was a master vocalist, so he could only manipulate a melody. She had some success with harmony, but was not as good as Ryl.

Terris began by pushing back the water knowing it was Safara's weakness. The sycops bore down on them hard as the way cleared. Safara rolled under a swing from a mace and stopped in a ready crouch. She listened for Terris' melody amidst the grunting, the creak of armor, and the pounding of approaching boots. She jumped up over the next swing and sensed something behind her. She twisted her body and let out a quick spurt of flame. The second sycop took the burn to the arm pausing for a moment. But it was enough; she ran back to Terris and picked up on his hum. He started a summoning call, but left the element up to her. She quickly filled in earth and a blockade grew ten feet tall and a dozen feet long between them and the two she had evaded. She shifted her harmony quickly to fire. Bolstered by Terris' own affinity, they summoned a cone of fire that immolated the two figures in front of them. Their pale faces melted, as the sycops fought on mechanically.

In the distance, they could hear the sound of two lightning strikes. Ayo could not conjure a storm on her own, so Marcus must have given her enough support to make one. Safara's relief was short lived, as one sycop flanked them and the other's arm burst through the wall. They had barely enough time to turn before Terris was knocked to the side and hit so hard he released the melody. His eyes widened, as he frantically tried to reestablish their attack for a second round. Safara pushed her harmony hard to meet his offering. They reached out through the Song for one another and felt a click, an alignment, just as the pale trooper head butted Terris into a tree knocking him unconscious.

Instantaneously, Safara was infuriated beyond anything she had ever felt before and simultaneously terrified for Terris. She screamed and the earthen bulwark crumbled crushing the third sycop. As she turned to face the last enemy, he stood over Terris's unconscious form with the mace ready to crush the life out of her newly established bondpartner. For the first time in her life, Safara was unable to make a sound or hear the Song.

A loud ringing sound hit her in waves drowning out her connection to the Song momentarily; she could feel herself losing consciousness. Safara threw herself at their assailant, placing herself between Terris and the sycop. The pale brute slammed into her and took them both to the ground, clamping a meaty paw over her mouth. Safara released a grunt of pain and welcomed oblivion.When his prey did not fight back, the sycop threw her over his shoulder and moved menacingly toward the unconscious vocalist lying nearby. From the trees, a loud clanging erupted and a bright light flashed directly into the monster's face. He threw up a hand to shield his eyes and dashed off into the forest the way he had come with Safara slung carelessly over his shoulder.

Nyx was tempted to follow, but stopped when a low growl sounded in the underbrush. Celeste raced after Safara leaving Nyx to rouse Terris. Ayo and Marcus returned to the campsite with Ryl to find Nyx desperately slapping Terris' cheeks and no sign of Safara other than the burnt corpses of the sycops. All three rushed to his side and worked to wake him up. In the meantime, Daichi arrived and began making a scene. Ryl sent the faerydae to calm both mounts. With some effort, the griffon stopped squawking, but both kept pacing.

Suddenly, Terris shot to his feet and screamed out for Safara while clutching his bleeding head. He spun in a circle hoping to see her. "Where is she? Where is she?" He kept repeating the question until Ryl pulled him over to the pool and heaved him in.

"She isn't here. You need to get yourself together and tell me what you know." Ryl rarely lost her temper, but she was a sight when she did.

"She was right there. The sycop came around behind us and head butted me into the tree. I was knocked out. She must have gotten that one because there were two left." His words tumbled out and he had to take a breath after every few words to calm himself. "No body. Either she ran or was taken. And she wouldn't leave us."

"Taken? Why would they take her?" Ryl pushed down her anxieties and tried to focus.

"She's a Canticle!" Terris ran a hand through his hair and tried to take it all in. His whole body vibrated with stress. "She wove a harmony into my song and amplified my abilities. We practically melted those two. I have never achieved that kind of result on my own." He gestured carelessly to the smoky piles of twisted armor and bone. He hesitated and added quietly, "And she is my bondpartner." He closed his eyes and let the tears track down his cheeks.

"*WHAT?!*" came the shocked response from all three.

"She doesn't have a designation. How could you bond?" Ayo looked skeptical. "Just because you sang together doesn't create a bond."

"I know what happened," he stated with assurance. He centered himself and reached out for Safara through their bond. He could feel her breathing, but that was it. She was alive, but he could not tell where or if she was in distress. "I can feel her if I concentrate. She is alive. We need to move though. If the sycop that got away finds another patrol, they will be looking for us."

They all broke up and saddled the mounts in record time. Terris told Ayo to ride Cerridwen and he moved to Daichi, who was still highly agitated. The griffon seemed to settle as he approached and allowed Terris to mount him without complaint. That alone proved his claim to the rest of them, as no one other than Safara was allowed to ride Daichi without her specifically instructing him to take the passenger.

"We will see what we can discover from the air, but we need to keep heading for Profana. That sycop will take his prisoner there for sure. It must have figured out what she is." Terris called from above. The horses and ram all thundered toward the entrance with little regard for noise. Daichi rose into the air like a shot and Terris took a moment to run his hands comfortingly through the soft feathery mane and whisper that they would get Safara back. Daichi let out a morose bark of agreement. There was no sign of either the sycop or Safara. He had not really expected to see any, but being up away from the distracting noises below allowed him to focus on his link. She was awake and distressed, but he did not sense much pain. Also moving quickly, but not in a discernible direction.

He asked Diachi to land near the others. They all galloped forward in a clump and shouted out what information they had. Ayo pulled together a good deal of water during their fight and Marcus augmented it with his wind to create a spectacular gale. It was concentrated over their location. The storm pelted the sycops and in their confusion, Ayo was able to add in a call for lightning. It blasted both badly enough that they were knocked out cold, if not killed. However when they rode passed later, there was only one body. Ryl's face was pale with worry and she leaned over Parsifal's neck desperately hugging him.

The horse also seemed distressed and tried to push them all on by refusing to rest when they were dropping out of the saddle near dawn. Finally, Ryl had to beg him to stop for her sake. He agreed and collapsed into an exhausted sleep. Nyx kept careful watch over his pet and her mount. Celeste had not made an appearance since they left the gully. Nyx informed Ryl that she was likely following Safara. When the lynx did not rejoin them, the group assumed that Safara was still moving and that Celeste was unlikely to leave her unprotected. That small hope was the best comfort they had.

CHAPTER 14

Scoria took a deep breath as she dismounted from her ram and set him loose to graze. They were right on schedule ten days out from Tark-Delve. Her ram would range around the mountain that they were on, but was unlikely to go far. Even if he did, she would summon him back using a fauna call. Fairn did the same. Both rams took off up the side of the mountain and they hid the saddles and bridles deep in the undergrowth of a nearby tree. The tall elf strapped the Basin on his back like a large turtle shell and gave Scoria a knowing look when she giggled.

"Laugh if you wish, but I have never felt so odd," he looked at her affectionately as she shouldered their pack of food and gear. "Carrying the Basin Octet around as if it were an everyday bowl instead of one of our most sacred relics. Do you see this?" He gestured to his back. "Beyond ridiculous. I look like a hunchback turtle."

"This view alone made this trip worth it for me," she returned good naturedly. "Lofty goals and rescue missions aside, it isn't every day you see an elf being less than formal. It's good for your soul, my love. Now come on. Into the cave while I still have *my* dignity."

"Dignity, indeed," Fairn followed her, thankful they were headed downhill, as he was weighed down by the heavy silver of the Basin. "Your dignity is always intact, while mine is under constant attack."

"If you didn't make it such a target, you wouldn't have to worry about it. Now do you want me to light a torch or should we save them for a bit? I think your night vision will work for a while and I can't call myself a dwarf if I get lost in a cave. We will need them eventually. Days underground is a lot even for me."

"No torches for now. We should save them."

They stopped at the mouth of the cave and peered in before proceeding. It looked like any other on the side of the mountains. The opening was jagged and rough. Several large boulders marked the entrance, but the passage cut away sharply to the left and down almost as soon as they entered. The air was crisp and cold as they descended down the path, which was worn smooth by years of dwarven expeditions to the lake to explore and note the changes to the water table of the mountains. Springs all over the area were fed from this source. The initial passage opened up into cavern after cavern. They could hear the sounds of cave animals like bats closer to the entrance, but as they moved forward the drip of water and the hum of the Song in the mountain were the only sound other than their breath.

They spoke occasionally, but usually remained silent so that Fairn could concentrate on his vision and Scoria needed to hear the mountain to make her way safely. The first day underground passed into night without any fanfare. They rested for a few hours and set out again long before sunrise on the outside.

They stopped for a meal at the top of a cliff. A steep switchback trail cut into the face of the fifty foot drop. Safara lit a torch and they moved carefully down taking extra time as needed. The weight of the Basin was starting to take a toll on Fairn. Scoria offered to trade with him, but he refused until they were safely down. The next two days continued in the same way. Both would march for hours in silence, sleep briefly, and then march again. They made it to the lake without incident other than exhaustion and stress about their plans.

Scoria called up a pillar of fire over the lake. It was huge, more of a subterranean sea, deep and disquieting. The water lapped against the shore with a rhythmic slap. Although the water was fresh and clear, there was a tinge of salt in the air, but no breeze. Outside of their small circle of light, silent darkness loomed and the shore stretched out in either direction until it was eaten again by the void. Yet, the very bottom of the lake glowed a bright blue refracting and augmenting the fading light cast by the flame.

Fairn set his burden down near the water and called some of the water from the lake into it while Scoria refilled all of their canteens. The clock for escape would start the second they began their song and they would need to move as soon as they were finished.

"Ready?" Fairn asked. It was the first word he spoke all day.

Scoria's face was lit by the dying cloud of fire over the lake. "Always," she answered simply.

Fairn began a clear, simple call, his favorite summoning melody. It moved up and down an arpeggio scale smoothly. Scoria was very familiar. He left the focus of the summoning to her. Unsurprisingly, she picked earth, as that was her greatest affinity. She focused on a small pebble sitting beside the Basin Octet and picked it up. Fairn nodded taking in the size, texture, color, and composition of the stone through their bond. They moved to the same side of the Basin and placed it between them and the lake. Facing the water, they let their song sink into the Basin until they felt it vibrating in the center. Like a gong, it took a moment to prime and suddenly became all they could hear. They locked eyes and focused on keeping their tones exactly unison as they ran through the melody over and over. After what seemed like an eternity, they heard a small plink as something hit the water of the relic in front of them.

Slowly, they let their song fade and Scoria bent down to retrieve a pebble exactly the same as the one locked inside her other fist. They were a perfect match. Their pure unison melody matching perfectly in tone and timbre had achieved an act of simple creation.

She let out a squeal. "It worked! This is a new rock. It feels brand new and WE are echoing in it!" She threw herself at Fairn, who caught her in an enormous hug and kissed her.

"Lyssanna will have felt that. As much as I want to celebrate, my love, we need to go." With that he released her and reverently emptied the bowl. By the time it was wrapped and strapped back on, Scoria had stowed both stones and was ready to go. It would be a long haul up hill and they had little time to make it out.

❋ ❋ ❋

Rasulo was in the vault visiting his silent project when he felt it. For a moment the Song sounded fragile and thin, as though made of spun glass. It pulled back farther from his senses and faded in a way that seemed familiar, but hard to place like a memory of a smell from childhood. All of the sudden the normal force of the Song rushed back into place flooding his senses and left him reeling. He staggered and caught himself on the table and forced his knees to support the rest of his body weight. His ears throbbing with the thooming sound lingering from its return. He blinked frantically trying to remember the feeling.

It was a creation! Someone had used the Song to create a completely new mass. He replayed the feeling in his memory to pull out as much information as possible. He oriented himself on the place to which the Song was pulled. It was directly to the east of Profana and had sounded resonant. The easiest way to make anything was to access the Pond. He began to pace back and forth across the vault. It had to be the Pond, some moron from Sonaris must have found and tested it. He took off up the stairs at almost a run, barely remembering to tamp down the lights and reseal the door. He made straight for the barracks and began calling out orders left and right. Most of the sycops on site were off duty, so he had a guard roused and summoned two of his lieutenants to organize supplies and mounts. Speed within the mountains required special mounts, lizards he had recently bred for such a purpose. Long, lithe, and scaly, the basilisks were not easy to ride or train, so the party was small consisting of Rasulo and five others. They were headed to the mountains as the sun rose. By evening, they were camped deep in the foothills of the Spina Ardus.

Rasulo instructed the group to stop and make camp, while he scouted ahead to center himself on the echoes of the creation act. It was louder here. He angled himself a bit to the north and felt more aligned with the sound, so he oriented himself toward that new direction and then returned to camp.

"Mason. Greyfinger," he barked as he got closer. Both lieutenants jumped to attention and dropped what they were doing. He gestured east and slightly north. "That is where we need to go. We will be looking for a cave with signs of recent traffic. Feel for the echoes of an earth melody and let me know if you so much as *think* you feel something. If we lose the chase, I will personally flay both of you alive. Understood?"

"Yes, sir." Both answered, wide eyed and nervous. Rasulo seemed perturbed for the first time in their memory. Normally, he was calm and unruffled, but that day he was agitated and pacing back and forth. Continually glancing over his shoulder in the direction he indicated earlier. No one slept that night. Had they been in any terrain other than the Spina, they would have marched through the night to avoid the tension. But even the Angelic knew better than to travel in the mountains at night, so they waited impatiently for morning.

Travel was difficult to say the least. Without the basilisks, they would have been almost a week getting to the cave. On the second day out of Profana, they came upon a jagged opening in the rock. Even Mason and Greyfinger could feel creation reverberating here. The sound was fading, but still noticeable if one was carefully listening. Rasulo charged into the mouth of the cave and his guards tumbled through in his wake. The darkness did not slow him, but the rest of the party required torches to see anything after the first few turns. Mason lit one at the front and the rear of the company, as they toiled along behind their leader. He was possessed, never stopping to rest and charging forward unafraid. Within minutes, he outstripped the rest of the party and they were left to follow after as best they could.

❋ ❋ ❋

"Give me the Basin, Fairn." Scoria stopped him at the base of the rock face and tugged the straps off his back. "Here. You take this." She handed him what was left of their food, keeping only her canteen hanging from her belt. "Rest down here for a bit. I'm going to get a start on this monster. I'll see you at the top." She squeezed his hand and kissed him quickly. The sooner they got out of the cave the better. Elves were not meant to be underground and away from the wind for so long.

"Boss me again and see how it turns out!" Fairn called up after her and heard her laugh in return. He waved at her back and sat down to catch his breath. The Basin was not a small or light object and he was tired from toting it around for the last two weeks. Truly, he was exhausted and relieved to be free of the extra weight. He rolled his shoulders and gave himself several long minutes to gather himself, then moved to follow his mate. She practically ran up the path and he smiled at her boundless energy. It was so like her to push herself forward and make him catch up. She knew he would follow wherever she led and the best way to get him to move was to give him something to chase.

When he finally reached the top of the cliff, his eyes automatically searched for Scoria. He saw her near the wall of the cave motioning him to be silent and to come quickly. He scanned out into the darkness and saw a figure moving their direction at a frightening pace. It flashed an odd shimmering light between the stalagmites moving their direction determinedly. Only one thing could have made it so far so fast. Fairn did a quick mental calculation and knew he could never reach Scoria and the Basin in time. With a thrust of air directed at her, he pushed her into a tight crevasse between two stalagmites and blew her a kiss as he met her horrified eyes. Their bond had never been filled with such tension. Her first duty must be to protect the Basin, but every fiber in her being rebelled at the thought of separating from Fairn. He pushed back into their connection and filled it with his determination and desire for her to remain where she was. For once, she did as he bid.

Within seconds of cresting the precipice, Fairn turned and retraced his steps. He jumped from straight down the trail, from level to level with no thought for safety. He just needed to reach the ground without dying. Rasulo picked up his pace when he sensed the wind melody and was an iridescent blur rushing onward never noticing the small dwarf huddled over a bulky pack off to the side. He reached the edge as Fairn hit the bottom. Immediately, Fairn began summoning earth and built it as he waited for Scoria to pick up his melody. It was markedly similar to the one they used to encase Rasulo into the heart of the mountain. But instead of focusing on the Angelic, who was descending the switchbacks to face him, it focused directly on the elf alone.

Scoria pressed herself back into the gap in the wall and tried to resist the song Fairn was building. But his desire to produce a song resonated so strongly that within seconds she gave in. She knew what he wanted and added her earth harmony. Every molecule of her heart cried out against his plan, but her mind understood his intentions and honored his request. Her bondmate could never survive a direct solo confrontation with the Angelic in his condition. This approach gave Fairn control of the encounter and would keep Rasulo from discovering the Basin. The roof of the cave began to shake and the stalactites let go of their moorings. Fairn pushed a large boulder in front of Scoria's position with a determined blast. His song was ear piercing as all air flow in the cave was used to propel the ceiling toward him at a faster and faster rate. Rasulo recognized the melody and belatedly attempted a disruption, but Fairn's determination resisted all attacks and manipulations. He summoned enough of the mountain to obliterate the entire path to the lake under a hundred feet of solid rock.

Scoria felt the first pebbles hit his face and arms followed inexorably by larger and larger debris. She supported his efforts from her enclosure even as his melody suddenly ended and echoed away. She felt a rock gash her check. The sting of salt in the wound was the first indication she had of her tears. Even after her mate was gone, she kept on calling to the earth. It rumbled under her feet and crumbled above her with the weight of her loss. She wanted to be with him no matter the cost. The handful of sycops lead by Mason and Greyfinger turned to flee back out of the cave. All but Mason were caught and crushed by Scoria's continued attack.

When her voice finally gave out, she was covered in rubble and dirt with a tiny crack of light several dozen feet above her head. Her voice was gone and she was trapped without a way to move more than a few feet. She felt herself begin to pass out and welcomed the darkness.

Miles away, Lyssanna urged her mount on. She set off for the cave less than a week after her sister. Pern would send a raven to Marcus in her place. Two days before, she felt the creation with a sinking feeling. They had all agreed on the risk, but that did not mean she would sit idly by as her son and sister took on all the danger. There was a rumble within the ground that felt like an earthquake and in the distance she saw the top of a mountain implode with a sudden pop. It inverted on itself and she felt the residue of an earth-wind song fading across the distance. Her ram struggled to maintain its footing and floundered along a ridge of flowing earth until it found solid rock again. Fearing the worst, Lyssanna pushed on through evening and into the greying darkness only stopping when the stars came out. Her mount was exhausted, but they eventually made it to the cave entrance days later, which was littered with the crushed decomposing corpses of several sycops and one mer commander. Truthfully, it was no longer an entrance. It was completely filled in with rubble.

"Scoria! Scoria Tark! Answer me!" Lyssanna called out into the night as she dismounted and ran toward the collapsed opening. Knowing the path, she ran in the rough direction of it along the surface. Trees were down everywhere and slowed her progress. She stumbled on during the deepest reaches of the night stopping to call and listen for her sister. The echo of the earth melody was greatest which gave her some hope. She followed the echo as it got stronger near its source and found a crack not more than two feet long. She put her mouth near the opening and screamed her sister's name over and over. A shallow groan was her only response.

Unable to see the origin of the noise, Lyssanna began an earth song. She had only a fraction of her sister's ability, but she pressed on. One stone at a time, she widened the crack and slid down into it carefully. At the bottom, she found the pathetic figure of her semi-conscious sister huddled around the Basin. Lyssanna pulled her sister to her side and attempted to warm her cold, shivering form under a cloak. Praising Stahd for the opportunity to do so as she waited for morning.

CHAPTER 15

Safara woke slowly; her head was pounding and her eyes refused to focus. There were voices nearby. Her left side felt warm and had a slight purr to it, but with no visible origin when the girl attempted a peek. Slowly a pair of vertically slitted eyes came into view and the warmth turned into a pressure on her chest. Celeste quickly scooted under a nearby bench as voices approached.

"I say we take her back to Profana. Too bad this idiot sycop can't tell us where he found her. If she isn't Sonaran, I'll give you my next assignment," said the first voice.

"That's a bad bet. Look at her clothing. Of course she is Sonaran. The better question is, 'What is she?'" replied the second.

"I gagged her to be safe, but she can still use the Song with enough focus. We should keep her unconscious."

"Agreed. You check her and I'll see about moving her into the compound in the morning."

The first voice came closer as it spoke. She faintly heard a sleep melody and then passed out again.

When she came to, Safara was starving and tied to a metal chair inside a cell with no reassuring warmth pressing against her. At least Celeste was able to stay with her for part of the way. Dreadfully thirsty and lonely, she had never despaired so much about her lack of affinity with water. She twisted her head. On a sideboard behind her, there was a pitcher and she could almost smell the water. Condensation gathered and slipped away on the outside of the brass surface. She whimpered and tried to edge that way. She called earth and for the first time in her life, it refused to answer. Her eyes widened and she suppressed her rising panic. Quickly, she tested fire and wind. Both of those responded normally, but the earth was muted and far away. A relieved sob almost set the sideboard on fire.

"Ah. So you are awake," a voice came from the barred window at the top of the cell door. "I wondered how long you would stay out once we released the sleep spell. You have been out for days." A short, gangly man pushed the metal door open. He was basically all arms and legs and had the look of a spider: skittish, cruel, and hungry.

"I am Faustus and I have been sent to perform an assessment on you." He casually wandered over to the pitcher and poured himself a glass of water. He raised it in a silent toast and took a long draught. "Now, I wonder what you would do for this?" He set the glass down in front of her and Safara could not help but lick her chapped lip below the gag as a droplet sloshed over the side and hit the oak plank of the table. "Whatever else you can do, water is out. So show me something worth seeing and I'll give you that. Attack me and you will die for it." He stated the last in such a matter of fact tone that it did not occur to her to disbelieve him. He removed the gag roughly managing to pull out several strands of hair that were caught in the knot. The girl bit back a whimper and used the pain to help focus her foggy senses.

Safara called on a draft of wind through the opening of the door. Shouting to the wind and making a bigger show than necessary, she used words to call a gentle breeze. "Wind to me! I would feel you on my face." She sang it over and over with much more volume than necessary, while only focusing enough to summon a small breeze. She hoped this arrogant man would fall for her ploy and decide that she was not valuable enough to watch closely.

"Wind, eh? Not particularly impressive though. If you had fire, you would have burned me or at least made the torch flare. You seem the type to try." He considered her a moment longer and pushed the glass to the edge of the table near her before leaving. The thud of his boots echoed back down the hall as he stormed back off to his chambers.

She pulled against her ropes and got as near the table as possible before biting at the edge of the cup and tilting it slowly toward her. It worked at first, but as the water level went down it became harder to balance the cup. She eventually had to grit her teeth and dump it up over her head. Some of the remaining water went into her mouth, but most of it splattered all over her face, neck, and shoulders.

The water woke her up a bit more and she finally heard a familiar sound. It was a light buzzing in her optimal range. Her bracers! On the other end of the table. She could hear her daggers. She spent the next few moments tuning the weapons, which were unsheathed and lying carelessly on the other end of the table. Her mind began working on a plan. She was definitely in Profana, which was good and bad. Good in that Iyna must be here. Bad in that she was locked up and alone.

She felt another pull. It felt like something was calling her specifically and it was outside the compound. Terris! Her memory of their fight by the waterfall came flooding back as she remembered that they bonded. Now he was somewhere near looking for her. She felt relieved that he was uninjured when he was knocked out and guilty that it took her so long to remember. She pinged a note of consciousness back to him and immediately felt him focus on her location. Her senses flooded with relief, some of it hers and some of it his.

With the knowledge that Terris and likely the others were somewhere close, Safara shifted back to considering her imprisonment. She considered burning off the rope, but did not want to risk singeing her wrists. She had no way of knowing the time of day or how long she had been unconscious. She used her song to drag the daggers slowly in her direction and positioned them at the end of the table with the point facing her direction and hanging over the edge several inches. She leaned back in her chair and balanced on two of its legs. Her ankles were tied together, but not to anything else. She lifted both legs and brought one booted foot down on the end of a dagger while slamming the chair back onto all four feet. The silver weapon arced up in the air over her head as she directed it, spinning as it descended. It ripped through the outside of the rope missing her wrists by a hair's breadth and clattered to the ground.

Between the chair and the clatter of metal, the guards were running toward her cell, fumbling with the keys as she repeated the move with her second dagger. As they opened the door, she rolled to the floor and collected her daggers taking her stance just as they both bore down on her from opposite sides of the table. She feinted to the right and then ducked around the chair using it to block that attacker's approach. She called out fire from the torch on the wall, but her throat was so dry that she managed little more than a squeak, which burnt out the torch rather than burning the sycop. The room plunged into semi-darkness and she used the distraction to move under the table as her eyes adjusted to the light spilling in from the passageway. She crawled under it as her captors searched for her. The table flipped over her and slammed against the wall. Her bracers clattered to the ground in front of her and she scooped them up hurriedly jamming a dagger into one. She heard the spring cock while shifting onto her back and aiming at the closest sycop. She pressed the trigger and her dagger struck it true in the neck, ripping clean through. He let out a garbled scream and crumpled to the floor with his wound hemorrhaging. The second sycop did not slow and swung his mace directly at Safara's head. She rolled toward his feet and felt the side of her tunic shred away with the swipe. She stabbed her remaining dagger into the top of his foot and through to the floor briefly pinning him in place as she summoned back her other blade. The sycop wrenched the dagger from his foot and threw it at her as she attempted to load the first dagger again. Instead of firing, she called on the second blade, slingshotted it around her head, and buried it directly in his eye. As with the first sycop, he fell with a short agonized scream.

Safara quickly gathered and cleaned both blades and before loaded them into her bracers after she buckled them on her forearms. Her second priority was taking a long, welcome drink from the pitcher miraculously still on the sideboard. She quit the room as quietly as possible, shocked that no other guards were around to investigate. When she gained the hall, she realized it must be the middle of the night, as torches were lit along all of the passages and no natural light crept in through any of the high, narrow windows above the cells. A few of the cells were occupied, but none of the pitiful creatures within would even respond to her questions. Most lay huddled in their beds and refused to look at her. She went up a few more levels, dodging the few guards she encountered and checked each room as she went.

Finally, she encountered a cell with two occupants, a mer and a dwarf. She tapped on the bars and begged the occupants to speak with her. The denizens of this floor seemed to be in better condition. Their rooms were airier and had multiple occupants for company.

A soft watery voice answered her plea immediately. "Iyna? Fish, is that you? Where have you been?" The mer moved immediately to the door and thrust her partially webbed hands out to Safara, who worked to control her cry of excitement.

"Iyna? You? You know Iyna? I'm Safara. Where is she?" Questions tumbled out of the girl's mouth as fast as her mind formed them. Terris must have sensed her excitement because she felt him reach out with a question. She paused and calmed herself, which also allowed a response to her questions. She focused just in time to see a guard rounding the corner. She ducked behind a column and willed herself invisible in the shadow. It took the sycop an eternity to pass, but finally he moved around the corner.

By this time, the dwarf was standing at the door with the mer. "I am Darek Delve and this is Samal. Who are you to ask about Iyna and how do you know that name?" The questions were asked carefully and Safara instinctively trusted both of them. Her trust bolstered by the Delve surname.

"Iyna is my sister. She was lost from our home eight years ago near Loch Fel. Our parents were killed and Ryl and I escaped to Sonaris. Iyna has been calling to Ryl over their bond for years, but we only recently learned her location. Please! Where is my baby sister? She has lighting white hair and clearest blue eyes. Please." Her voice broke as her words tumbled out rapidly. She grasped at their hands through the bars her eyes begging them to guide her.

Samal answered quickly. "She was taken for personal training with Rasulo this three days ago and she has not returned to us. She has lived here in this cell with us for the last eight years." At Safara's muffled cry of alarm, Samal continued. "Never fear. I heard a lullaby echoing down the halls not an hour ago. I taught it to her years ago and some of the others picked it up and passed it on to us. While she is not here, she is near. There is one level above this one. Rasulo keeps his most powerful slaves up there. Get her out. Do not let her come back for us. She will try, but she must leave. Whatever Rasulo has been doing to her in training is killing her. He left two days ago in a great rush, so this may be her only chance of escape."

Safara tested the bars, but could not get them to budge or burn with her voice in its current state. Frustrated she kicked at the door. Darek's gravelly voice broke through her outburst. "Patience, girl. Your sister is the priority."

"Lyssanna Tark would want us to free you." Safara shot

back at his startled look.

"Did you get the map?" he asked softly.

"Yes. Celeste brought it a few weeks ago. Lyssanna thought you might be the sender."

"Clever woman, that." The dwarf ghosted a smile in the moonlight. "Your sister can tell her all about it. I cannot leave here and Samal has no way of fleeing either. So we are back where we started…get your sister out. Now." He reached through the bars and gave her a light shove.

Safara stumbled and released Samal's hands looking at them both in horror. "But if I can't open your door, how will I get Iyna out?"

"Tell Iyna to shatter the lock. It will bring every sycop in the building, but she could do it." Samal answered quickly.

Darek cut in. "Or just knock out the patrol on her level. They will have the keys for that floor."

"Then why not do that for you?"

"Because, daft child, the patrols are timed to pass the stairs at regular intervals and they call up and down. If this floor misses its call, you will be trapped on the top of the mountain with a thousand foot fall. What are you going to do? Jump?" Darek responded almost affectionately.

"Can we get out onto the mountain side?" Safara asked a plan forming in her mind.

"Yes, there is a skylight in the upper hall." Samal's voice cut out. "GO! Now, the guard is coming back."

Safara turned and sprinted for the stairwell just as the guard noticed Samal at the door. He kicked at her vengefully, but did not notice the long dark braid disappearing up the spiral steps to the next floor. She waited between the two floors until she heard the guard at the top send down his call before returning to his patrol. As she waited, she reached out to Terris and pulled at their bond forming as clear a picture as she could of her location praying to Stahd he would understand to send Daichi. Usually she could feel her familiar, but either he was far away or her bond with Terris was so strong that it felt easier to call him. Reassurance flooded their connection and she could feel her bondpartner moving toward her.

The sycop moved away along the hall and Safara moved silent as a shadow behind him. He was larger than the last guards and all visible skin was covered in puckered scars. Some were a faded white with age, but several of the larger ones were pink and angry looking. She let him get several paces ahead of her. Then she ran at his back and jump-kicked off the nearest wall. The kick aimed at a fresh wound on his neck. As she landed, she hooked her arm around his neck and used her momentum to slam him into the ground. It was not a quiet attack, but it was effective. Faces appeared at several of the cell doors. Before the guard had a chance to recover, she hit hard with a sleep song using her affinity for fauna to knock him unconscious. His hand hit the floor with a soft thud as he sank into a deep sleep.

Safara rifled through the pouch at his waist and found the keys. "Iyna! Iyna!" She called in a desperate whisper.

"That is the girl's cell." A dwarven arm shot out across the hall and pointed to the cell at the end below the skylight.

"Thank you. I promise to leave you the keys, but I have to get my sister out." Safara rushed to the end of the hall and tried several keys before finding the right one. The iron cell door swung open and she called her sister's name again.

The figure on the bunk stirred, but did not wake.

"Come on, sleepy. We have to go." Safara sobbed out as she recognized her sister's unique coloring.

Iyna awoke with a start and stared at the unfamiliar

face that housed a distantly familiar voice. She choked back a scream as Safara's hand covered her mouth.

"Please, Iyna. Come with me. Questions later. We have to move now."

"Fara?" Iyna started crying in relief as her sister hugged her tightly and pulled her out of bed in the same move.

"Yes, Squirt. Get dressed. We have less than five minutes before there are guards all over this hall and we need to be on the roof by then."

Iyna pulled on her boots, as she was still dressed. She grabbed her cloak and they left the cell. Safara told her to stand below the skylight and bounded down the hall to the dwarf. She quickly handed him the keys and pressed his hands through the bars. Iyna heard her murmur, "Stahd's Blessings. If you get out, please take the mer, Samal, and dwarf, Darek, with you. They are one floor down."

At that Iyna went rushing for the stairs, only to be stopped by her sister. "Darek will have my head faster than the guards if I let you go down there. He and Samal both want you out of here and quite frankly, our ride can't carry them, too."

"NO, Safara! They are my family."

"I know, Iyna, I truly do, but we will never make it out of this mountain if we don't go out the roof. No matter how well you know this place. Do you know what Ryl and I risked to get this far?"

"Where is Ryl?" Iyna asked with a hiccup that sounded suspiciously like a whimper.

"She is fine. Later." Safara reassured her and pulled her under the skylight.

It was just big enough to squeeze through. Safara had Iyna climb to her shoulders and use her as a ladder to stand and hoist herself onto the roof. Iyna lay on her stomach and reached down to help Safara, who jumped and pushed off the wall, twisting in the air to catch her sister's forearm. Iyna let out a yelp of pain at the sudden weight on her arms. Safara pulled herself up over the edge and they huddled as far away from the opening in the shadows as they could. Within a minute they heard a commotion coming from the hall below and grunting from several sycop guards when they found their compatriot out cold and a cell empty. The alarm was raised all over the compound. The head of a body too large to fit poked out through the skylight and surveyed the roof. Iyna threw up her hood and turned her back hoping her black cloak would blend into the rocks. Safara huddled behind her and hid her face. The guard let out a call and Safara cautiously peeked over to see it staring straight at them. Fortunately, he was wedged in the skylight and had a hard time getting back down. As his head disappeared, Safara felt and then saw a familiar white shape streaking toward them from the west.

Safara felt Terris and Daichi approaching. She grabbed her sister's arm and yelled, "Trust me!" as she started running doggedly to the edge of the cliff. She could feel Diachi zero in on her location. Iyna followed without thinking and let out a shriek as they leapt off the edge. Safara gave her sister a push toward Terris' outstretched arms. "Catch her," she commanded, as she angled her body below the griffon and called his name just as loud grunts were heard from Terris and Iyna. She spread her arms to make as large a target as possible. Within seconds, she felt Daichi's claws digging into her leather vest. She almost threw up when he jerked her upward and took off to the west.

A call of wind warned them of the danger from the roof. Silhouetted against the moonlight, two white cloaked lieutenants gathered their focus into a gale force storm. Daichi pushed into the wind with all his might trying to gain altitude over the storm, but it was focused on their small group drawing them backward to the mountain top. The distance from the cliff was shrinking every second and the powerful white wings beat against the current. Safara did what she could and created a small windless pocket at the center of the storm so that the griffon would not exhaust himself.

Far below, Ayo and Marcus watched as the white blur of the griffon floated in the middle of a pocket storm. They approached from the west urging Mynock to cover the ground as fast as possible. A golden shimmer appeared out of nowhere and yowled at them demandingly. "Celeste!" Ayo called in relief to the lynx, who continued in front of them, weaving conspicuously between trees guiding them to a hidden track up the mountainside until they were directly below their missing friends. Without missing a beat, they dismounted and assessed the situation. The pair could see the griffon struggling against the wind to move forward. Daichi had the strength to carry two adults, but with three riders and the storm he was fading fast. Working in tandem, they built a rival ice storm to cancel out the first using the same melody and harmony as they had in the gully. The storms met furiously pushing against one another and covering the mountainside in wind and rain. Ayo thrust her song forcefully against the other and froze the water forming several large icicles. They whipped around the storms several times gaining speed with each pass. Marcus pushed hard behind them forcefully embedding the missiles deep in the chest and sides of their opponents. Both Sonaran students felt an odd click and alignment as they hit. The first storm dissipated suddenly and Daichi shot forward. Ayo and Marcus looked at each other in shock realizing that they, too, had bonded. The dwarf quickly threw the mer up on the ram and they nimbly raced down the craggy mountain side eyes wide and disbelieving. Neither was inclined to talk, but their bond radiated the confusion they were both feeling.

Profana receded rapidly behind them. As Daichi recovered his bearings and flew directly toward a pair of horses galloping away to the west. He bent his head down and squawked at Safara in alarm chiding her for their impulsive boarding.

"I agree with him completely," came Terris' voice from above. "Next time let us land."

Safara coughed in response trying to get her breath back feeling suddenly lightheaded and desperately tired. She could hear Iyna sobbing above in shock.

"I'm free, Fara! Free! For the first time in eight years, I can go wherever I want and be with my family! And...no buzzing out here!" She sounded elated, bordering on hysterical. Terris hugged her and introduced himself. Iyna returned the hug and began to calm.

Safara felt the tension slowly ebb out of her bond with Terris as he leaned over to see her hanging from Daichi's claws. She twisted her head and tried unsuccessfully to see him. Instead she stuck her arm out to one side and flapped it a little to prove she was alive.

They were losing altitude quickly and the sound of pounding hooves rose to meet them. Daichi swooped in low above the horses, neither flinched. Ryl was on Cerridwen and called a warning to Parsifal as Safara was deposited on his back. She immediately slumped over and hugged his neck letting out a cry of relief. Parsifal snorted, but did not break his pace. They kept on for an hour and crossed the River Fel finally stopping on its far side. They dismounted in a deep grove of pine trees.

Iyna leapt from Daichi's back the moment his feet touched down. She called out Ryl's name as loud as she dared and shot straight for her, pulling her down off Cerridwen's back. The two locked in an embrace, which Safara soon joined unsteadily, dropping them all down in a heap. All three were crying and holding each other. Trying to cram eight years of history and news into the shortest time possible. Iyna kept repeating that her headache was gone. Parsifal was impatiently awaiting his turn to greet his girl. Nyx was flying around their heads tinkling out a happy noise and checking Ryl and Iyna for injuries. He kept resting his head against one or the other of them and looked content. Out of nowhere, Celeste joined the group loudly insisting on Iyna's attention.

"Celeste! You brave, smart girl." Iyna released her sisters and threw herself toward the lynx. "You brought them to me. You knew they were mine!" She fondly petted her and wiped her tears against the silvery coat. Celeste did not mind the moisture for once and pressed herself against Iyna purring loudly.

Terris hung back a moment to allow the sisters space. When Iyna broke away, he pulled Safara to her feet and into his arms. All scolds went unsaid as he held her close and she held him back. Safara released a breath, unaware she was holding it in, and pressed her face into his chest. Terris almost laughed in relief and pulled back to look at her face. He froze as his hand met the exposed skin on her side and she sucked in a gasp of pain.

"Fara. You are bleeding. We need to take care of this. Choirs above! What happened?" He asked incredulously while bending to inspect her wound.

With all the excitement of the last hour, she had not even noticed that the swipe from the mace tore more than her shirt. It shredded a hand's width of skin across her torso. Everything from her ribs to her knees was covered in blood and she suddenly felt nauseated from blood loss and hunger. She fought the fatigue that was settling over her to reply, "Oh, just a sycop with a mace, you know. Standard rescue stuff." The attempted joke fell flat as she sank to the ground unevenly. Terris managed to catch her as she crumpled. Ryl and Iyna both hovered anxiously.

Choking back his own alarmed reaction, Terris did what he could to staunch the blood with his cloak while Ryl retrieved the bandages. He made quick work of cleaning the wound and binding it up. Safara fell asleep just as Marcus and Ayo joined them. She did not wake up despite the commotion made by the recent arrivals and introductions to Iyna. Food and water were passed around. Terris cradled Safara gently as he explained their bond to Iyna and answered what questions she had about Sonaris and the school. Ryl was content just to be beside her twin as they continued to work on Safara's wounds. The other pair kept their bond to themselves, but eventually moved to the edge of the campfire light to discuss what happened in low tones.

And still Safara did not wake. The cuts were not especially deep, but there were a lot of them. Combined with her lack of real sleep and sustenance over the past days, it was no wonder she was exhausted on top of her injuries. As the sun was coming up, they broke camp. Terris held Safara in front of him on Daichi; Ayo covered her as best they could to ward off a chill. Iyna and Ryl refused to be more than two feet from one another and rode Parsifal, who was elated to have both of them even as he cast concerned glances at Safara. Ayo and Marcus managed the other two mounts and they all headed back around the southern end of the Spina Ardus as quickly as possible. Marcus took the lead on Mynock with Daichi again at the rear. They traveled for most of the day, with Safara waking occasionally only to resume sleeping as soon as she took a head count and ate a little. Terris was concerned as she developed a fever and was growing warmer by the hour, so the decision to split up was made. Terris and Safara would fly over the Spina to Tark-Delve and wait for the rest of the group.

Ayo pulled Terris aside whispering furiously as she did. "I agree that you and Fara have to go, but I don't like being left out here to babysit. Send someone to meet us as soon as you get to Tark-Delve." Unfortunately, she was not as quiet when whispering as she assumed.

"Babysit?" replied Marcus in a strangled voice. Ayo did not need to test their bond to feel his confusion and disappointment. She froze and turned slowly. Marcus' face flushed dark as he swallowed whatever he meant to say. He sprang into

Mynock's saddle and thundered off.

"What was that?" Ryl turned on Ayo. "He wouldn't normally give a copper for your snark. What happened?"

Ayo looked at her feet and scuffed her toe in the dirt a few times before looking up and admitting that they bonded on Profana.

"But that is great news. The school will have three bonded pairs for the first time in decades." Terris was clearly excited at the prospect.

"Neither of us wanted to bond with the other. It just happened. Repetition of the same successful feat combined with an intense amount of focus and we clicked. But we don't know what to do about it. And now he is furious with me and off riding around to settle down. Worse yet, I think I meant to make him mad. He can sense in our bond that I am reluctant and it feels like a rejection." She paused and leaned against a tree with a sigh. "I'm an idiot. I have the gift of a lifetime and I'm rejecting it because he wasn't what I expected."

"So stop being an idiot. Keep an eye on the girls and apologize to him. My grandparents could never stay mad at each other no matter what the other did. Besides he is your bondpartner, not your bondmate." He smirked. "At least, not yet."

Ayo threw a stick at him and told him to take Safara and get in the air. Ryl and Iyna roused their sister long enough to say goodbye, but the fever had set in and she barely acknowledged them. The four of them got her settled as comfortably as possible astride the griffon's snowy back. Terris held her tight and called to Daichi. He took off at a run gaining speed until he could lift into the air, pumping his wings. The trio wheeled twice over the heads of the others before they shot off north over the mountains.

Within two days, they arrived at Tark-Delve with Daichi

landing right outside Council Hall. Terris gathered up Safara and rushed into the building causing a ruckus, which thankfully attracted Pern Tark's notice. He quickly moved the pair to his home one level down and summoned a healer. Masters Parke and Deckard had arrived the week before and welcomed the pair. Parke hugged his son so tight, Terris feared his ribs were bruised and Deckard fussed over Safara when she awoke. Both seemed shocked that Terris and Safara bonded, which grew to almost disbelief when they learned of the other two pairs en route. Deckard left immediately to join them.

The next days were hard on Safara and Terris. He could feel her pain and frustration with her wounds. The healer was confident that she would return to full strength with rest and care, but she required absolute vocal rest for a while to ensure the strain was not permanent. Daichi was allowed to stay in the courtyard of the Tark family compound and made friends with all of Marcus' young relatives, who all thought him great fun.

After Safara recovered from her fever, she wrote a note requesting to see Lyssanna and was informed that she had been away for well over a week. Pern was growing concerned, as he had no word of her. Safara hauled herself to her feet and stumbled to the courtyard with Terris' help and Pern followed. Daichi was allowing the children to climb all over him, but carefully extricated himself when Safara approached him.

She fell against his neck in a big hug and he swatted her affectionately with his tail a few times. Safara's smile was as brilliant as the sun at being able to see her familiar. She ruffled the feathers in his mane before pulling on his beak to bring his forehead to hers. She closed her eyes briefly and leaned into him. Daichi pulled back and made a deep snort while shaking his head and stomping at the stone pavers with his back paws. Again Safara repeated her movement with his beak. He let out a squawk and suddenly took off to the south with Safara waving him on encouragingly.

"Where is he going?" asked the older dwarf, his shaggy eyebrows were raised almost to his hairline.

"She told him to go get Lyssanna," responded Terris, who looked to Safara for confirmation. She responded with a short nod as she watched her familiar soar up and out of sight.

"Thank you," Pern stated simply. "I sent the raven out to Marcus when we felt the change in the Song, but it must have arrived after you separated."

"They will have plenty of news when Deckard reaches them. He is an excellent tracker and faster than most mounts when he wants to be. They will arrive safe and probably mothered to death." Parke commented with one of his wry smiles before insisting Safara go back to bed. At her mutinous look, Terris offered a compromise of a nap on the terrace and helped her to a cushioned lounger in the sun leaving her briefly to retrieve a blanket and a book.

❈ ❈ ❈

The next week was nerve wracking for all three groups. Deckard arrived back with the two bonded pairs one evening as the sun was setting. The party looked haggard and relieved. He found them slogging around in the foothills near the Myrti occasionally beset by dog sized lizards, which had left them alone on the initial trip because of the griffon. Without a large predator as a deterrent, they were a plague, sneaking in to camp to steal food or stalk Nyx. The faerydae hid in a pack for most of the journey. The three sisters slept in a pile together for the night and did everything together. The twins were relieved to see their sister up, moving around, and quietly vocal.

Lyssanna appeared the next morning cradling Scoria in front of her and the Basin strapped on her back. Daichi had to range over the southern half of the Spina to find them, as Lyssanna had been unable to move Scoria on her own. The group landed in the courtyard and Daichi let out a screech that woke the entire city level. Safara came rushing out of her room and latched on around his neck. Pern and Parke appeared next and helped the dwarven sisters dismount. Scoria was barely conscious and Lyssanna was holding on to her control by a thread.

Safe with her family, she let the tears track down her cheeks and asked that the healer attend Scoria, who had only managed a few words since being found. All Lyssanna knew was that Fairn was gone and Scoria seemed unwilling to talk about it. Once the older sister had some rest, she insisted on summoning the Dwarven Council and invited Parke, Deckard, Safara, and Terris to attend.

* * *

Dwarven High Council meetings were traditionally held inside the rotunda of Council Hall. The center of the dome was open to the entrance hall below and the marble table spanned the circumference of the dome and was carved out of the same rock as the walls. Eight council seats circled around at regular intervals with two smaller chairs to either side for emissaries or aides with the center open to the hall below. The entire building was sealed from within during every session; all doors and windows save those in the rotunda itself were blocked.

With a shuffle and generally murmurs, seven council members took their seats. Nanus Delve began a light hum which was picked up by each member and echoed in a round. All over the buildings doors slammed shut and windows shuttered until the opening at the center of the table was a giant black hole and nothing could be seen below. The only light in the room came from the windows of the rotunda behind each chair. Lyssanna stood up. Her short hair was ragged, but clean, and she was clearly still exhausted. She addressed the council in a strong, if scratchy, voice.

"Few know what I am about to reveal and I apologize for the secrecy with which we have acted. However, it was necessary. Developments have made it impossible to move forward without a wider knowledge of our situation." She paused for a drink and ran a hand through her hair. "Two weeks ago, Fairn and Scoria left the city with the Basin Octet in an attempt to draw Rasulo away from Profana for a short time. They were successful and as a result a young vocalist was rescued by a group of Sonaran trainees."

Grumbles of protest broke out around the table voicing conflicting opinions, all but Nanus Delve seemed infuriated to have been left out.

"Order!" called Lyssanna. "You must allow me to finish, as we have gained and lost much in this venture. Safara, this young human canticle, was able to reach her sister inside the compound and free her with help from her bondpartner and her familiar. While this is important, we also have confirmation that Darek Delve is alive and being held at Profana with a group of Users." This pronouncement ended the few grumblers that were still making noise. "Darek was able to smuggle out a map sketched by Rasulo himself using the familiar of the young girl that was saved. We know what he is looking for and we need to find it first."

"Enough dancing around. What is he looking for?" came a gruff voice from the other side of the room.

It was Scoria that answered taking the remaining council seat, her eyes were dull and her voice listless. "The Pond. He is looking for the source of the Song."

The other council members looked shocked at her statement and her appearance. She was so altered from her normal demeanor that Petra Delve moved quickly to her side and offered her some water. She asked what was wrong and why

Fairn did not have his usual place by her seat.

"He sacrificed himself for me and the Basin. And he made me help." Scoria's voice cracked, but she held her watery eyes steady meeting the gazes of all present. Her pain was palpable and many tears were offered up, as hers were gone for the moment. "I will not allow that...that thing to take Fairn from me for no reason. No more cycles. This has to be the last." She stated in an emphatic whisper that echoed across the chamber. "I will not be left to wither and serve no purpose. We will find the Pond and defend it. And he will suffer for all he has brought on this land."

"Agreed, Scoria," replied Nanus in an unsteady voice. "My brother has been held for too long and we will suffer it no longer. We will need to discover what is being planned at Profana."

"As to that, we should ask one who has been there." Lyssanna motioned to Safara to stand and address the council.

"Iyna was imprisoned for the last eight years at Profana, so she is the true expert. However, I did speak to Darek. He said he was trapped and from the tone of his voice and my experiences I think he meant more than just the bars of the jail. Any User with an affinity for earth could have tunneled out of there by now and half of the cells I checked contained dwarves. When I tried to summon earth on the mountain, it would not respond. At all. There is something very odd about that place. Iyna keeps repeating that it is quiet outside of Profana. I think I heard what she meant, but I can't be sure, as I was focused only on finding her and not reconnoitering for information. As for what I saw, no Sonaran canticles were present and none of the lieutenants seemed to be pairbonded; although, they do try to work as duets. I do not know what that means, but it does seem like Rasulo is collecting Users from anywhere he can find them...I think he is building an army of Users to supplement his sycops. Those that do not join him are used as laborers. As for the map Celeste brought, it shows all of the places where Rasulo did NOT find the Pond."

She motioned to Terris and he used his affinity for form with her help to create a map in the empty space at the center of the rotunda. Lyssanna took over from here and Safara gratefully sank back into her seat while maintaining the image before them.

"It appears that he checked over the Low Plains, the Great Marsh, and even inside The Band at some point. The High Mesa and Spina Ardus have been checked in a few places, as well."

"The resources of Sonaris are available. I have no doubt that the mer and elves will join in the search, as well," offered Parke.

"For now, we may be wise to keep the search quiet. I am not opposed to informing the others, but should Rasulo learn of our plans he may become more unpredictable," Nanus returned. Parke nodded his head in agreement.

"Rasulo will not be going anywhere soon," Scoria cackled hysterically. "He is buried under a mountain. But he will worm his way out soon enough."

Lyssanna moved to her sister and urged her to accompany Petra from the room. "We should end this meeting now and reconvene tomorrow. I will send word of a time. Consider our options, but keep the information discussed secret for now." She rushed to follow her sister without further comment while Nanus lifted the lockdown on the building.

❋ ❋ ❋

Safara found herself on the balcony of Scoria's home having elected to change locations to free up space in the Tark compound. Her hostess soon joined her to watch the sunset. The similarities of the evening stood in stark contrast to the last happy evening they had spent in that house. They both sat in silence, curled up in matching chairs and covered in blankets to ward off the evening chill. No words were needed; as they watched the inky shadows chase away the colors of the sun.

"I wouldn't change a thing, you know." Scoria's voice sounded off to the left in the fading light. "Even had I known this was the outcome, I would have chosen him again and again. He allowed me to be more than myself and I hope I gave that to him, as well." She let out a cough that almost sounded like a laugh. "I guess this will help my focus."

"I am sorry about Fairn. I don't want to imagine what you are feeling." Safara did not know what else to say for fear of hurting her host, both knowing that Scoria's loss could easily become her own one day.

"Do not fash yourself. Worries find us in this life without taking on extra. I do not begrudge you your sister's rescue. We all knew the risks going in. Apparently, that blasted Angelic has some basilisks that are nimbler than rams in the mountains. He was there two days after we created that pebble. No one could have foreseen that. I am just relieved that you managed your end, or my loss truly would have been for nothing." She rummaged around in her pocket. "Would you like to see it?"

The dwarf snapped her fingers and a spark of light illuminated her fingertips casting her face into deep shadows. In the other hand, she held out two identical stones. Both were unremarkable grey and only about the size of an acorn. But they were exactly the same, down to the divot on one side and a black discoloration on the other.

"May I?" asked Safara, holding out her hand.

"Just don't touch them with your affinities. I can still feel Fairn in it." With visible effort, Scoria dropped both stones into the waiting palm below.

Safara was careful to only feel for the Song. Her eyes popped open wide. "They are exact. But the one on the left is new. So amazing! What did it feel like?" She passed them back and cuddled into her chair.

"I never thought to try anything like that before. But it was perfect unison. Our physiology being different makes blending our tones difficult, so producing a perfect tone with our vibrato melded was difficult. Once I felt our voices align, it was so easy. Perfect. Almost no effort actually. Just us working toward a common goal. And it felt right, you know?" She brushed away a stray tear summoned with the memory. "I had never felt so aligned like we were coexisting in the same exact space at the same exact time. I will never regret that experience with him."

Safara did not have a response and they went back to sitting in the dark until Lyssanna showed up and packed them off to bed. "You two will have plenty of time to bond later. For now, this is enough. Rest and we will sort this out eventually."

Off to the south, a low rumble was heard that grew louder and louder. The bass notes ringing off of every peak and echoing across the range. All three women moved to the edge of the terrace unable to see what was happening. Within a minute, Daichi landed by Safara and Terris reached down a hand to help her mount in front of him. Without explanation, they soared off into the night gaining altitude and whipping around to face the source of the disturbance. The southern end of Spina Ardus was shaking from an earthquake. Dust spouting into the air in multiple geysers. From their vantage, the pair saw several peaks quiver and fall taking out anything in their path.

"I don't think Rasulo is under that mountain anymore." Terris muttered into Safara's ear. She shuddered and nodded.

"Take us back, Daichi. We should warn the others."

To be continued...

ABOUT THE AUTHOR

J. G. Flora

Honestly, there isn't much to know. I do my thing and live my weird. I hope you do, too.